TEXAS SECRETS, LOVERS' LIES

Karen Whiddon

D0102726

HARLEQUIN® ROMANTIC SUSPENSE

If you purchased this book without a cover you should be aware
that this book is stolen property. It was reported as "unsold and
destroyed" to the publisher, and neither the author nor the
publisher has received any payment for this "stripped book."

Recycling programs
for this product may
not exist in your area.

ISBN-13: 978-0-373-27843-5

TEXAS SECRETS, LOVERS' LIES

Copyright © 2013 by Karen Whiddon

All rights reserved. Except for use in any review, the reproduction or
utilization of this work in whole or in part in any form by any electronic,
mechanical or other means, now known or hereafter invented, including
xerography, photocopying and recording, or in any information storage
or retrieval system, is forbidden without the written permission of the
publisher, Harlequin Enterprises Limited, 225 Duncan Mill Road,
Don Mills, Ontario, Canada M3B 3K9.

This is a work of fiction. Names, characters, places and incidents are
either the product of the author's imagination or are used fictitiously,
and any resemblance to actual persons, living or dead, business
establishments, events or locales is entirely coincidental.

This edition published by arrangement with Harlequin Books S.A.

For questions and comments about the quality of this book,
please contact us at CustomerService@Harlequin.com.

® and TM are trademarks of Harlequin Enterprises Limited or its
corporate affiliates. Trademarks indicated with ® are registered in the
United States Patent and Trademark Office, the Canadian Trade Marks
Office and in other countries.

Printed in U.S.A.

™ www.Harlequin.com

Books by Karen Whiddon

Harlequin Romantic Suspense

The CEO's Secret Baby #1662
The Cop's Missing Child #1719
The Millionaire Cowboy's Secret #1752
Texas Secrets, Lovers' Lies #1773

Silhouette Romantic Suspense

*One Eye Open #1301
*One Eye Closed #1365
*Secrets of the Wolf #1397
*The Princess's Secret Scandal #1416
Bulletproof Marriage #1484
**Black Sheep P.I. #1513
**The Perfect Soldier #1557
**Profile for Seduction #1629
**Colton's Christmas Baby #1636

Harlequin Nocturne

*Wolf Whisperer #128
*The Wolf Princess #146
*The Wolf Prince #157
*Lone Wolf #103
*The Lost Wolf's Destiny #167

Silhouette Nocturne

*Cry of the Wolf #7
*Touch of the Wolf #12
*Dance of the Wolf #45
*Wild Wolf #67

*The Pack
**The Cordasic Legacy

Other titles by this author
available in ebook format.

KAREN WHIDDON

started weaving fanciful tales for her younger brothers at the age of eleven. Amid the Catskill Mountains of New York, then the Rocky Mountains of Colorado, she fueled her imagination with the natural beauty that surrounded her. Karen now lives in north Texas, where she shares her life with her very own hero of a husband and three doting dogs. Also an entrepreneur, she divides her time between the business she started and writing. You can email Karen at KWhiddon1@aol.com or write to her at P.O. Box 820807, Fort Worth, TX 76182. Fans of her writing can also check out her website, www.karenwhiddon.com.

First and always, to my wonderful husband. Thanks, Lonnie, for making my dreams come true. Second, a shout-out to all the dedicated and hardworking people who volunteer in animal rescue. You work so hard and give so tirelessly of not only your time, but your wallets and purses, to help those creatures who have no voice. Hats off to you for all you do—especially you, Legacy Boxer Rescue, Inc.

Chapter 1

I wish you were here.

In her mind Zoe Onella replayed the last words her best friend, Shayna, had said to her before disappearing. *Or maybe I could visit there. I really need you right now.* The entire cross-country trip from New York to Dallas, Zoe wished she'd have probed or, even better, agreed to let Shayna visit.

Instead, she'd rushed Shayna off the phone so she could meet a couple of friends for happy hour. And then, two weeks later, the next phone call had been from Shayna's mother, Mama Bell, worried because she couldn't locate her daughter. Mama had actually believed Shayna might have been with Zoe.

With guilt churning inside her, Zoe collected her luggage and stepped outside. The scorching air blasted her like a furnace. Ah, yes. Dallas was still the same as she remembered. Hot and miserable. She slipped on her dark glasses before she looked around for her ride.

No one on the sidewalk even looked familiar. Which was odd, since Mama Bell had promised to send someone to collect her. Fine. Squaring her shoulders, Zoe hefted her suitcase and began the trek to the cab area, lifting her chin and making her stride confident despite the towering heels she wore. This was her New York persona, one she planned to hang on to while here in Texas, to remind herself of the person she'd become.

She could handle this. Would handle it, exactly as she'd done a hundred times before at home in the city. So what if the cab fare from DFW to Anniversary would be outrageous?

"Zoe," called a voice—deep, masculine and unforgettably familiar. The sound of it reached inside her, echoing old longings. "Over here."

She stiffened. Brock McCauley. The one person from her past she didn't want to see. Not now. Not ever.

For the space of a heartbeat, she debated pretending not to have heard him and striding down the sidewalk as fast as she could. Away from him. Just like before. Instead, she took a deep breath, pasted her best "I am all business" smile on her face, and turned to face the man she'd practically left at the altar long ago.

The instant she saw him, all the jangling noise inside of her went still. He looked the same—tall and broad shouldered, blond hair cut in the same sexy-shaggy cut. As his piercing blue eyes met hers, her entire being vibrated. Though her heart hammered out a welcome, she schooled her expression to nothing but pleasant surprise.

The man she'd once needed with every fiber of her being wasn't the one she wanted now.

"Mrs. Bell sent me to pick you up," he said. His blank expression let her know he took no enjoyment in the task. She nodded, unable to summon up a response. After all, what did one say to a man after you'd broken his heart?

He led the way to his truck, a new Chevrolet painted shiny red. She flashed back five years to his beat-up old pickup, which had also been red, remembering the way they'd celebrated their love in his front seat.

As her face warmed in a blush, she climbed up into the cab and turned away, pretending a sudden interest in everything outside her window. Guilt be damned. She had nothing to say to him, nothing at all.

Everything that had happened between them was in the past. She refused to look back.

Brock started the truck and they began the long drive from DFW Airport to Anniversary. Keeping his gaze on the road, Brock apparently felt no need to fill the awkward silence with meaningless words. She appreciated that, also unable to give voice to the thoughts taunting her. Might-have-beens that could never be. All they had in common now was Shayna, the only reason Zoe had returned.

Still, they had to speak eventually, didn't they? About Shayna. Especially since Zoe's former fiancé and best friend lived together and planned to marry.

Life in small-town Anniversary had gone on just fine without Zoe. Her gut reaction after Mrs. Bell's frantic phone call had been to panic. She'd been standing by the window in her Manhattan apartment, watching the traffic below do its thing, the same as it did every morning. The hustle and bustle of other people starting their day had always fascinated her. The gray sky promised rain, which meant outside would be muggy and a sticky, frizzy hair day. And then the phone call from the woman Zoe considered her mother, saying Shayna had disappeared and asking Zoe if her daughter was with her. Apparently, Shayna had mentioned she was planning a visit.

When Zoe had told Mama Bell no, her answer had been greeted by silence. She sensed she'd dashed Shayna's mother's last hope. And Zoe thought back to the last conversation she'd had with her best friend, wishing she'd paid better attention.

Though Mama Bell hadn't come out and asked, Zoe knew she was needed back home. She'd instantly volunteered to fly to Texas and sort things out.

In all the years since Mrs. Bell had taken Zoe under her wing, raising her with as much love as if blood bound them together, she'd never asked for anything.

She didn't have to ask this time.

Though Zoe hadn't actually seen Shayna since she'd left, and even though they'd lost that best friend need to talk every day, they'd still spoken occasionally by phone. In her heart of hearts, Zoe knew the connection was as strong and unbroken as if they were actual sisters.

Even when Brock and Shayna had gotten together and Shayna had tentatively asked Zoe if she minded, Zoe had tried to be happy for the two of them. In the tangled mess her leaving had created, someone should be happy. Truth be told, she'd missed Shayna and actually welcomed a chance to see her again. Brock, however, was another story. Zoe had never gotten over the agony or the guilt of practically leaving him at the altar.

She'd missed Anniversary, she realized. It would

always be home, the place where she'd grown up. If only the town didn't hold so many dark, bloodstained memories. Here, in a dark alley behind a seedy bar, a younger Zoe had watched her mother die.

Glancing again at Brock, she wondered how he was dealing with Shayna's disappearance. After Zoe vanished on him five years ago, this must feel like a twist of the knife. She ached for him, even as she tried not to feel anything at all.

Did she want to know? Was it relevant to figuring out where Shayna had gone? More uncomfortable than she'd been in ages, Zoe tried to figure out the best way to ask.

While she considered, after clearing his throat, Brock brought up the subject first, still not making eye contact, instead focusing on his driving.

"Now that we're face-to-face again," he said. "Why don't you tell me why you left?"

Dread filled her even though rationally she knew he had a right to know. He deserved an explanation, or at least part of one. Five years had passed, after all. "When my mother was killed in that alley behind her favorite bar, I was there. She'd called me, drunk, and asked me to meet her. When I got to the scene, it turned out her drug dealer was also there, and she owed him money."

Though her voice broke, she continued. "She'd told him I'd bring that money. When I didn't, he slit her throat. Right in front of me." Remembered horror made her shudder.

His steady gaze stayed on her, but he made no move to touch her. "I knew about her murder, but not that you were there. Why didn't you tell me? I would have helped you."

"That's just it. I couldn't. Not only did he give me twenty-four hours to get the money, he told me if I didn't, he'd find me and kill everyone I held dear." She took a deep breath.

"At first, I ran because I was in fear for my life. Later, I was messed up. Seeing such a thing…I couldn't handle…"

"Me?" he asked, sounding wounded, his grip tight on the steering wheel. "You couldn't handle me?"

"We were so young, Brock. And you kept pushing to get married. It was too much. So I stayed in New York." Even after all this time, her voice shook. There was more, but she wouldn't tell him the rest of it.

"So you ran and then kept running, from this town, from your friends and your family, and from me." No emotion in his voice. No condemnation or sympathy, disbelief or commiseration.

Oddly enough, this gave her strength. "Yes."

Expression like granite, he didn't respond.

"Tell me about you and Shayna," she said, breaking the silence. After Shayna had confessed to Zoe that she'd always had a thing for Brock, Zoe'd spent months trying to adjust to the idea that her best friend had gotten together with her former fiancé.

"Shayna was moving out," he said, the bluntness of his words matching his unemotional tone. "These past few months have been…difficult for both of us."

Trying to hide her shock, Zoe stiffened. For the past few months, every time she'd talked to Shayna, her friend had been full of cheerful plans about her and Brock's upcoming wedding. Until the final phone call, when she'd clearly reached out to Zoe for help and Zoe had been too self-absorbed to notice. "Moved out? What happened? I thought you two were getting married?"

Now he looked at her, not bothering to hide his shock. "Shayna and I never even discussed marriage."

Not wanting to betray her friend's confidence, Zoe simply nodded. Right now, it was more important to find Shayna. After, they could straighten everything else out.

"When did you last see her?" Zoe asked.

Brock sighed, drumming his fingers on the steering wheel as he drove. "It's been a few days. This past Friday, we discussed her moving out, and I offered to help find her a place to live. She went out that night with her friend Cristine and never came back home."

Again she nodded, as though none of what he said came as a complete surprise when, in fact, she was stunned. Did Brock know more about Shayna's disappearance than he was saying?

"Where do you think she's gone?" she finally asked, even as she knew she wouldn't be here if the answer were as simple as Shayna telling her fiancé where she'd be for the next few days.

He shook his head. "I have no idea. I've been trying to reach her. So have her parents and her friends. She hasn't shown up for work and her cell phone is turned off."

At least he and Shayna's mother were telling the same story since Shayna had disappeared. But was he the one who'd provided this set of facts?

"She'll come back," Zoe said, speaking with a confidence she wanted badly to feel. "She's probably just taking a break from everything. As soon as she finds out I'm in town, she'll make contact."

"You think so?" His tone told her how unlikely he found that possibility. But then, he didn't know what Shayna had said the last time she and Zoe talked.

No matter. "She has to," she replied, hoping it would be true. The alternative was unthinkable, that Shayna Bell had truly gone missing. If that was the case, who knew what might have happened to her then.

Inwardly, Zoe winced. She could only pray that the darkness of her past, after so many years, hadn't caught up with her best friend. Surely not. The killer was still in prison and appeared to have totally forgotten the young woman he'd threatened to kill. As far as he knew, there was no connection between Zoe and Shayna. On top of that, Shayna wouldn't make the kind of foolish choices that would place her in harm's way.

Silence fell again. Odd, between two people who'd never been at a loss for words. Of course, that was in the past, before Zoe had set fire to every bridge that tied her to people she'd loved in Anniversary. Now, Zoe couldn't blame him for wanting to ignore her.

Weirdly though, with Brock she'd expected…more. Accusations, finger-pointing, something reminiscent of the passion that had once blazed between them.

Of course, five years had passed. There was no passion left. He'd gotten over her by now, just as she'd… refused to let herself even think about him. At first, doing so had hurt too badly. Later, she'd bowed to the inevitable and tried with all her iron will to move on.

As had he. When Shayna had called Zoe, her voice full of a tentative sort of joy, to ask if she minded the two of them dating, Zoe hadn't hesitated to tell her friend not at all. Grab happiness with both hands and don't let it go, she'd urged Shayna. After all, that was how Zoe had learned to live her life in the big city.

Life went on. Old hurts, old loves, while never completely forgotten, were buried, moved past. There was no reason at all now why she and Brock couldn't be civil. After all, they both wanted the same thing—Shayna to be found safe.

As the silence dragged on, Zoe snuck a glance or two at Brock, reminded of his old nickname—Brock the Rock. Judging from the size of his biceps and the breadth of his chest, he hadn't given up lifting weights. He would have been able to protect Shayna if he'd been in their home when someone came for her, but more personal thoughts tried to break Zoe's focus on her missing friend. She'd never been able to picture Brock and Shayna together—they hadn't even seemed to like each other back when Zoe and Brock had been an item.

"Why?" she asked, finally breaking the silence. "Why was Shayna moving out?"

"That's kind of personal," he replied lightly, still staring straight ahead. "And none of your business."

That hurt more than she'd expected. Still… "Maybe it isn't, right now," she replied. "But if the reason has something to do with her disappearance, you'd better believe I'll ask you again."

"Fair enough." This time, he swiveled his head to face her. His blue eyes flashed sparks, causing heat to flare low in her belly. This, she squashed with the ease of years of practice. She might not have been able to completely forget him, but she had managed to stop loving him a long time ago.

A few minutes later he exited the highway and the streets began to look more and more familiar, making her sit up straighter. She hadn't been back at all since she'd fled everything and everyone as though pursued by demons.

She might as well have been. She'd changed everything about herself, from her hair color and cut to the way she dressed and spoke. She'd worked hard to lose her Texas drawl, adopting a hint of a Midwest accent, so no one would realize where she was from. These days, though, she looked much the same as she used to, albeit with a much more expensive haircut.

Originally, Zoe had planned to return. To apologize to Brock, explain what had happened, and step right back into the life she'd been destined to have. Especially since she'd learned, a few weeks after leaving, that she was pregnant.

She'd lost the baby in the first trimester. That had been bad enough, but she'd learned that the endometriosis and the horrible scarring to her fallopian tubes meant she would never be able to have children. She'd realized then, in the middle of her grief, that she could never go back to Brock or to her old life.

It had taken this, Shayna's disappearance, to bring her back home. Back to the place she'd grown up, where most of her happy memories had been replaced with dark and bloody ones.

She shivered. Had she honestly believed she'd never have to revisit Anniversary?

And this. Confronting Brock McCauley—the man she'd left—again hadn't figured into her plan. Of course, never in her wildest dreams would she have imagined Shayna would go missing and she'd have to return home to try to find her.

As for facing Brock—what had she thought? He'd

been engaged to her best friend and Anniversary wasn't a large town. She'd been bound to run into him eventually. The past always found a way to catch up. She only hoped the rest of it—the stuff of nightmares part—stayed away.

As they pulled up in front of the white brick ranch house where she'd been raised by a family that wasn't her own, Zoe felt her tension ease. Staring, she inhaled. Swamped by a wave of nostalgia so strong it clogged her throat, to her surprise she found herself blinking back tears.

As if he sensed this, Brock cleared his throat. "Are you okay?"

Crap. Temporarily unable to speak, she nodded, careful to keep her face averted. Showing emotion would reveal weakness, and she couldn't have that. Not with him. Especially not with him.

One second, then another ticked by before she got herself under control. "I'm good," she said, her brisk, self-assured tone giving credence to the lie. Shoulders back, she pushed open the door and climbed out of the truck.

With her head high, she started up the sidewalk, noting the neatly maintained flowers lining it—that much hadn't changed—and her world began to slip back toward the past. She pushed aside her worry and picked up her pace as the front door opened.

"Zoe!" Mama Bell appeared, her plump arms open wide. She still smelled the same—of freshly baked cookies. Her curly hair might be grayer now, but she still wore it in a long ponytail.

Zoe flung herself into the other woman's hug—her mama, she told herself fiercely. No matter that they weren't related by blood. After all, Mrs. Bell had stepped in and raised Zoe when her real mother had gone to jail. Even after, when Zoe's mother had been released and wanted her back, Zoe had spent more time at the Bells' than in the cramped apartment her mother called home.

Actually, Zoe had come to rely on the Bell family long before her drug-addicted mother had been killed. Ever since Zoe'd met a five-year-old Shayna in kindergarten and the two girls had become best friends Mrs. Bell had recognized Zoe's desperate need for family and love and had welcomed her as if she was one of her own. Zoe had called her Mama Bell ever since.

"Come inside," Mama Bell managed, openly crying. "Oh, I'm so glad you could make it home." Catching sight of Brock, the older woman brightened. "Brock, don't just stand there like a stranger. Get on in here, too."

But Brock shook his head. Zoe wasn't surprised. "I've got to head back to the store," he said. "Take care, Mrs. Bell." His carefully blank gaze touched on Zoe briefly before he dipped his head and climbed back into his pickup.

Zoe watched as he drove away. Then, allowing Mama Bell to shepherd her into the living room, she soaked in the familiar chintz furniture and floral-scented candles, while the other woman closed the door and engaged the dead bolt.

"You lock up now?" she asked. In the old days, no one in Anniversary had locked their doors.

Mama Bell nodded, her expression sad. "Crime has gotten worse. Especially during tourist season, when all those city folks show up with their fancy cars and bored teenagers."

The lake had always been a popular destination. As soon as the weather grew warm, wealthy people from Dallas, Austin and Houston headed to their huge vacation homes on the large, inviting body of clear, calm water. And then there were the weekend tourists, people who came for Saturday and Sunday, clogging up the two-lane roads and spending much-needed money, before returning to the city and their jobs, leaving their litter behind.

"Sit, sit." Wiping at her still-streaming eyes, Mama Bell gestured at the couch. The bright floral-patterned sofa had occupied the place of honor facing the television ever since Zoe could remember. The sight of it made her heart clench. She'd come home now. This felt like—no, *was* home.

Chest tight, Zoe sat.

"Can I get you something to drink? Cola? Sweet tea?"

"No, thanks." Patting the cushion next to her, Zoe tried to smile. "Please. Let's talk. Tell me what's been going on with Shayna."

Mama Bell nodded and hurried over, nearly tripping over her feet in her rush to get to Zoe. Zoe noted the older woman still wore her favorite outfit, sweatpants and a T-shirt with a saying on the front—today's advertised a restaurant in town—and brightly colored sneakers that tied it all together. Her trademark dangling earrings completed the picture.

"Don't ever change," Zoe said impulsively, hugging her. "You look the same as ever."

"Thanks." Mama Bell tried to smile. "I've even lost

a few pounds since Shayna..." Her smile wobbled and she finally gave up and bit her lip instead.

"Tell me." Zoe touched her arm. "I talked a little to Brock on the drive from the airport. I'd like to hear your take on what was going on with Shayna."

"That's just it." Mama Bell shook her head, sending her silver earrings flying. "I have no idea. When Shayna started acting strange a few months back, I tried to talk to her about it. She got angry at me. Told me to quit trying to poke my nose into her business."

Zoe blinked. "That doesn't sound like Shayna."

"I know." Again Mama Bell's large blue eyes welled with tears. "She and I were always so close."

"So what happened?" Zoe leaned closer. "What made her change?"

"I don't know." Mama Bell actually wrung her hands. "She seemed happy enough when she moved in with Brock, but I guess the two of them were having troubles. When I asked her about it, she told me she didn't want to discuss it."

"Several months, you said?" Zoe couldn't imagine. "Why didn't you call me and let me know?"

"How could I? Shayna made it plain she felt I was being pushy. Calling you just would have made things worse. Shayna even stopped coming to Sunday suppers. To be honest, when she went missing, I didn't even know." She hung her head, her rounded shoulders shaking. "I hadn't talked to my own daughter in over a month."

Shocked, Zoe didn't know what to say. Over a month? And Mama Bell hadn't seen fit to call her? This stung. "I last talked to her two weeks ago," she said, keeping her voice gentle. "Our usual phone call. She told me she and Brock were engaged."

"What?" Mama Bell gasped, as though in pain. "How could she have gotten engaged and not even told me?"

Zoe stroked the older woman's arm to soothe her. "That's the thing. Brock says they weren't. He says they never even discussed marriage." She took a deep breath. "He told me Shayna was moving out."

This time, Mama Bell moaned. "Oh, Zoe. That's the other thing. I've caught Shayna in quite a few outright falsehoods."

"Do you think she lied about the wedding?" Zoe could hardly wrap her mind around that.

"She had to." Mama frowned. "Brock wouldn't lie. That man's never done anything but told the truth." She sighed. "I'm so worried. I don't know what to do."

"We'll get through it together," Zoe said. "What about the police? Have you contacted them?"

"Yes, of course. But since Shayna's been telling everyone in town that she wanted to leave, their hands are tied. The sheriff did add her to the Missing Person's Database. Brock let Shayna's father look through her bank records and there was nothing out of the ordinary. But she hasn't used her cell phone since she vanished."

Biting her lip, Zoe tried to think. "And the last time she was seen? Brock said he saw her this past Friday."

Mama Bell nodded. "She and Cristine went out. The two of them have been doing that a lot lately. Hanging out in bars, dating strange men. I know she's a grown woman, but I've been worried sick."

Zoe didn't blame her. None of this sounded at all like

the Shayna she knew. "Anything you can tell me about her behavior will help."

"She was jumpy. Nervous, always looking out the window."

"Do you think she was on something?"

"I… No." Mama Bell stood and crossed her arms. "I think she was afraid," she finally said. "Zoe, she told me what happened to your mother and how you got messed up in it. Even though the man responsible is still in prison, I think she was scared the same thing might happen to her."

Chapter 2

Ever since Shayna vanished, Brock had felt unsettled. Guilty, too, as if he'd failed her. After all, she'd been living with him. He'd always tried to watch out for her as best as he could. He'd been the person she'd call if she was going to be late home and vice versa.

Even though their relationship hadn't worked out, he considered himself an honorable man. He'd tried to do right by her, lately more like a friend than a lover, a relationship status on which they'd both agreed.

Though he was understandably worried, he knew Shayna better than most. He didn't really believe she was missing. Given her new lifestyle, she'd probably met someone and taken off for a little private recreation vacation. This disappearance was so like her— or maybe more like the person she'd become these past few months. He barely even recognized her. Though he'd tried to tell himself it wasn't his fault, Shayna had completely changed after Brock told her he could never love her the way she deserved to be loved.

To say she'd gone wild would be an understatement. She'd gone from a careful, studious, at-the-library-every-weekend woman into a let's-do-a-pub-crawl-every-Friday partyer. In addition to dressing like a streetwalker, she'd changed her hair to some spiky, vibrant color not found in nature and caked on the makeup so heavily she was nearly unrecognizable. No matter what happened between them romantically, they'd always been good friends, at least since Zoe had left. These days, they didn't even have that. He didn't like the woman she'd become.

Shayna didn't care what he thought. She and her friend Cristine Haywood had become thick as thieves. Long before announcing her plan to move out, Shayna had taken to vanishing immediately after work on Friday, refusing to answer her cell and finally straggling in late Sunday afternoon, looking as if she'd spent the entire weekend in a drunk tank.

At first he'd worried, but even attempting to broach the subject had made Shayna react with out-of-proportion anger. She'd thrown things, screamed, cursed and generally carried on so loudly he'd figured the neighbors must have thought he beat her.

Finally, he'd simply told her he was there if she needed to talk and left her alone. She was a grown woman, after all. And he wasn't her keeper.

He figured this disappearance, though much longer than her usual disappearing weekends, was the latest stunt. A means of getting attention. Because if there was one thing Shayna thrived on these days, attention would be it.

He also didn't believe Cristine when she claimed to have no idea where her new best friend had gone. He'd talked to Mama Bell, and Shayna's mother had conveyed her own worries over the changes in her daughter's behavior. Evidently the older woman had grown so concerned that she'd called Zoe Onella. And now even Zoe had returned to town to try to help, though he had no idea why. As far as he could tell, Shayna and Zoe hadn't been chummy since Zoe took off five years ago.

Zoe was one person he would have preferred to have gone the rest of his life without seeing again. How in the hell she still had the power to make his heart clench, he didn't understand.

When she'd left, mere weeks before their wedding, his hurt had blossomed into hate. This had sustained him through the dark nights when, more than once, he'd found himself looking into the bottom of a bottle. Gradually, the hate had faded, though the pain had never left him. He'd convinced himself he was over her, tried like hell to make himself forget.

Then he'd seen her striding through the airport, her long-legged beauty taking his breath from him.

That image was still burned on his mind. He knew when he closed his eyes to try to sleep later, he'd only see her impossibly long-lashed brown eyes staring at him as if she didn't know him. Had he truly been so easy to forget?

"Hey, Brock." Ted Williams sauntered into the feed store, his red tractor cap turned backward. "Cristine asked me to put these up." He slid a paper across the counter. "Is it all right if I hang one up in your store?"

A photograph of Shayna stared up at him. Her bright smile and windblown hair proved it had obviously been taken in better times. Brock grabbed the paper and read. "Cristine wants to be in charge of the search?"

Ted shrugged. "No one else is doing anything. Even the police don't really think she's disappeared. What could it hurt?"

The bell over the door tinkled, saving him from answering. When he saw who'd come into the feed store, his gut clenched. Marshall Bell, Shayna's father.

Before Brock could tell Ted to put the paper away, Mr. Bell caught sight of his daughter's photo. Immediately, he looked ill. All the color leached from his face. He opened his mouth as if to say something, then closed it and wiped his hand across his lips. "Brock," he managed, and then had to clear his throat. "I'd like a word."

Brock nodded, glancing at Ted, who apparently chose not to take the hint and continued standing there. "Alone?" Brock asked, more to clarify things than anything else.

"Please," Mr. Bell rasped.

Still Todd didn't move, as though his feet had grown roots.

"Todd?" Brock prodded him with his elbow. "Do you mind?"

Looking disappointed, Todd finally shuffled away.

"What's with him?" Mr. Bell grumbled. "Was he one of Shayna's new boyfriends?" Then, realizing he was talking to the man who'd lived with his daughter, he appeared contrite. "Sorry, son," he said, squeezing Brock's shoulder. "No harm meant."

Grimacing, Brock nodded. He still hadn't gotten used to people making comments to him about Shayna.

Her sudden disappearance made everyone in town think it was all right to say just about anything to the man she'd been cheating on. He could only imagine what kind of remarks they made to her parents.

Mr. Bell looked left and then right. Besides him and Brock, there were three other people in the feed store. Brock's sister Eve, who worked part-time at the store while attending junior college, Todd, and Anna Perilli, who raised Arabian horses. She was looking at bits and bridles, so she would be all right for a few minutes by herself.

"Come with me," Brock said, leading Mr. Bell toward his cramped office. The room remained exactly the way it had been when Brock's father had occupied it, with the exception of a hanging wall calendar that Brock changed out every year.

Once inside, Brock closed the door and indicated a chair across from his at the desk. "Have a seat."

Sighing heavily, Mr. Bell sat. "I'm worried about my daughter," he said.

"I understand." His fingers steepled in front of him, Brock waited to see what else the other man had to say.

"What do you think?" Mr. Bell peered at him with bloodshot eyes. "Do you think our Shayna just ran away?"

Our Shayna. On the verge of telling the truth, Brock hesitated then decided not to. No sense in hurting Shayna's father any more than he had to. "I honestly don't know, Mr. Bell."

"Call me Marshall," the other man said, surprising Brock. He'd known Mr. Bell his entire life and never addressed him by his first name.

"I'll try," he said, meaning it. "Though I might forget. Force of habit. As far as Shayna leaving, I don't know." He took a deep breath, aware his next words would probably be a shock. "Marshall, did Shayna tell you that she and I were breaking up? She was planning to move out of the apartment soon."

Marshall recoiled, clearly stunned. "I suspected that would happen. Do you have any idea where she was planning to live?"

"She was talking about moving in with Cristine," Brock said, dodging a direct answer. "Those two had gotten to be pretty good friends."

"Cristine." The other man's voice conveyed his disgust. "I wish she and Shayna had never started hanging around together. She's nothing but a bad influence on my baby girl."

Again Brock had to bite his tongue. He was of the opinion that Shayna and Cristine egged each other on. Who was the worse influence, he couldn't tell. He really believed they sort of fed on each other's energy.

Suddenly, he realized Shayna's father was eyeing him with suspicion, making him wonder what his expression had inadvertently revealed.

Torn between wanting to laugh or simply shake his head, Brock decided the direct approach would be best. "Despite the fact that our relationship was over and her plans to move out, I bore no malice toward Shayna, I assure you," he said. "I promise you I had nothing to do with her disappearance."

Instead of appearing relieved, Mr. Bell narrowed his eyes. "That's a strange thing for you to say. I never accused you of anything like that."

"No, you didn't. But I wanted to set your mind at ease in case you were wondering."

"I wasn't." Mr. Bell sighed heavily. With apparent difficulty, he focused on Brock again. "But I know you. I'm certain you'd never do anything to hurt my daughter."

"Thanks."

"How are you doing with all this?"

Surprised, Brock shrugged. "I can't help but think Shayna will be found when she wants to be found."

Marshall cocked his shorn gray head. "I didn't mean about that. I'm talking about your former fiancée. Zoe's back in town. Though I'm not sure why, my wife seems to think if anyone can find Shayna, Zoe can."

Brock shrugged. "I don't care either way what Zoe does. That relationship was over long ago." As far as Zoe being able to find Shayna, anything was possible. Though Shayna had lately made a big effort to prove she didn't care about anything or anyone, Brock figured maybe Zoe would prove the exception.

"Apparently, the two of them have kept in touch all this time," Marshall continued. "My wife even thought maybe Shayna took off to go visit Zoe."

"I see," Brock said, though he really didn't. He hadn't even known Shayna and Zoe still talked to each other these days. Shayna had said Zoe'd been backing away, abandoning her friendship the same way she'd deserted him.

Marshall nodded, his faded brown gaze far away.

Though Brock understood the older man's concern and worry for his only daughter, his intuition told him that this roundabout conversation wasn't the entire reason Mr. Bell had come to see him. He checked his watch. "I'm sorry, but I've got to get back to work. Is there anything else I can do for you?"

The other man nodded, a muscle in his cheek working. "I'm leaving," he blurted. "Tomorrow."

Stunned, Brock wasn't sure how to respond. "You're leaving? What do you mean?"

"I'm leaving Mrs. Bell, Anniversary, everything." He waved his hand vaguely. "All of this is way too painful. I can't take it anymore."

"But what about your wife?" Brock sputtered. "She's already hurting over Shayna's disappearance. Think about what this will do to her."

The other man's face seemed to close in on itself. "I have thought of that, believe me. But I can't help thinking it will hurt her worse if I stay."

"Worse? How can it be worse than that? And what about when Shayna comes back? How's she going to feel when she finds her daddy has taken off?"

"*If* Shayna comes back," Marshall said, his voice full of the same weariness revealed by his rounded shoulders and defeated posture. "As to that, I can't help but feel if she didn't care enough to say goodbye, what will it matter to her who's here when she returns? Look after them for me, will you?"

He waved away any comment Brock might have attempted to make. Moving laboriously, as though he'd aged twenty years in the space of minutes, he gave Brock a bleak smile.

"Why are you telling me this?" Brock asked as he followed him to the door.

"Because you care," Mr. Bell said. "I have to let someone know, and you're the closest thing I have to a son. As far as I can tell, you might be the only one holding this family together by the time all of this is over."

Those words haunted him. For the rest of the afternoon, as he loaded pickup trucks with bags of feed, sold bridles and bits, hay and birdseed, Brock tried to figure out what the hell Mr. Bell was thinking. If he did leave, the fallout would be tremendous. Poor Mrs. Bell, who was one of the nicest, kindest women in town. She would be devastated.

And Zoe? She considered the Bells her family. Mr. Bell was the closest thing to a father she'd ever had. How would she take his desertion?

Just like that, the old pain came roaring back. Zoe'd left him, and he'd foolishly believed he'd recovered. Now he realized what he'd done was survive, nothing more. And despite the fact that his and Shayna's relationship hadn't worked out, he didn't understand how she could do the exact same thing. To him or to her family. And now this. Marshall Bell was beating a fast track out of town.

Wherever she'd gone, Shayna needed to come home now. If she didn't, she might return to Anniversary some day and find she had nothing left to come back for.

The rest of the afternoon dragged. After finally turning the Open sign to Closed, Brock locked up the feed store and tried to decide whether he wanted to grab some fast food for dinner or cook something himself.

Or he could make another trip to the sheriff's office and see if there was anything else they could do to help find Shayna. He'd been there several times already, as had Mama Bell. He'd learned that adults have the right to leave without telling anyone where they are going, who they are with or why they left. According to Roger Giles, the sheriff, without evidence of foul play, they had to balance the missing person's legal right to do what they liked and the family's natural desire to make sure their loved one was all right.

In other words, the information would sit in a file and, beyond the occasional phone call to see if Shayna had come home, little else would be done.

While Brock didn't like it, he could see Roger's point.

More weary than he'd been in ages, he decided he'd figure something out on the drive home.

Instead, he found himself turning onto the Bells' street. As he coasted to a stop in front of the neat ranch-style house, he debated whether he really wanted to go inside. Not only was Mr. Bell's secret weighing him down, but he wasn't sure he was up to seeing Zoe again.

The decision was taken from him when the front door opened—Mrs. Bell, heading to the mailbox to get the day's mail. The instant she caught sight of him, she smiled and waved.

"Brock! What are you doing sitting in your truck? Come on inside. I was just about to cook up some of my famous fried chicken." Her smile wavered slightly. "Who knows, maybe Shayna will smell it and decide to come home."

Despite himself, his mouth watered and his stomach growled. Mrs. Bell was known all around town for her chicken. It was the best he'd ever had.

Any reservations he might have had vanished, just like that. His stomach won out. He cut the engine and pocketed the keys.

Retrieving her mail, Mrs. Bell chattered all the way up the sidewalk. Apparently, Mr. Bell hadn't yet told his wife of his plans to leave. Brock wondered if he would.

He held the door open so Mrs. Bell could go inside. Zoe glanced up as they entered the room. Surprise flashed across her face when she saw Brock, but almost immediately she schooled her features into an expression of polite interest. "Brock," she said. "What are you doing here?"

"I stopped by after work to check on ya'll, and Mrs. Bell invited me to dinner." He kept his response equally civil. "When she mentioned she was making her chicken, I couldn't pass it up."

"Oh, look at this!" Mrs. Bell held up a flyer, passing it to Brock. "Looks like Cristine is having a get-together tomorrow over at the high school."

Brock nodded, reading the leaflet quickly. Maybe if he kept himself busy while he was here, not only would he not have to wonder if Shayna had left because of him, but he also wouldn't have to look at Zoe and wonder what might have been.

"A get-together?" Zoe's voice jolted him out of his thoughts. "Why on earth—"

"Wrong choice of words," Mrs. Bell said, lifting one shoulder in apology. "Cristine is calling a meeting to organize a search for our Shayna. Even if she took off on her own, maybe Cristine can help locate her."

Closing her mouth, Zoe nodded. To Brock's surprise, she glanced at him, almost as if seeking his opinion. The instant her vibrant brown eyes met his, he felt a slow burn begin in his blood. Did she feel it, too? How could she not?

But her glance flitted away almost as quickly, and he knew he'd been wrong. Zoe didn't feel anything for him. She never had.

"Are you going?" Mrs. Bell asked, taking the flyer from him and passing it to Zoe.

"We'll go," Brock found himself saying, replying for both of them even though he had no right.

"Of course, we'll go," Zoe interjected. "We all want to help find Shayna as quickly as possible."

Since there was nothing Brock could add to that, he nodded.

"Well, I'd better get busy frying up some chicken." Mrs. Bell headed toward the kitchen.

"I'll help," Zoe said, letting the flyer flutter to the floor as she jumped to her feet. She hurried away, leaving him alone in the oak-paneled living room.

He picked up the flyer and read it again. While he'd never really liked Cristine, he found it commendable that she cared enough about her friend to do something to try to find her. The skeptical part of him wondered if Cristine just missed having someone to party with, but in truth, her motives didn't matter. Finding Shayna was what mattered. Even if she had just climbed onto the back of some guy's motorcycle, she needed to understand the worry she'd caused her family.

Again, he questioned how it could be that Shayna hadn't at least told Cristine where she was going. The two women had been best friends, so close that Shayna had planned to move in with her.

The thought twisted his gut. This one little fact, his belief that Shayna would have clued Cristine in, worried him more than anything else.

Glancing again at Zoe, he couldn't help but wonder how she and Cristine would get along. Both women thought of themselves as Shayna's best friend. They couldn't be more dissimilar, except for the fact that they both loved her.

Cocking his head, he listened to low murmur of

voices as Zoe and Mrs. Bell talked in the kitchen. The sound brought back old memories. As teens and young adults, he and Zoe and Shayna had spent a good bit of their time hanging out at the Bells' house. Partly because of Mama Bell's amazing cooking, and partly because the place always felt warm and welcoming, Brock had come to consider it his second home.

As nostalgia filled him, he grimaced. He hadn't even realized how much he'd missed those days. Or that part of them, at least. He was over the Zoe part. Completely.

A few minutes later, he heard the sizzle of the frying pan, and then the heavenly smell of Mama Bell's fried chicken filled the air.

On cue, his stomach growled, making him grimace at himself. Suddenly the delectable fried chicken had become a gateway to a past he'd put behind him. Life had been…good. He had a routine, a rhythmic sameness to his days that felt soothing, and maybe just the tiniest bit boring.

Not anymore. Now that very same peaceful existence had been turned on its ear. He didn't like change. Never had. But starting with Shayna's abrupt disappearance, his ordinary life had been thrown into upheaval. He'd tried searching for her, just as he had for Zoe when she'd left. Both times, he'd found nothing but heartache.

Now Zoe was here. Zoe, whom he'd loved more than life itself.

And, though she had no idea, he owed her. It had been because of her prodding that he'd gone to broadcast school after graduating high school, because of her bugging him that he'd applied for an internship at a radio station in one of the largest markets in the country. He'd been accepted right after she abandoned him before their wedding. Of course, fate had other ideas. As he'd been packing to move to New York City, his father had suffered a massive heart attack and died, leaving Brock to pick up the pieces. Someone had to run the feed store and take care of his younger sister Eve, who'd only been thirteen at the time.

Reluctantly, Brock had given up his dreams. He worked occasionally on the night shift at a local country music station, when he wasn't running the feed store. Unlike Zoe, he'd stayed right here in Anniversary, where he had family and responsibilities. His aging mother and baby sister depended on him, as did the local farmers and ranchers who relied on the feed store for their supplies.

While it wasn't the life he'd wanted, it was the life he had. Brock believed he'd made the best of it. He'd even managed to find a sort of happiness. Or so he'd thought, until he'd seen Zoe's face again.

He could only hope Shayna showed back up. Maybe then Zoe would go home, Mr. Bell wouldn't feel compelled to leave, and life around Anniversary could return to normal.

Except for one thing. Seeing Zoe again had reopened that aching, empty space inside his heart, the place only she could fill. He'd managed to forget how much he missed her. Until now.

And he sure as hell didn't like it. Not one bit.

If not for the tantalizing scent of the chicken frying, he'd have already made an excuse to leave. Instead, he was still lost in thought when Mrs. Bell reappeared in the doorway. "We're just about ready. Are you going to join us?"

"Yes. Sorry." He set the flyer down on the coffee table. "I was just…thinking."

Mrs. Bell smiled sadly and touched his arm. "You miss her, too, don't you?"

Startled, he swallowed. It took a second, but he realized she meant Shayna, not Zoe. Again, guilt squeezed his chest. Instead of answering, he ducked his head and headed toward the kitchen.

A heaping platter of perfectly golden fried chicken sat in the middle of the table. Keeping his gaze locked on that rather than Zoe, who stood at the stove stirring something, Brock took a seat. His mouth watered.

"That looks wonderful, Mrs. Bell."

"I made rice and butter beans to go with it," she said, glancing at her watch. "Marshall's late. He'd better get here soon or he's going to miss his favorite meal."

Brock debated whether or not to mention that Marshall had been in to the feed store, but kept his mouth shut. He wasn't running interference for the man.

Zoe moved closer, taking a seat directly across from him. He looked up, unable to help himself, and his mouth went dry. With her delicate features and full mouth, she'd always been beautiful—now she was exquisite. Her skin glowed against a soft curtain of sable hair. She was polished and fashionable in a way that only served to remind him she didn't belong in Anniversary.

"Help yourself." Mrs. Bell pulled out her own chair, passing Brock a bowl full of plump butter beans. "You'll have to take a plate to Eve. Her apartment is on your way home. I know how your sister loves my fried chicken."

"Everyone loves your fried chicken," Zoe teased. Her lighthearted tone reminded him of the old Zoe, the one who'd spent the day at the lake with him, worn old cut-off shorts and one of his ratty T-shirts, and let the sun warm her freckled nose. Now, as far as he could tell, not a single imperfection marred her perfect, creamy skin.

"I wonder where Marshall is," Mrs. Bell mused again. "It's not like him to be this late without calling."

"Try his cell," Zoe said, wiping her hands on one of the paper napkins piled in the center of the table.

"No, that's all right." A shadow crossed the older woman's face. "He'll come home when he comes home."

Zoe stared hard at her, then returned her attention to spooning rice and butter beans onto her plate. When she'd finished, she slid the bowls over to him, taking care not to accidentally touch his fingers.

He was glad, he told himself. Damn glad.

Silence fell while they all dug in. The crispy chicken had been cooked exactly right, and the seasoning made the flavor explode in his mouth. He had three pieces and could easily have had more, but he didn't want to appear gluttonous.

"That was wonderful," he said, putting down his fork and pushing his plate away. "I'm stuffed. Thank you so much for inviting me."

"Oh, you're welcome, dear." Mrs. Bell looked from him to Zoe and then back. "So." Her smile looked a bit forced, and her voice sounded overly bright. "Zoe tells me you and Shayna were splitting up."

He glanced over at Zoe, who shrugged.

"We were." He cleared his throat. "She was planning on moving out. I'm sorry she didn't tell you."

"Apparently there were a lot of things she didn't tell me." Her mouth twisted and for one awful minute he thought she might cry. "I just wish she'd told me where she was going, if she did leave town like everyone seems to think. She sure didn't take an awful lot with her."

Brock nodded. Only a few of Shayna's clothes were missing. A weekend's worth, both he and Cristine had estimated. Not enough to account for the amount of time she'd been away, but indicative of the fact that she hadn't intended on returning to the apartment right away.

Zoe reached over and covered the older woman's hand with her own. "Don't worry, Mama Bell. We'll find her, I promise."

Her words had Brock clenching his jaw against the urge to tell her not to make promises she couldn't keep. But Zoe had always been impulsive and passionate. She truly believed what she said, he could tell. And who was he to say she was wrong?

Assuming Shayna wanted to be found.

Zoe jumped to her feet. "I'll take care of the dishes. You go and rest, Mama."

"Oh, no. That's not necessary." Mrs. Bell waved her away, her expression sad. "You're a guest in this house. You should be the one to go sit down. I imagine you and Brock have a lot of planning to do. Though I'm grateful Cristine is organizing things, I have more faith in the two of you."

Brock watched with interest as Zoe's blush deepened. "You did all the cooking. Now go sit. I insist," Brock said.

Her refusal to look at him felt like a knife twisting in his gut. He knew there was more to why she'd run off, virtually leaving him at the altar, despite her partial explanation. And now she'd come back, believing he was marrying her best friend, and treated him like a stranger.

Worse, now Shayna had gone missing right after he'd broken things off between them. He, more than anyone, knew the awfulness of that.

"I've got to get going," he said, pushing to his feet. "Thank you so much, Mrs. Bell. Your chicken is still the best in Texas."

The older woman's eyes narrowed. "Thanks, but why are you in such a hurry to run off? I thought you and Zoe could compare notes and maybe work out a plan to find Shayna."

His chest felt tight. Careful to keep his gaze trained only on Mrs. Bell, he shook his head. "We'll do that tomorrow, at Cristine's thing."

He wasn't sure how he felt about the way she eyed him then. As if she could see his torment, knew his guilt.

"I understand." She patted his cheek. "I'm so glad you could stay and eat."

"Thank you again." He couldn't get out of there fast enough. As soon as he got home, he planned to pop a beer, make a few more phone calls trying to locate Shayna, and work on forgetting Zoe had ever come back to town.

Chapter 3

One of the bad things about having an extremely popular blog, Zoe thought, was the need to update it every single day. Though that had become easier since the blog's advertising revenue had enabled her to quit her day job. She'd divided her site into sections, calling one "Observations," another one "Fashion Picks," and a third "Things I Like."

According to her stats, most people visited the site for the "Observations" section, where she let herself go, writing about whatever topic interested her at the moment. Since she wrote *City Girl* anonymously, she never held back, whether writing about matters of the heart or sniping at life's minor irritations.

About a month before Shayna disappeared, Zoe had acquired a literary agent who'd been shopping a proposal based on her blog posts for a book deal. So far they'd garnered several rejections, but the agent remained hopeful.

Zoe already had the outline finished for a second book, in case the first one sold. She was glad she'd gotten that done before Shayna disappeared.

Now she had a few hours before she had to attend Cristine's gathering. She wrote a quick blog post, one from the heart, talking about the value of best friends and how one doesn't always appreciate what one has until it's gone. After she'd finished and published it, having written it with Shayna in mind, she could only hope her friend would somehow see it and come home.

Then Zoe closed her laptop and prepared to leave. Mama Bell waited in the living room, dressed and ready.

As they arrived at the time stated on the flyer, Zoe couldn't believe the packed parking lot. She circled until she found a space, parked and then hurried around to open the door for Mama Bell, who waved her away.

"Cristine sure got a good turnout," she said.

Mama Bell nodded. "Everyone loves Shayna. Even though most everybody thinks she took off of her own free will, they all want to do what they can to help."

Stunned, Zoe nodded. This made no sense. If Shayna was anywhere in town, she'd have put in an appearance before now. Together they went inside. Immediately, Mrs. Bell spotted a group of her church friends. "Excuse me, honey," she said, patting Zoe's arm. "You go ahead and mingle. I'm sure a lot of folks will be glad to see you."

Though Zoe doubted that, especially since she'd left without a word to anyone, she gave a fond smile and moved away, listening to snatches of conversations as she wove through the throng. The parallel between her disappearance five years ago and Shayna's now was worrying her. Not because she believed it, but because she didn't. Everyone in Anniversary appeared to think Shayna had simply taken off. Zoe hoped that was true. The alternative was unbearable.

A woman came up, tall, wearing skintight jeans and a low-cut T-shirt. Smoothing her sleek cap of shoulder-length hair, she gave a faint smile and wrapped her arms around Zoe. After a second of hesitation, Zoe hugged her back.

"Zoe! So good to see you. I'm glad you were able to make it back and help bring Shayna home."

Zoe nodded, wishing for name tags. "Of course. I'm sorry, you are…?"

At her words, the woman's smile widened. "You don't recognize me, do you?"

"No." Zoe frowned. "You do look familiar, but I just can't place…"

"Cristine, where are the sign-up sheets?" Brock said, as he came up to them.

"Cristine?" Stunned, Zoe tried not to show it. "Cristine Haywood?"

The woman's smile widened. "That's me."

"Shayna's best friend," Brock supplied.

The sound of his voice sent a pleasurable shiver through Zoe. To hide her reaction, she focused on Cristine, who looked nothing at all like the awkward girl she remembered from years past.

"I don't know what to say," Zoe began. "You look totally different than you did in—"

"High school." Dipping her head as though Zoe's words had embarrassed her, Cristine smiled shyly before turning her attention to Brock. "The sign-up sheets are on the table by the refreshments."

He gave a curt nod before turning away. Unable to keep from watching him go, Zoe wondered why she got the feeling he didn't much like Cristine.

When she looked up, she noticed Cristine also silently watching him walk away, her expression a mixture of regret and dislike. Apparently the feeling was mutual.

"He can be such an ass," Cristine said, catching Zoe eyeing her. "Seriously. If Shayna were here, she'd tell you."

"Is he always like that?" Zoe asked, before she thought better of it. The Brock she remembered had been happy-go-lucky rather than irritable.

"Sometimes." Cristine shrugged. "He's pretty moody. I honestly don't know how Shayna put up with it."

Interesting. Zoe filed that bit of information away. She'd ask Shayna about it later, after she was found. Which she would be, Zoe had no doubt. Whether to deal with the pain of realizing her relationship with Brock would never be more than friendship, or something else, eventually Shayna would tire of hiding and return home.

The only troubling detail with this scenario was the apparent fact that either Brock was not telling the truth, or pretty much every word Shayna had told Zoe in their last few conversations had been a lie.

So what was going on? Maybe Cristine would know. Zoe just had to figure out how to ask her.

While she considered this, someone called Cristine

away. "We'll catch up later," she told Zoe, and hurried off.

Zoe continued on, still listening rather than interacting with people. She needed to talk to Brock. See if she could get a feel for whether or not he was telling the truth.

Searching the crowded room, she found him on the other side. Somehow, their gazes locked. Even now, when she wasn't entirely sure he hadn't had something to do with Shayna's disappearance, a shiver of wanting ran through her, all the way from her heart to the soles of her feet.

Damn. She'd told herself a thousand times she wouldn't let this happen. But she no more knew how to stop it than she knew how to quit breathing.

Giving herself a mental shake, she wished she could avoid him totally. But she couldn't. She needed to talk to him, to try to discern truth from lies. Despite the fact that the old attraction still lingered, she had no choice. As Shayna's former boyfriend, he would have a better insight than others.

She caught up with him near the sign-up table. "Do you have a minute?" she asked, after carefully penning her name directly underneath his.

He gave her a decidedly unfriendly look. "For what?"

Refusing to let his attitude bother her, she took a deep breath. "I wanted to ask you a few more questions about Shayna, if you don't mind."

Apparently he did. Just like that, his expression shut down. Alarm bells went off inside her. Why was he acting like this? Did he have something to hide?

"Why are you here?" he asked, sounding stiff. "And don't tell me you and Shayna were still as close as you used to be, because she told me how you'd cut her out of your life."

Dumbfounded, Zoe was too stunned to hide her shock. Slowly, she shook her head. "I never cut her out of my life. Sure, we didn't talk as much as we used to, but we were still close. Or so I thought."

He crossed his arms, giving her a look that told her he didn't believe her. She didn't care; she wasn't entirely sure she believed him, either.

"What happened?" she finally asked. "I know you said you two were splitting up. What else was going on that would make her want to go into hiding like that?"

"First off, let me reiterate again—Shayna and I didn't work out. We were never engaged. She was moving on and moving out. As to what else was going on in your *best friend's* life, I can see you have no idea," he muttered. "Really, if you're basing your information on what she was like in the past, you didn't know Shayna at all."

If he thought his harsh tone and narrowed eyes would scare her away, he had no idea how far she could go.

"Then tell me," she pushed, wishing she dared touch him. She considered herself a brave person, but even she wouldn't go that far. "Fill me in on what was going on."

But he simply shook his head and walked away, his entire body stiff and unfriendly. Despite that, she ached to go after him, if only for the simple excuse of touching his skin.

Damn. This yearning for the past needed to stop. Obviously, she wouldn't be getting any help from him without a battle, which was understandable. She couldn't blame him for still holding a grudge against her for what had happened between them five years ago.

Though she hadn't stayed in touch with him—her heart had been too broken—Shayna had kept her filled in on what was going on in Brock's life. As far as she knew, he was happy and content with his life. He didn't seem the type to be carrying a torch for anyone.

Unfortunately, she was definitely the type to pine for someone. Brock McCauley had been the love of her life. She'd never met anyone else who even came close to measuring up.

He'd obviously moved on. It had to be something else, some other reason he refused to discuss Shayna with her.

Again, the prickling sense of unease. No, she told herself. Not Brock. It had to be something else. Maybe whatever had driven a wedge between him and Shayna had hurt him. He had to be saying there'd been no engagement to mask the pain he must have endured when Shayna broke things off.

That made sense. Zoe looked once more for Brock, unable to find him in the crowd. He had to be lying. Because the Shayna she'd known all her life was giving and generous, happy and carefree. And she didn't tell her best friend outright lies or keep secrets.

"Wow. What'd you do to set him off?" Cristine appeared again, right behind Zoe, as though she'd been watching and waiting for the opportunity. "Then again, it doesn't take much these days."

Trying not to show her irritation, Zoe shrugged. "I have no idea. I simply asked him something about Shayna."

A shadow crossed Cristine's face. "Oh. That would do it. He and Shayna weren't getting along at all."

Debating, Zoe decided against asking Cristine if

Shayna had told her she and Brock were engaged. In view of Brock's denial, and Mama Bell's shock, that particular bit of information could wait.

"You and Shayna were good friends?" Zoe asked.

Cristine's sallow complexion lit up. "*Best* friends," she emphasized. "We ran around together every single weekend."

Zoe cocked her head. "What did you two do?"

Cristine's smile widened proudly. "Party. Though I tried to keep up with her, Shayna could drink me under the table."

"Oh." Zoe wasn't sure how to respond to that. "So do you have any idea what might have happened to her?"

"Zoe, Shayna was worried." Cristine looked around, her furtive behavior making Zoe tense up. "You might as well know that we—she and I—experimented a little with drugs."

At Zoe's dismayed expression, Cristine shook her head. "Oh, nothing serious. A little X, some weed, the occasional hit of crank."

Nothing serious? While Zoe was still trying to process this, Cristine took her arm. "She was worried about something, but she wouldn't tell me much more than that."

Damn. Zoe's heart skipped a beat. Yet again, the last conversation she'd had with Shayna replayed in her mind. She should have listened, should have done something. Maybe if she had, Shayna would still be here.

Guilt flooded her. Then, as blood rushed to her head, she inhaled deeply, trying to catch her breath.

"Zoe?" Cristine leaned in, peering at Zoe's face. "Are you all right?"

"Yes. No," Zoe said, taking a deep breath. "Cristine,

what's the deal with the sheriff's office? Mama Bell says they're not exactly helping to find her."

Cristine grabbed her arm. "They say since Shayna's an adult and has been talking about leaving town, she probably just took off. They won't take us seriously." She sounded bitter.

Zoe shook her off. "Why the hell not? Shayna is missing. How can they dispute that?"

"According to them, an adult has the right to go anywhere they want without telling anyone where they went. Without evidence of foul play…" For a second time Cristine looked around, lowering her voice. "Part of it might be that Shayna was seeing Roger Giles, the new sheriff."

Dumbfounded, Zoe narrowed her eyes. "Recently?"

"Yes."

Oh jeez, this really didn't sound like the Shayna Zoe knew. "You're telling me she was seeing someone behind Brock's back. Was this before or after they broke up?"

"Who knows?" Cristine gave a brittle laugh. "Honey, Shayna was seeing lots of people behind Brock's back."

"Brock told me they'd become like roommates."

"Okay." Cristine gave a short bark of laughter. "But she was still living there. I told her to wait until she moved out. For Brock, I think it was a slap in the face."

Gut twisting, Zoe nodded. "So you're telling me Shayna was…cheating?" She could scarcely say the word. The Shayna she knew despised both liars and cheaters.

"No, not cheating. Shayna wasn't exclusive with anyone. She made that clear up front. Roger Giles was aware he wasn't the only one. Brock knew it, too, though he wasn't too happy about it."

Zoe had to give Cristine credit for sticking by her friend. In fact, Cristine actually managed to sound indignant.

"What about Brock?" Zoe asked. "You say he knew she wasn't exclusive, but was he aware of all this?"

Cristine shrugged. "It wasn't that way in the beginning. The two of them tried, they really tried. All I know is Shayna was pretty devastated when she and Brock didn't work out. At first, I think she started fooling around trying to make him jealous." She shrugged. "Or maybe she was getting even. Who knows?"

Zoe didn't know what to say.

Again, Cristine leaned closer. "Think whatever you want to about her, but I can tell you this much. Shayna sure knew how to live life to the fullest. She and I had a lot of good times together." Wiping a tear from her eye, she looked away. "That's why I don't believe she left willingly. She has to be in trouble. Otherwise, she would have let me know. We were best friends."

So were we, Zoe added silently. *Once.* Only now she was finding out she really didn't know Shayna at all. The woman she thought she knew was turning out to be a remnant of the past.

Scary thought. Just like with Mama Bell, Shayna had shut Zoe completely out of the truth about her life.

Drugs. Alcohol. Sex with random men.

Zoe's mother had been a party girl. Zoe could only hope Shayna hadn't gotten mixed up with the same type of people. After all, that was the reason Zoe's mother had ended up dead, with her killer in prison.

Zoe made a mental note to check online later and

make sure nothing had changed. The last time he'd come up before the parole board, he'd been denied.

Meanwhile, Cristine watched her like a hawk. A concerned, slightly ditzy hawk, but closely nonetheless.

"I'm still going to talk to the police," Zoe repeated. "Now, please excuse me."

Cristine stared and then nodded. "Let me come with you."

Glancing around the crowded room full of people she should recognize but didn't, Zoe shook her head. "Thank you, but that's not necessary. You've got plenty to occupy you here. I'll handle this on my own."

Cristine dipped her chin, swallowing hard. "But you are signing up to help search, right?"

"Of course." Zoe forced a smile and gestured to the line at the sign-up table. "Judging from the size of this turnout, you should have a ton of people show up tomorrow to assist."

Cristine bit her lip. "About that. Will you help me organize it?" she blurted. "I want Shayna found, and no one else besides you and Mrs. Bell is taking her disappearance seriously."

Surprised, Zoe considered. What Cristine said made sense. Still, until she got a better feel for things, Zoe preferred to go it on her own. "I don't know," she finally said. "It looks to me like you have everything pretty much under control."

Then, before Cristine could say anything else, Zoe turned and hurried away.

Rushing outside, she nearly ran into Brock. Immediately, she felt a tingle of excitement low in her belly, which she ignored.

"Leaving already?" he asked, blocking her way and making no effort to move.

She tried to catch her breath, nodded and kept her expression impassive. It wouldn't be a good thing if Brock learned how her body still reacted to him. "I thought I'd head over to the police station and see if I can light a fire under them."

"Good idea." He fell into step beside her. "It's a short walk. Do you mind if I go with you?"

Would wonders never cease? Suddenly everyone wanted to go with her to the police department. First Cristine, and now Brock. She had to wonder if ulterior motives might be involved.

Glancing at Brock, his ruggedly handsome profile strong and rigid, his massive shoulders stretching the cotton of his button-down shirt, Zoe again quelled her inner quivering. She tried to be objective—as if they hadn't shared a past—and debated asking him if he knew about Shayna and the sheriff. In the end, she decided against it. She wasn't yet positive it was the truth.

"If you want," she answered, turning away, unable to keep looking at him, hating how badly that hurt. "Though judging how you've been acting since I got here, I can't help but wonder why you'd want to go anywhere with me."

He touched her shoulder, making her jump and face him. From his expression, he wasn't too happy about her statement.

Tough. She'd only spoken the truth.

"Look, Zoe," he began, his husky, Southern-accented voice both familiar and exotic. "Though I'm of the opinion Shayna took off with some guy for an extended vacation, I still want her found. Just because we weren't getting along doesn't mean I'm not worried about her."

Interesting. Now she definitely had to wonder what he was hiding. And he *was* hiding something, of that she had no doubt. "I'm glad to hear you say that," she said, deciding to test his veracity. "The way I see it, we're going to have to put our differences aside so we can work together. Don't you agree?"

His face revealed his surprise, and he slowly nodded. Of course, he had no idea that the look in his eyes plainly communicated the opposite. Work together? He might as well have given her a hell, no. At least that would have been truthful.

"I have to admit I could use your help sometimes," she continued, again speaking only the truth. "I'm getting too many conflicting stories."

He gave a heavy sigh. "I have a feeling I know what you mean."

"Do you?" Now would be the perfect time to find out his version of the truth. "What exactly happened between you and Shayna?"

"That's private, between me and her. None of your business."

"It is my business if it has something to do with her disappearance. What happened, Brock?"

He took a deep breath and then shook his head. "Look, Zoe, you turned your back on me, on us and on this town. People around here might be more forgiving, or they might tell you all of this is none of your business. I don't know why Mama Bell called you or even why you came. As far as I'm concerned, you've amply demonstrated you don't give a damn about any of us."

His words hung there, lodging in the empty space

inside her heart. She shriveled a little at his tone, but then she'd known coming back wouldn't be easy. He might not like it, but she knew she needed to probe into the relationship between her missing friend and her former fiancé. If she wanted to gain insight into what had happened to Shayna, she would have to ask difficult questions. And if Brock wanted her found, he'd have to answer them.

They started walking, side by side, close but not touching in any way. She felt unsettled, as though his body exerted some sort of gravitational pull on hers. "What do you mean, you know what I'm talking about?"

Not looking at her, he responded. "Shayna had gone wild. Cristine was her partner in crime. They were into drugs, alcohol and one-night stands. I couldn't exactly stop her, but I could make her keep it out of my apartment. She couldn't wait to move out."

Again, nothing should have surprised her, but she found it hard to reconcile the Brock she'd once known putting up with the kind of behavior Cristine had ascribed to Shayna. And what had her best friend been thinking? None of this even remotely made sense.

But then again, people changed. Everyone did. Including her. Except for one thing. Who would have guessed that she'd still get that internal zing straight to the heart every time she even looked at Brock?

As they neared the building that housed the Anniversary police station, Zoe had to wonder if it wasn't entirely possible Brock knew about Shayna and the chief and had come along to enact some sort of testosterone pissing contest.

But then again, pulling something like that off surrounded by armed officers of the law would be more than foolish—it would be downright suicidal.

She needed to calm her overactive imagination and find out what the Anniversary police department was doing to help find her friend.

And she suddenly realized this was one thing she'd be better off handling by herself. As it stood, she suspected Brock's motives for the abrupt about-face. After all, why would he want to work together with the woman who'd basically left him at the altar? Especially if—she shot a quick sideways glance at him—Shayna had been cheating on him constantly?

"Wait." Without thinking, she touched his arm, nearly gasping at the sizzle that ran up her fingers straight to her heart. "I think I'd rather do this alone."

"Of course you would," he responded, the crease between his brows revealing his displeasure. Though he didn't move, she could see him visibly withdraw.

Fighting the odd urge to apologize, she nodded. Good. Maybe now she could breathe. After all, there was no sense in letting him get too close. He might be the man who'd made her friend disappear—and still she was attracted to him.

"Look, Zoe," Brock said. "Whatever went wrong between us, Shayna matters now. Nothing else."

"You're right," she said. "But I honestly think this is something I need to do on my own."

"Fine." Crossing his arms, he gave her a hard look. "Call me if you need me."

After a second of hesitation, Zoe agreed.

Once inside, she saw several people she recognized, more proof that life in a small town remained essentially the same.

"Can I help you?" a woman asked, her voice cool. Great. Agnes Caliburton from high school. She'd been part of a gang of girls who'd tormented Zoe to no end, simply because Zoe had been pretty.

Zoe pretended not to recognize her. "Yes. I'm here to see the sheriff." In the old days, when Renee Beauchamp had run the place, Zoe could have just walked right in. Apparently not anymore.

Agnes stared, her expression hard. "Do you have an appointment?"

Zoe met her gaze and held it. "No. But I'm sure he'll see me. Tell him Zoe Onella is here to see him."

Agnes didn't move. "Regarding?"

"Shayna Bell." Crossing her arms, Zoe waited, practically daring the woman to say anything else.

Instead, Agnes spun on her heel and headed toward the back.

Leaning on the counter, Zoe waited.

A moment later, Agnes returned, the downward twist of her mouth showing her displeasure. "Follow me," she said, lifting a part of the counter so Zoe could go through.

A few paces behind Agnes, Zoe kept her gaze straight-ahead, well aware of the curious stares of the half-a-dozen officers milling about in the common room.

When they turned left, into a short hallway, Agnes stopped short of knocking on the closed door. "Here you go," she said, and beat a hasty retreat, leaving Zoe unannounced.

Fine. Rapping sharply on the door, Zoe waited until the man inside spoke before turning the handle and entering.

She stopped short at her first sight of Shayna's lover, assuming what Cristine had told her was true. Blond and deeply tanned, he had the look of a Colorado ski instructor or golf pro. His sparkling blue eyes were friendly and his smile warm. Not at all what she'd expected.

But then what had she thought? That Shayna would cheat on Brock with a man who was ugly?

"What can I do for you, Ms. Onella?" he asked, his Texas drawl completely charming.

"Please, call me Zoe," she said automatically.

"Fine, Zoe. I'm Roger." He held out his hand and she shook it. "Agnes tells me you're here to talk about Shayna?"

"Yes." She searched his face for some hint of emotion at the name. "I don't know how else to put this, so I'm going to be blunt. I understand you and she... intimate?"

One corner of his mouth quirked as she felt her face redden. "We were friends with benefits, if that's what you mean. But I'm curious. Surely that's not what you came to talk to me about?"

Despite her discomfort, she held his gaze. "Isn't that a conflict of interest?"

"In what way? Shayna hasn't been charged with a crime."

"Actually, I came here to find out what your office is doing to find her."

"Everything we can, Zoe," he assured her, leaning back in his chair with his hands behind his head. "We have a missing persons report on file. Our hands are tied. Shayna is a grown woman who told many people she wanted to get out of town. There's no evidence of foul play or anything suspicious—"

"Something happened to her," Zoe interrupted. "Why can't you just consider that a possibility?"

He took a deep breath. "She never stopped talking about the fact that you did exactly what she longed to do. Not only did you get away, but you were living what she considered a glamorous life. I think she was envious of you. I think she left to try and make it on her own away from here."

Damn, that hurt. "Glamorous? I worked as an executive assistant. Plus, even if that was what happened, Shayna would never disappear without telling anyone where she was going."

"And how do you know she didn't?"

He wasn't taking her seriously and that infuriated her. "Because she had no reason to. Everyone she knew and loved is here. On top of that, her bank accounts haven't been touched. I'm willing to bet if you checked, you'd find the same with her credit cards."

"First off, we can't. Shayna has a right to privacy just like anyone else."

"What if her parents insist? Or Brock, since they were living together?"

"Shayna would have to give permission, whether verbal or otherwise. Since she did not…" He spread his hands. "We can do nothing."

"She would have called me," she insisted. "There's no way she would have left without at least letting me— or her mother—know."

"You can't be sure of that. Zoe, the Shayna I know is a restless, unhappy woman. She was, whether you knew it or not, insanely jealous of you and your success. She wanted to escape this town, this life." He shrugged. "That's one of the reasons why the relationship between us didn't work. I left Houston to escape the big city. I love Anniversary. She'd come to despise everything about it."

Despite herself, she recognized the validity of his statement. "You have a point," she grudgingly admitted. "But still…"

He stood, indicating the discussion was over. "I can promise you this, Zoe," he said. "The instant we have any reason to think differently, we'll expend every resource to make sure Shayna is found. But as it is…"

She dipped her chin. "I understand."

The sad thing was, she did. But on the other side, she wasn't sure she trusted Shayna's former lover to be in charge of searching for her.

Unfortunately, she was beginning to think the search would be pointless. All indications seemed to point to Shayna leaving town on her own, in much the same way that Zoe herself had done five years earlier.

Still, a niggling doubt remained. Mainly because no matter what Shayna might have become, Zoe knew she wouldn't have taken off without talking to her and she'd have put on a show for Zoe, at the least, which means she cared what Zoe thought. Whether Shayna lied or not, she'd clearly needed some kind of help all along. Now she was missing. Zoe's heart ached for her troubled friend.

So she would continue looking, no matter what. And, until she knew more, she'd hope for the best but suppose the worst.

Chapter 4

As Zoe left the police station and stepped outside into the bright sunshine, her cell phone rang. She didn't recognize the number but answered anyway.

"Zoe, it's Cristine." The other woman's words were rushed, as if she was nervous. "I need to talk to you."

"Okay." Zoe checked her watch. "I'm just leaving the police station. I can be back there in a few minutes."

"Oh, not here." Cristine coughed delicately. "It's too crowded. I'd like someplace a little more private."

Interesting. Zoe sensed it could be important, but still needed clarification. "Is this about Shayna?"

"Yes. I'm tied up with this until late this afternoon. We've already started organizing some searches, though the big one will be on Saturday, when everyone is off work. How about we meet for breakfast tomorrow morning? How about Joe's coffee shop?"

"Joe's is still there?" Zoe and the Bell family had spent many a Sunday morning at that diner. "From what I remember, it's always really crowded."

"On weekends, yes," Cristine said. "But since tomorrow is Friday, if we go right after the morning rush, say about eight-thirty, it will be fairly empty. We should be able to have a private conversation with minimal interruptions."

"Sounds good." Ending the call, Zoe didn't see the need to head back to the high school. At this point, it appeared she was on her own. She texted Mama Bell, letting her know to take the car whenever she was ready to go. Mama replied almost immediately with an okay and a smiley face.

Relieved, Zoe popped into the corner gas station and purchased a bottle of water. She set out, glad of the alone time, planning to walk back to the Bells' house at a leisurely pace. It was probably just over a mile and she knew she could use the exercise. She walked a lot in the city and not only was the movement therapeutic, it always helped clear her head.

And she certainly had a lot to think about.

As she left downtown behind, she realized she'd always considered Shayna fragile. Zoe loved her like a sister—and always would, no matter what. The woman Shayna had apparently become proved that point. From what Zoe had heard, Shayna was more fragile than ever, doing drugs, sleeping around—and disappearing.

What the hell had happened to make her change so completely? Had it been Brock, as Cristine had hinted? Or jealousy over Zoe's life, like the sheriff thought? Or was it something more, something no one yet realized or understood, that same something that had made her tell Zoe she needed her? Zoe suspected if she learned the secret to that, she might find out what had become of her friend.

Emotions—chief among them jumbled regret and longing—swamped Brock as he'd watched Zoe stride into the sheriff's office. Was she playing some sort of game with him? First she'd asked for his help and then, barely a minute later, told him she'd changed her mind.

And she'd claimed they needed to *put their differences aside?* As if what had happened between them was that simple.

Did she not understand that she'd freakin' ripped out his heart? That every time he saw her and she gave him that patently false smile, he wanted to haul her up against him and kiss her senseless, before shoving her away and then daring her to tell him that he meant nothing to her. Did she not realize she was the reason he couldn't love Shayna the way she deserved, and, worse, that Shayna had guessed it, too?

Of course, he couldn't. Not when the *only* reason Zoe had returned was because her friend Shayna had gone missing.

Another twist of the knife in his heart, knowing she hadn't come back for him. Worse, Zoe couldn't see the parallel between how she'd behaved then and what Shayna appeared to have done now.

Disappeared without a word to the ones who loved her.

He'd tortured himself for months after Zoe left. Searched high and low, hounded Shayna and the Bells for some hint, any hint of where she'd gone. He'd planned to find her, demand an explanation, ask her to look him in the eye, kiss him on the mouth, and then tell him she didn't love him, didn't want to be his wife.

After a while, tired of spinning his wheels, he'd tried to drown his sorrows in the bottle. His sister Eve had been the one to pull him from the abyss when he'd hit rock bottom. With both their parents dead, she needed him more than he needed oblivion. So he'd returned home to raise Eve and nurse his broken heart. As the years had passed, he'd come to believe that, even if not entirely whole, he had healed as best he could.

He'd been wrong.

Her mere presence had brought it all rushing back.

Cursing, he felt like punching something. He wanted Shayna found as much as anyone else did, but for sanity's sake, he needed to spend as little time around Zoe as possible.

Instead of going home, he headed for TJ's Brew Pub. Though he hadn't been to the place in months—no, make that years—the bartender Jason, who was the *J* in TJ's, welcomed him as if he was an old friend.

Which he sort of was, since they'd gone to high school together.

"What'll it be?" Jason asked, only his narrowed eyes indicating how apprehensive he was about the answer. He rubbed his bald head quickly, the gesture born of habit. Even back when he'd had hair, Jason had always rubbed his head.

"Club soda," Brock told him, giving him a twisted grin. "Don't worry, I'm not falling off the wagon any time soon." He'd been sober three years and counting.

"I'm glad," Jason countered, grinning back. He brought the club soda and placed it on the counter.

"Though I had to wonder, man. I mean, you coming into the bar and all."

"I wanted to test myself." Brock picked up the club soda and took a drink. "Plus, sometimes I miss the atmosphere." To his surprise, the words rang of truth. He hadn't thought of anything beyond going inside the pub, as if the dim light and the seventies-style paneled walls represented a safe haven.

In the old days, they had. But then, so had alcohol.

"Hey, I'm hearing things." Jason leaned closer, lowering his voice to a conspiratorial near whisper. "How are you dealing with Zoe Onella being back in town?"

Brock stifled a groan. Even here, he couldn't escape her.

"Fine," he said. "Just fine."

TJ's was empty, the after-work crowd still glued to their desks and computers. A few die-hard souls dotted the interior, intent on the beer or their laptops, mostly alone, though Brock spotted one couple snuggling in a back booth, giggling over a pizza and a couple of brews.

He'd always loved the taste of beer. Even now, though he hadn't drank one in years, his mouth watered.

With the ease of much practice, he pushed the craving away. He'd heard it never left you, this almost obscene yearning for alcohol. Kind of like the way he felt about Zoe.

Damn. Cursing under his breath, he took another drink, glad Jason had moved away to help another customer. He'd just gotten his world whipped into shape. While he couldn't say he was truly happy, he was content. He had the feed store, his mother and sister, and his weekend gig at the college radio station. That was enough. It had to be, because that was all he had.

He cursed the day Zoe had come back into town and started him once again wanting more.

Morning arrived silently in Anniversary, the only hint of its arrival a shaft of yellow light. Stretching, Zoe reflected on how she missed mornings in Manhattan. There, the noise built like a crescendo, rising in waves and pulling you from your nest under the covers. She found it invigorating, emerging from her apartment onto the bustling street, the sounds of the city a shot of adrenaline straight into her veins.

Here, she had to rely on coffee. Strong coffee. She had a cup at Mama Bell's before driving into town to meet Cristine. She took the cup with her, sipping as she drove.

Still she felt half-asleep as she negotiated the surprisingly crowded downtown area. It took her a few minutes to find a parking spot. Once she had, she slugged back the rest of the coffee, aware there'd be more.

Stepping into the coffee shop felt like hopping backward in time. A blast from the past at Joe's. It ought to be their slogan. Glancing around, Zoe could swear the same people in the various red vinyl booths had been here the last time she'd come, over five years ago.

"Well, I'll be... Zoe Onella?" Hand on one cocked hip, the other holding a steaming pot of coffee, Patsy O'Brien flipped her long, gray braid out of the way and grinned. "Have a seat anywhere, sugar. Let me guess, cheese blintzes with blueberries, right?"

Zoe nodded. Though she'd originally planned on having a sensible breakfast of scrambled egg substitute with turkey bacon and wheat toast, she suddenly craved the comfort food of her youth.

"Zoe, over here." Cristine waved from a booth near the back. Today, she'd lightened up on the heavy black eyeliner, though apparently she still favored low-cut shirts and push up bras.

Zoe hurried over and slid in.

"Coffee?" Cristine passed a cup over to her. Accepting gratefully, Zoe caught Patsy's eye. The older woman bustled over, filled the cup and sighed. "Look at you, all sophisticated and everything. Maybe when the breakfast rush slows down, I'll have time to chat." And she hurried off, to Zoe's relief.

"You do look different," Cristine mused. "Of course, you were always pretty, even back in high school. But now you look so…citified."

Not sure if the statement was an insult or a compliment, Zoe only sipped her coffee and nodded. Then, because she wanted to focus the conversation where it belonged, she leaned forward. "How was Shayna acting these last few weeks? Did she say or do anything unusual?"

"You mean something to let me know she was planning on running off?" Pursing her lips, Cristine considered the question. "Well, she had been acting worried. She had a bit of a run-in with a drug dealer. That's never good. She owed him money and wasn't sure how she'd come up with it."

At the words, Zoe's stomach clenched and she closed her eyes. Again, it was hammered home to her how much Shayna had changed. Shayna had known the adverse effect drugs had had on Zoe's life. Zoe's mother had been an addict and had done prison time, before being released and then murdered by her dealer in front of Zoe.

She couldn't believe Shayna had sunk that low.

"Are you sure?" she heard herself ask, even though she knew Cristine had to be.

"Yes." Cristine bit her lip. "But no worries. I covered it for her. I loaned her the money and she'd already started paying me back."

"Did she?" Zoe felt a flash of anger and let it show in her voice.

Cristine looked down. "Yes."

Hurt and angry and confused, Zoe sighed.

"Hey." Cristine's sweet Southern drawl brought her out of her thoughts. "Are you okay? You looked kind of out of it for a minute there."

"I was just thinking about the past." Before she could say anything else, Patsy appeared with their food.

"Here you go, sugar." She set a plate with three cheese blintzes covered with blueberries and whipped cream in front of Zoe. "Now you try and eat all of this, you hear? You are looking way too skinny these days."

Zoe nodded, unable to keep from smiling. In New York, everyone she knew was obsessed with remaining svelte. Hearing Patsy call her too thin was like balm on her soul.

Obligingly, she dug in. Across from her, Cristine stared at her omelet before finally picking up a piece of crispy bacon and crunching it between her teeth.

At least the arrival of their breakfast had saved them from further conversation. Zoe still had no idea why Cristine wanted to meet with her privately. Though she knew things moved much slower here in Texas than they did up north, she needed to try and pry that out of her.

Eventually, Patsy cleared their plates, refilled their

coffee and left the check, expressing her regret that she was still too busy to stay and chat.

Taking a deep drink of coffee, finally feeling caffeinated, Zoe glanced at her watch before extracting a twenty from her wallet to pay for the meal. Funny how this exact same breakfast in Manhattan would have cost twice as much. "Cristine, was there a reason you wanted to meet me for breakfast? If not, I've really got to get going."

Leaning back in the booth, Cristine arched her brows. "Yes, Zoe. I did need to discuss something with you. I'm sorry I didn't bring it up sooner, but it's difficult for me to say."

Watching her, Zoe waited.

After getting no response, Cristine continued. "I think I know what happened to Shayna, though I don't know if she ran off or was abducted."

"Abducted?" Zoe sucked in her breath. "Why are you telling me this? Don't you think you should go to the police?"

"I don't have concrete evidence." Cristine grimaced, looking uncomfortable. "Only my suspicions."

Crap. Torn between wanting to believe her and demanding Cristine march right down to the police station this instant, Zoe leaned close. "Tell me what you know," she said. "Then maybe we'll go talk to the sheriff together."

"Okay." Relief colored Cristine's voice. "Shayna was friends with a lot of men, you know?"

Zoe nodded. "Go on."

"Well, she'd been hanging around with this biker who did a lot of work for the local dealer."

Could this get any worse? Somehow, Zoe suspected it could and would.

"What's the biker's name?" she asked.

"Mike." Cristine sighed. "I haven't seen him around at all since Shayna disappeared. That dude is really good-looking, but jealous as hell. And like I told you, Shayna doesn't make any long-term commitments."

"What about Brock?" Zoe pointed out. "Shayna moved in with him."

"Yeah, but once she realized it was going nowhere, she got bored." Cristine gave a soft laugh. "She likes to keep things free and easy. Like me. We just want to have fun."

"Do you think Mike ran off with her?" Zoe asked.

"Ran off?" Cristine's heavily made-up eyes filled with tears. "It's possible, but like I said, Shayna didn't make commitments."

"We need to tell Roger. Even if there's no real evidence, this is something he needs to know."

"I already told him an amended version." She shifted in her chair, clearly uncomfortable. "I couldn't tell him about the drugs. I didn't want to get Shayna in trouble."

Or herself. "What did he say?"

Cristine sighed. "He promised to put it in his file."

"And now you're telling me?" Zoe leaned forward. "Why?"

"Because someone needs to go talk to Mike—and probably some of the others Shayna was involved with."

Someone, meaning obviously not her. Zoe found that slightly odd. "Cristine, you know their faces. Who better to dig for information?"

"That's just it, I can't." Twisting her hands together, Cristine leaned closer. "You see, Shayna wasn't the only one who owes money. After I covered her debt, I thought she'd be paying me back. Instead, she disappeared. Meanwhile, I sort of owe a couple of other guys money and..."

"If you show up, they'll expect you to pay it."

Cristine nodded. "And I can't. At least not until I get paid. What about you? No one around there knows you. You'd be perfect. Shayna and I hung out at several places, but there's one bar in particular, the one where Mike hangs out. We were there the night Shayna disappeared."

"Where is it?"

Cristine named a bar in a bad part of town. The Hitching Post. Of course. Zoe shouldn't have been familiar with it, but she was. She'd witnessed her mother's murder in the alley behind there.

The idea of going back to that bar, near that dark alley, made Zoe break out in an uncomfortable sweat.

She had no choice. If she wanted to find out what had happened to Shayna, she had to go back to the place that haunted her nightmares.

Unfortunately, she couldn't go alone. She'd have to ask Brock. At least she trusted him. He was and always would be the most honorable man she'd ever known. But then again, Shayna had changed completely. What if Brock had, too?

Still, she'd ask him. At the thought, her insides churned. Still, maybe they could figure out a way to work together for Shayna's sake. "I'll let you know," she told Cristine, pushing up from the table.

Instead of going home, she took a deep breath and headed out to the one place she knew she could find Brock. McCauley's Feed Store.

Several pickup trucks were parked in the lot. She pulled in between two of them and killed the engine. Taking a deep breath, she squared her shoulders and got out.

Inside, she blinked. The store had changed dramatically. She remembered a homey place of disorganized chaos. Saddles had been mixed in among bird feeders, dog food next to fertilizer. Customers had to hunt to find the items they wanted.

Now, everything had been arranged in logical order. Saddles were grouped with bridles and halters and bits. There was a bird section, a wildlife section, and a gardening section, among others. Hunting was big business in these parts and come deer season McCauley's would sell out of deer stands and feeders. There were even two entire rows of fishing rods and reels, along with lures and various other angler items. The concrete floor appeared clean and well swept, and the checkout counter had been relocated to the opposite side of the store.

Again, she scanned the interior, almost feeling as though she was in another place entirely. She didn't see Brock anywhere.

Two men were standing by the shelves containing sacks of dog food, hotly debating the merits of particular brands. They fell silent and turned to stare as she walked by. She gave them a friendly smile and tried to move past.

"I know you," one man said slowly. "Zoe Onella, right?"

She stopped, searching his face, hoping for a hint to tell her who he was. Though he looked vaguely familiar, she didn't recognize him. "I'm sorry," she began, "I don't—"

"Marvin Smith," he interrupted, holding out one tanned hand. "I was two grades ahead of you in school."

She shook his hand. "Great to see you."

The other man, who until now had stayed silent, spoke. "Aren't you the one who ditched Brock right before the wedding?"

Her embarrassment deepened. She tugged her hand free and flushed. "I—"

"Yeah, she is," Marvin put in. "The whole town was talking about it for months after. So tell us, why'd you do it?"

At a complete loss for words, she glanced around wildly, hoping for rescue. It came in the form of Brock. Judging by his frown, he'd heard everything.

"Zoe." Brock stepped between them, his flat tone at odds with the raw emotion glittering in his eyes. "What are you doing here?"

He didn't sound friendly. What had she expected, him to welcome her with open arms?

"Maybe she came to buy feed," Marvin put in. Judging from the avid interest on his and his friend's faces, news of her visit to Brock would be all over the town by morning.

"Maybe she did," Brock said. His impersonal tone could have been a greeting for a total stranger.

She knew she should have felt relieved, but it stung.

"I wanted to talk to you," she said, aware of the other two men's keen attention. "In private."

He nodded, his expression shuttered. "When I have a chance. I have customers."

Marvin laughed.

Ignoring him, Zoe forced a smile and shrugged. "No

worries. Whenever you get a minute. I'll look around until you're free."

But he'd already turned away, dismissing her. She noted the stiff set of his broad shoulders. Maybe she'd been wrong to come here. Apparently, this was a bad idea.

Then she thought of Shayna, who had been there for her so many times, and Zoe knew she had no choice. If the police wouldn't help, she needed backup. Brock was an honorable man. She had to ask for his assistance. If he truly cared about Shayna, he'd manage to put their differences aside and help Zoe find her.

"Looks like it's not gonna be a friendly reunion," Marvin commented to his friend.

Ignoring him, Zoe moved off.

At least thirty minutes passed. Zoe had inspected every birdhouse and dog collar, and she'd moved over to the saddles.

"What are you doing here?" a soft voice asked. Eve, Brock's younger sister. Zoe would have known that voice anywhere, even though it was five years older.

"Eve!" Delighted, Zoe spun around and enveloped the slender girl in a hug. "I haven't seen you in forever." Pulling back, she noted Eve's long, straight blond hair and gorgeous blue eyes. "I can't believe how grown you look! How are you?"

"I'm fine. And I'm nineteen now." Holding herself as rigidly as her older brother had, Eve eased out of Zoe's arms. "Are you here to see Brock? Does he know you're here?"

Noting Eve's troubled expression, Zoe guessed she was worried about Brock's feelings. "He does." She hoped her friendly tone would provide a measure of reassurance. "I need to talk to him when he finishes with the customers."

Eve glanced around and frowned. "The store is empty except for you."

Turning, Zoe saw Eve was correct. And still no sign of Brock. "That's weird," she said.

"Maybe he doesn't want to talk to you," Eve suggested, her blue eyes wide. "I think you should go."

In the past, a younger Eve had idolized Zoe, following her and Brock around like a puppy. She'd been fourteen when Zoe had left and all dreamy eyed over some boy band. For the first time, Zoe realized her sudden departure had hurt Eve, too.

"Eve, listen I—"

"Are you ready, Zoe?" Brock appeared suddenly, making her wonder if he'd been lurking and listening again. At her nod, he took her arm. "Good. Come with me to my office. I've got a couple of minutes to spare." He glanced at Eve, frowning. "Eve, can you watch the floor for me?"

She nodded, her expression still troubled. "Of course."

"Good." His gaze found Zoe. "Follow me."

The coldness in his bright blue eyes turned her insides to ice. Giving Eve one last look, Zoe turned and went after him.

His well-worn Wrangler jeans fit him like a glove. She couldn't help but admire his backside—that, at least, was one thing that hadn't changed.

They reached the double doors marked Employees Only that separated the retail part of the store from the storage and offices. They headed toward the office that used to belong to Brock's father. It, too, had been cluttered and disorganized. Now, it was as tidy and neat as the rest of the store.

Brock went around to sit behind the gunmetal-gray desk. "Take a seat," he said, indicating a folding metal chair across from him. "And then tell me why you're here."

Taking a deep breath, she supposed she should be relieved he wasn't pretending to be friendly. At least this way, she knew exactly where she stood.

Still…that desk. She tried like hell to avoid looking at it. Because when she did, she saw images of their bodies intertwined and she remembered the inventive, carnal things she and Brock had done on that very same desk.

Her face flamed as she wondered if he remembered, too.

"I need your help," she said, trying to sound assertive, as if she was in New York and meeting with a prospective backer.

Brock leaned forward, his expression unchanged. "With what?"

"Finding Shayna."

A flicker of impatience crossed his face. "And?"

Zoe took a deep breath. "I've been talking to Cristine. She says you're aware that she and Shayna went out partying together a lot."

He nodded. "I know."

One brow raised, he waited. His chiseled features looked both stern and sexy. Her mouth went dry and she had to swallow hard, aware she wasn't sure how he'd receive her words.

In a rush, she told him what she'd learned. "Not only did Shayna have a fling with the sheriff, but apparently she and Cristine made a game out of picking up random men in bars."

He grimaced. "I'm sorry you had to learn about your friend that way. I was hoping that part of her lifestyle would stay quiet."

Shocked and surprised, she found herself at a loss for words. "You knew everything?"

"Yes." He made a sweeping gesture with his hand. "How could I not? Shayna didn't bother to hide what she was doing, and everyone in town was talking."

Once the gossip got going in a small place like Anniversary, it was hard to stop it.

"They were? Even to you?" The instant she asked the question, a sudden, horrible suspicion seized her. "That must have made you feel…awful. Pissed off."

He gave a slow shake of his head. "More like embarrassed for her. We had already ended our relationship. She was still staying with me, until Cristine could upgrade to a two-bedroom apartment so Shayna could move in. We were more like roommates at that point."

Roommates. Blinking, Zoe tried to reconcile that with what Shayna had been telling her for the past eighteen months. "Wow. Considering what she said to me, I'm thinking she felt more connected than just roommates."

"I doubt it." He gave her an amused look. "Especially since we had separate bedrooms and she paid half the rent."

Again, Zoe had the unsettling feeling that she'd stepped into some sort of alternate reality. "Okay, I guess I'm going to have to take your word for it. Tell me this—how long has Shayna been such a…party girl?"

If she hadn't known him so well, she would have

missed the guilt that flashed across his handsome face. "A few months. Ever since she and Cristine started running around together."

"So before that, she was…normal?"

Again the guilt. "I guess."

Zoe knew she had to press. "Do you know why she changed?"

Though he didn't answer, she could tell he knew.

Chapter 5

"What are you not telling me?"

Instead of answering, Brock looked away and Zoe knew he wasn't going to say. "I'm not sure why she changed. She claimed life was just too boring. She wanted to experience more, she said. More fun, drinks and drugs and, of course, more men. Life on the wild side."

Yet again, he'd managed to bewilder her. "You and she…discussed this?"

"We lived together, Zoe. And while in the end we'd decided we weren't soul mates, or even lovers any longer, Shayna and I were still good friends. In fact, except for Cristine, I probably knew her better than anyone. I cared about her, too."

A confusing mixture of relief and uncertainty flooded her. She had to curl her fingers into fists to keep from touching him. "We don't have any facts, just a lot of supposition."

He nodded. "That's right. Shayna isn't here, that's all we know. Whether she left voluntarily or not, we have no way of knowing."

Finally back on familiar ground, she nodded. "What do you think has happened to her?" Leaning forward, scooting up to the edge of her chair, she didn't bother to hide her frustrated anger. "Half the town seems to think she just up and took off."

She couldn't bear the flash of pity in his eyes and had to look away.

"Zoe, it's entirely possible Shayna did exactly that."

"But why would she? I don't understand."

"Like I said, she was bored. Tired of life here in Anniversary. Maybe she did take off, looking for adventure and excitement."

Puzzled, Zoe tried to give serious consideration to the possibility. "Cristine said she didn't have much money. Where would she go?"

With a sigh, he leaned back in his chair and put his arms behind his head. "To find you, Zoe. She thought you were living the kind of life she wanted. I don't know if you were aware, but she's jealous of you."

"Roger said something similar." Zoe sighed. Not a single time in the entire five years since Zoe had run away from Anniversary and all she held dear, had Shayna even given her a hint of her unhappiness, restlessness or dissatisfaction. Not once had Shayna even *mentioned* the possibility of coming for a visit.

Somehow, Zoe managed to give Brock a halfhearted smile. "While that's certainly possible, I doubt it. All Shayna had to do was ask, which she never did."

A horrible blankness came over his face. The expression both terrified her and caused her pain. "I wasn't aware you and she spoke much anymore. At least from what Shayna told me. She said you'd been backing away, as though you wanted to shed the last few people who connected you to your old life."

More lies. For a moment, Zoe was struck speechless. Had Shayna made a habit of lying, or was Brock the one telling falsehoods as a means of gaining some sort of petty revenge? The Brock she'd known would never have done such a thing, but then neither would Shayna.

"Cristine has another theory," she said, her voice cool as frost. Without pulling any punches, she relayed what Cristine had told her about Mike and the bar.

Brock listened in silence. Trying to remain aloof, she found herself watching his features for a reaction—good, bad or in between. "Well," he finally said. "We're still no closer to finding her than we were before."

"That's why I came to see you. We should go to the Hitching Post and try and find this Mike."

"We? How about I ask Roger Giles to take care of this? He or someone in his office would be better equipped to deal with trouble."

"Will he? When I talked to him, he didn't seem willing to do anything."

"I'll ask him and let you know." The maddening hint of arrogance in his profile should have angered her. Instead, she wanted to reach across the desk and cover his mouth with hers.

Damn. What was wrong with her?

"Let me know what Roger says." Getting up, she moved slowly to the door, careful not to look at Brock, stunned at the sheer strength of the simmering desire she felt for him.

Her body ached for his touch, filling her entire being with a fierce and urgent wanting. Even now, when every ounce of her focus should be on finding her friend.

She'd already lost so much when she'd had to leave town—her fiancé, her family, her friends and her home. She couldn't bear losing Shayna, too.

Brock didn't call after her or follow her, and even though she hadn't expected him to, she told herself she was glad. What had she expected? Nothing she was learning about Shayna added up.

Zoe needed to regain her objectivity—about Brock, Cristine and Shayna. Until her friend was found—alive or…God help her…dead.

Unfortunately, the more time that passed, the worse things were beginning to look. Zoe wasn't even sure who she could trust. In five years, they'd all turned into strangers.

Especially Shayna. As soon as she found that girl, Zoe was going to let her have a piece of her mind. After she apologized for not paying attention during that last, apparently desperate, phone call.

Again, Zoe wondered if this was all her fault. As she got back inside Mama Bell's car, she speculated. Had Shayna really gone looking for her without telling her? Or was Cristine's theory more accurate? Had Shayna taken off with some biker named Mike?

Instead of driving home, Zoe went to the public fishing pier, parking in a shaded spot, and walked out onto the wooden structure to sit on a bench near the edge. At that time of the day, only a few fishermen occupied the pier, intent on their lines. Though they nodded a greeting, no one spoke.

Another blessing, for which she was glad. She needed silence, time to digest what Brock had told her, and to pick out truth from the increasingly tangled web that Shayna's life had become.

Fact one. Cristine had said Shayna had expressed fear and worry about the drug dealer to whom she'd owed money. Even though Cristine claimed to have satisfied the debt, Zoe needed to check that out.

Fact two. Shayna had been seeing multiple men, apparently heedless of any emotions they might have toward her. Any one of these men, the sheriff notwithstanding, could have done something to Shayna in a jealous fit of rage.

Fact three. Shayna had apparently confided in Brock her desire to leave town, possibly to find Zoe. Zoe wasn't entirely sure what she thought about this statement. The last several times she'd spoken to Shayna, her friend had been full of talk about her wedding plans and the goings-on in Anniversary. She hadn't sounded like a woman ready to leave town. At all.

And honestly, if she were going in visit Zoe, wouldn't she at least have said something? If Shayna had, Zoe would have told her to buy a plane ticket to come in at JFK or LaGuardia.

Shayna had never asked. She'd never even hinted.

And then there was Brock's story. Zoe hated suspecting him, but his story made him seem as if he was trying to give Zoe a reason to give up the search.

She had to wonder. Given what she'd learned about Shayna, had Brock done something to hurt the woman he claimed to view as only a friend? Even thinking such a thing hurt and felt like betrayal, but Zoe owed it to Shayna to find out the truth.

She wouldn't abandon her plan to visit some of the bars Shayna had frequented. If Brock wasn't willing to accompany her, then she'd either go on her own or ask Cristine to go with her, even though the other woman claimed she couldn't.

Decision made, she pushed to her feet and went back to the car. She'd let Mama Bell know she'd be staying in town a while longer.

She could work on her blog from here.

Her blog! That would be a start. She could post Shayna's picture, tell an abbreviated story of her disappearance and invite people to post possible sightings.

Perfect. In a hurry to begin, she started the engine and backed from her parking spot. Her spirits felt higher than they'd been since she'd arrived back in town. Doing something, no matter how small, was always better than doing nothing.

Watching Zoe walk away, Brock swallowed back the riot of emotions threatening to swamp him. All he could think about was her.

Zoe. Zoe. Zoe.

Hellfire, he was doomed. All this time, he'd been telling himself he was over her. He'd convinced himself that he didn't care that she'd never called or written to apologize or explain. Five years had passed.

The first few months after she'd left had been rough. He still remembered the raw agony, the aching certainty that she'd kept something from him. He had to believe she would never have left him if something hadn't happened that had forced her to leave the town and the people she'd loved. Turns out, he was right. Still, the fact that she hadn't come back when the danger was over, still rankled. Zoe belonged here. She'd loved this town.

Unlike Shayna, who'd made no secret of her desire to leave Anniversary behind. While he didn't understand her apparent decision to take off without a word to anyone, if she was emulating Zoe, she'd done a damn good job.

Again, Zoe. It always came back to her, somehow. Her return had sent his world into upheaval.

Thanks to her, he no longer believed in love. He wasn't the same man who'd viewed life through glasses colored by his love for the woman who'd abandoned him without a word. Zoe had proved real and lasting love didn't exist. So he'd accepted his bland existence and learned to take one day at a time.

In the five years since she'd ripped out his heart, he'd made a life for himself. It wasn't perfect, but it was his. He valued stability, but in the blink of an eye, Shayna's disappearance had changed everything. Zoe, back in town, treated him like a casual acquaintance, which should have been fine but wasn't.

He needed her. No, more than that, he craved her. All he could think about was how badly he wanted to get her naked, to feel those silky limbs wrapped around his while he buried himself deep inside her.

Damn. Cursing, he fought to control his unruly body. He didn't understand his still overwhelming attraction to Zoe. By all that was right and just in the world, he should be able to find indifference. Especially now, when she'd shown back up and tried to pretend nothing had ever happened between them.

Had she erased their past from her mind, from her

heart? Maybe for her, that was an option, but Brock would never forget the happiest time of his life. Nothing since compared. He had a sneaking suspicion that nothing ever would.

Bad for him, but he'd learned his lesson. This time, he knew better. Zoe Onella would never hurt him again. During her no doubt brief stay in town, he'd consider her dangerous and do his damnedest to stay away.

Standing, he stretched, wishing he could will away the ache that had bloomed in his chest. It had been his ever-present companion ever since Mrs. Bell had called to let him know Zoe was coming back to Anniversary.

Even then, he'd believed he had a handle on his emotions. He'd thought he had himself firmly under control, that Zoe meant nothing to him anymore. He'd tried to hate her and, failing that, had worked hard to relegate her to nothing more than a memory. Until he'd seen her striding through the airport, all long-legged, beautiful confidence, and realized he was wrong.

He wasn't safe. He was in trouble. The less time he spent with Zoe, the better.

As he turned to leave the office, his phone rang. Shayna. For a second his heart stopped as he stared at the caller ID.

"Hello," he answered, his voice breaking.

"Brock, it's Cristine."

Cristine? He cursed. "What the hell are you doing with Shayna's cell phone?"

Apologizing, she sounded agitated. "She left it in one of the bars where she and I hung out. I was there last night and the bartender gave it to me."

His heart sank. Shayna without her phone would be

like him cutting off his right hand. "Why are you call-ing me?" he asked.

"I redialed the last number that she called." Cristine hesitated. "She called you, Brock."

He didn't understand. "So? She called me all the time."

"True." Audibly swallowing, she sounded strangely nervous. "That would make you one of the last people to talk to her on the night she went missing."

"So?" He didn't bother to hide his impatience. "What are you trying to imply?"

"Nothing," Cristine practically yelped. "I'm going to let you go. I need to call Zoe."

Before he could respond, she ended the call.

Slowly, Brock replaced the phone in its cradle. Had Cristine just suggested he'd somehow made Shayna disappear?

When Zoe saw Shayna's number on her caller ID, she nearly dropped her phone. Pressing the accept button with trembling fingers, she took a deep breath. "You sure have a lot of explaining to do, woman."

"Whoa. Zoe, it's Cristine. Sorry."

Listening as the other woman explained how she'd come by the phone, Zoe couldn't stop shaking. She couldn't believe Cristine could be so thoughtless to give her such a broken and utterly false hope.

Then, Cristine's words dawned on her. "What's the name of the bar where Shayna left her phone?"

"The Hitching Post."

Of course. Would fate never get tired of punching her in the stomach? "I thought you said you couldn't show your face in there until you got paid."

"I scraped together some cash," Cristine responded. "Though that was our favorite, Shayna and I usually hit a couple of other biker bars in addition to the one where she left her phone."

Great. Zoe closed her eyes. Just great.

"I should let you know," Cristine continued. "I called Brock, too. He didn't seem too happy."

"I'm not surprised," Zoe snapped. "He probably had the same reaction I did when Shayna's number came up on the caller ID. Tell me at least you didn't do that to Mrs. Bell, did you?"

"Of course not." Unbelievably, Cristine sounded indignant. "Look, I'm calling you because the night Shayna disappeared, she made a call from the bar. The call was to Brock, at nearly eleven."

Zoe rubbed her suddenly aching temple. "Surely you're not trying to imply—"

"I'm not implying anything," Cristine told her. "I'm just letting you know all the facts. You need to know everything, if you're going to be effective in finding Shayna, including the possibility that Brock might be a suspect."

Despite numerous small searches, the big one Cristine had organized was scheduled to begin at eight sharp in the morning. Since none of the others had turned up anything, an air of desperation fueled this one. It seemed the entire town had turned out, all massed together in clusters at Turner's Park.

Still dressed in her skin-tight clothes and heels too high to hike in, Cristine came up to her and handed her a huge silver whistle. Her long, perfectly manicured fingernails were painted a vivid scarlet, matching her lipstick. "Here you go," she said.

"What's this for?" Zoe asked as she accepted it, along with a typed list of names.

"Since I'm putting you in charge of your section, you'll need to blow it if any of your people find anything." Cristine gave an earnest smile. "Also, it'll be useful for calling your crew in when the search is over."

"While I applaud the sentiment, why here?" Zoe gestured at the forest. "Shayna hated the woods and camping and roughing it." She stopped herself just short of asking if that was still true.

"Why not?" Cristine's patently pleasant smile had begun to grate. "I mean, we've got to start somewhere, right?"

"True," she said, skimming the names on her list. A few sounded familiar, but out of the twenty, she didn't know most of them.

"Thank you." Leaning in, Cristine gave her a quick hug. "I really appreciate all your help in bringing our Shayna back."

Zoe stiffened. "No problem."

"By the way," Cristine continued as if she hadn't noticed how quickly Zoe moved away. "I read your blog. Thanks for posting the story of Shayna's disappearance. With all the readers you have, that should help a lot if someone happens to sight her. I shared it on Facebook and Twitter, too."

Her blog. Blogging had started as a hobby and ended up being the reason she'd been able to quit secretarial work, a job she'd grown to despise. Her blog had been her only outlet for letting off steam.

City Girl had begun as a slightly snarky insight into

the world of a single girl in the city. Over the years, the blog had evolved into so much more. She talked about favorite food, fashion trends and faux pas, as well as her hopes and dreams.

The only person in Anniversary Zoe'd told about *City Girl* was Shayna. It had long been their little secret, Zoe's way of filling her friend in on her life when things got too hectic for a phone call. Promising to keep it to herself, Shayna had taken great delight in being the only one in town to realize the popular blog *City Girl* was written by small-town girl Zoe Onella. Eventually, Shayna had shared it with her mother of course, but as far as Zoe knew, that was all.

Apparently, not any longer. It would seem Shayna had also shared that info with Cristine, her new best friend. Zoe wasn't sure how she felt about that.

Briefly she debated asking Cristine to keep *City Girl*'s true identity under her hat, but she figured that would be like setting a match to gasoline-soaked timber.

Instead, Zoe turned away and scanned the crowd. She spotted Brock, making his way toward them.

Cristine saw him a second later. "Here he is," she said, waving. "I hope you don't mind, but I've asked Brock to search with your team."

Mind? Every nerve ending in her body instantly came awake.

"All right," Cristine said, as soon as he'd reached them. "Let's get this show on the road." She walked away. She'd gone about ten feet when she began blowing on her whistle, which gave off a shrill, high-pitched sound. Immediately, all conversation ceased.

Once they were organized into the predetermined groups, Zoe led hers to the section of the forest they'd been assigned. Brock stayed close behind. Feeling apprehensive, she ordered them to fan out. They'd meet back at the starting point in one hour, sooner if they found something.

"I'm going to stick with you," Brock told her, leaving no room for argument.

Though her pulse rate had gone into overdrive, she simply nodded. What mattered was finding Shayna.

As they crashed through the woods, pushing aside underbrush and looking, Zoe alternated between determination to try her best and a hovering kind of dread. She figured they wouldn't find anything, but what the heck would she do if they did? The thought made her feel sick. Because finding Shayna here would mean she'd been killed. Zoe didn't even want to think about that.

Not possible, she told herself, scanning the leaves and the heavy bush as she pushed through, glad she'd worn jeans.

"Zoe?" Brock asked. "Are you all right?"

"I'm fine," she responded, trying not to look at him. "I just don't understand any of this. Why did Shayna change so drastically? I don't even know who my best friend was anymore. Finding her body without making things right would be unbearable."

Almost in tears, she took a deep breath and continued blindly pushing through the brush. "Shayna is alive, Brock. She has to be. To consider any other possibility is simply unacceptable."

"Hey." Brock touched her arm. To her deep and infinite shame, she nearly turned and went to him for comfort. Since she'd lost that right years ago, she did not. Instead, she swiped at her eyes with the back of her hand.

"I think I might be the reason Shayna changed," he said, his voice rough. "It wasn't until I broke up with her that she started hanging out with Cristine, going to bars and saying she wanted to leave town."

Her first instinctive reaction—shock—froze her in place. "You blame yourself?" she said. "What on earth did you do?"

Shadows of guilt darkened his blue eyes. "I told her I could never love her the way she wanted. I knew she thought our relationship had grown more serious than it was. I didn't have a choice but to be truthful. She deserved more."

A dull ache settled in close to her heart. "Then why were you living together if you didn't care for her?"

"We started out as roommates. Separate bedrooms and all. She was lonely, I was lonely...." He looked down. "One thing led to another."

"I see," she said, though she didn't.

"I doubt you do. It was good, as long as we both understood the parameters. But when she wanted more, I wasn't going to pretend, just to keep her there. Shayna deserved better than that. I was doing her a favor, though I doubt she saw it that way."

Again, Zoe found herself on the edge of tears. She pushed forward, beating at the brush, glad he was behind her and couldn't see her face.

They reached the end of their assigned search area. Glad she finally had her emotions under control, she turned. "We need to go that way," she said, and pointed.

"What about you, Zoe?" His lowered voice vibrated with intensity. "Are you ever going to tell me the rest of the reason you ran away? I know you saw your mother killed, but you're not telling me everything."

Her breath caught.

Throat tight, Zoe looked down.

"Don't you think it's time I knew the truth?" he persisted. "All of it."

"I can't." Determined to keep her emotions close from now on, she lifted her chin. "This is about Shayna, not about me."

"Us," he said. "About us. Sooner or later, you're going to have to face me and give me the facts. I deserve to know."

She didn't answer, couldn't answer. Instead, she pushed on, not waiting to see if he followed.

Two hours later, three sharp blows on a whistle called them all in. Both relieved and frustrated, Brock turned to make his way back to the park. As soon as they reached it, Zoe hurried off in the other direction.

"Brock!" Mama Bell hurried over. "I understand Marshall came into the feed store the other day."

Inwardly wincing, he nodded. "I take it you've talked to him."

"I have."

He couldn't tell anything from her expressionless face, so he simply waited to see what else she'd say.

"Marshall is leaving town. He's going looking for our Shayna." Her mouth twisted. "At least that's what he's calling it."

"I'm so sorry." He touched her arm, then pulled her in for a quick hug. "I don't know what else to say."

Her faded blue gaze searched his. "Why didn't you tell me?" she asked. "The other night at dinner."

"It wasn't my place," he answered softly.

She gave a slow nod. "I haven't told Zoe yet. She just got back home. Shayna's missing and now this." She sighed. "I feel like my entire world is falling apart."

He hugged her. "I'm sorry. If there's anything I can do, anything at all, let me know. I'm not going anywhere. You know I'll always make time for you."

"Thank you." Hugging him back, Mama Bell sighed again, her full lower lip trembling. "Well, I'd better find Cristine and see if anything turned up. I didn't really think it would, but you never know."

With that, she walked away.

He watched her go, her broad shoulders bent with the weight of her troubles.

Zoe caught up with her as she crossed the picnic area. Though he couldn't hear the words, judging by Zoe's animated gestures, she was excited about something. Mama Bell listened, nodding. Then Zoe kissed her cheek and rushed away.

Unnoticed, he tracked Zoe until he could no longer see her. The instant she disappeared from view, all the colors seemed to leach out of the landscape, the greens no longer as vibrant, and the violent blue of the sky going a dreary gray.

Shaking his head at his own bit of foolishness, he turned around and headed to the parking lot. He wished like hell Shayna would show up. Not only for everyone's peace of mind, but because after she did, Zoe would go back to whatever big city she'd come from and his life could return to normal. Which was, he told himself, exactly what he wanted.

Mama Bell cried every night. She probably didn't know Zoe could hear her, but the sound broke Zoe's heart. Open-ended sobs full of sorrow and agony. As if Mama believed her little girl was dead.

Even thinking the word pierced Zoe's heart. She couldn't imagine a world without Shayna, her best friend and the sister of her heart. Of course, the irony of these feelings didn't escape her. All the while the two of them had been living their lives, far apart. Zoe had believed they were still tethered by a connection forged long ago as children.

Unfortunately, the more she learned about the life Shayna had been living, the possibility of something happening to her became more and more viable.

She couldn't help but question Brock's role in all of this. He claimed he'd been honest with her, but then why the hell had Shayna told stories about their relationship? Cristine seemed suspicious of what went on between Shayna and Brock, but the possibility of him being abusive was something Zoe couldn't even begin to entertain. The Brock she'd known her entire life would never have raised his hand to a woman under any circumstances.

But then the Shayna she'd known would never have done any of the things she'd apparently done.

Which just showed she didn't know these people anymore. That thought made her wish that her life in Manhattan could have stayed the same. The crowded anonymity of the city was starting to look really good right about now.

Tossing and turning in her old twin bed, Zoe pounded the pillow. She needed to do something, anything, to bring closure to Mama Bell and this town. She *had* to find out what had happened to Shayna. Then she could leave forever. And if Shayna was ok, Zoe would take her away with her.

Chapter 6

The next morning, she wandered into the kitchen and found Mama Bell sitting at the table, an untouched cup of steaming coffee before her. She looked up as Zoe entered, apparently unaware or not caring that tears streamed silently down her cheeks.

Moving carefully, Zoe pulled out the chair next to her—Mr. Bell's chair. "What's going on, Mama?" she asked softly.

"My family is disintegrating," the older woman said quietly, swiping at her face with the back of her hand. "If you'd asked me a few weeks ago, I would have told you love was the glue that held us all together. Now Shayna has gone missing, and my husband has apparently decided to do the same."

Taking a big gulp of air, she turned her coffee mug

around and around in her hands, though she didn't take a sip. "I'm thinking the love was all on my part."

"Oh, Mama." Zoe captured her hand. "Shayna adores you, as do I. And Mr. Bell is just having trouble dealing with all this. He'll come around, you'll see. Just give him time."

But Mama Bell shook her head. "He won't have that option," she said, her voice grim. "He's abandoning this family—me—when we need him the most. What if Shayna—"

"Shh," Zoe interrupted. "Don't say that. Don't even *think* it." She jumped to her feet and began pacing. "I'll figure something out, make a plan. I'll find Shayna, I promise."

As Mama Bell's face cleared, Zoe felt a twinge of guilt for making a promise she wasn't a hundred-percent sure she could keep.

No, she told herself silently. She *would* find out what had happened to Shayna. This waiting around was ridiculous. Three days had gone by, three days in which no progress had been made.

That would end. Starting right now.

"What are you going to do?" Mama asked.

"I'm going into town," Zoe said, energized with her sudden sense of purpose. "Will you need your car today?"

"No, but don't you want coffee and something to eat before you go?" Mama Bell pushed to her feet and gave Zoe a tremulous smile.

"Nope." Zoe stepped forward and placed a quick kiss on her cheek. "I'll get something at the coffee shop. I've got plans to make."

On the way, Zoe took a slight detour. According to

Mama Bell, Brock lived in one of the recently renovated apartments over the shops downtown. Zoe was a little surprised he was still renting, but then who was she to talk? She paid an exorbitant amount for a tiny bit of space in Manhattan and wouldn't trade it for the world.

Yet the more time she spent in Anniversary, the more she realized she'd missed the place without even realizing it.

More than that, if she was honest, she'd missed Brock.

Whoa. Immediately she put the brakes on that line of thinking. She'd missed him, had in fact gotten used to living with a constant ache in her breast.

Driving slowly, she was surprised at the trendy look of the apartments. With their earth-colored, stucco exteriors and red shutters and doors, they would have fit in a larger city, like Austin or even Dallas. They looked like exactly the sort of thing a young and upcoming professional might want.

Unfortunately, Brock was none of these things. They didn't look like anything he'd want. A man like him belonged in a white frame house out in the country, with acreage and barns and livestock. He owned a feed store, after all.

Evidently, he'd changed too. Feeling like a foolish stalker, she pressed the accelerator and drove on. Her timing must have been an omen, because she snagged a parking spot right in front of the entrance to the coffee shop.

Strolling inside, she headed for the counter, not wanting to take up an entire booth all by herself. Halfway there, she spotted Brock, cell phone to his ear.

Stunned, she stopped in her tracks and debated making a hasty retreat. Too late. He'd seen her. Anniversary was just too small.

"Hey." Appearing distracted, he waved her over. Sitting next to him, hips close enough to touch, was the last thing she wanted or needed this morning. She went anyway.

Brock concluded his call and placed the phone on the counter next to his coffee. "That was Mama Bell," he said, unsmiling. "She asked me to help you. She says you have some sort of big plan to find Shayna. I assume it's the one you mentioned earlier—us going to the Hitching Post and talking to this Mike?"

Push and pull. The tug of him turned her insides to liquid. Furious with herself—and with Mama Bell for involving him—she slid onto the stool and gestured at Patsy for some coffee. "Yes, it is. And Mama Bell is right. We should stop playing games and put our heads together to find Shayna. While we've been worrying about feelings from the past, she may be in terrible danger. Or worse."

He nodded. "Eat first, then we'll talk." Picking up his phone, he began scrolling through his email. Though she tried to stare straight ahead, she could see him out of the corner of her eye. She couldn't help but watch him, admiring the way a shaft of sunlight turned his hair to molten gold. Did he ever think about her anymore, she wondered before forcing her gaze and her thoughts away. What did it matter, anyway? She was leaving again as soon as Shayna was found.

"What'll you have, honey?" Patsy asked, pouring a cup of coffee and placing it in front of her. "My new cook makes a mean Greek omelet."

Zoe nodded, wondering how on earth she was going

to eat with Brock next to her, giving off pheromones or whatever it was he did to make every cell in her body quiver. Damn the man. She would have thought, after five years, she'd be indifferent to him. Obviously he didn't have the same problem; when he looked at her she didn't see the slightest hint of desire in his blue eyes.

Which was good, she told herself, keeping busy with doctoring her coffee with cream and one packet of artificial sweetener. Exactly how it should be. For Shayna's sake, they'd have to work together.

Damn. There was no avoiding the woman. She'd even invaded his favorite breakfast spot. To his chagrin, Brock could scarcely choke down the remnants of his food.

She sat so straight backed she might have had a spine made of steel. He noticed she tried not to look directly at him, instead sneaking sideways glances. Each time she did, he felt as if she'd reached out and caressed him.

The silence stretched between them, canceling out the background noise of the busy café. He had to fight the urge to drink her in, to study any differences that might have changed her in the past five years, to search for anything about her that still felt the same. After all this time, Zoe shouldn't have this much power over him.

"So, tell me, what's your plan?" he asked despite himself. Though he really didn't want to know, he had a sense that brave, overconfident Zoe might even put her own life in danger if she thought it could help her friend.

Her chin lifted, a sure sign that he was right.

"Like I said, I'm going to try hanging out in the bar and see if I can locate this Mike."

"The Hitching Post."

"Right. Cristine said she and Shayna were regulars, even though it's in an area of town most sane people consider dangerous."

About to ask why, he stopped himself. The reason seemed obvious. Though he'd known Shayna and Cristine had gone out to have a good time, he hadn't been aware they were putting themselves in danger.

Again the guilt, mingled with anger. Then horror, as he realized what Zoe had just said. "You're going to the bar alone?"

"Yes, since you clearly didn't want to go with me. I'm going to do what Shayna did. Get dressed up and pretend to be looking for—"

"No," he interrupted, as if he had the right. "Absolutely not."

She stared at him, her eyes narrowed, apparently thinking he must have lost his mind. "Um, I wasn't asking your permission."

She had a point. Frustrated, he let his breath out in a puff of air and dragged his hand through his hair. "At least tell me you're taking Cristine with you."

"I'm not." She gave him an almost apologetic grimace. "I don't trust her. She may have been Shayna's last friend, but she didn't know the Shayna I knew and loved. I'd rather go alone."

Alone. The thought of what could happen to a woman like her, alone in a place like that, turned his insides to ice.

"You can't," he said. "You won't be safe."

She took a long drink of her coffee before facing him. "I don't have a choice. Too much time has passed since Shayna vanished. I've got to find out what happened to her."

Something in her voice, the slightest quiver, told him she too had begun to entertain the possibility that Shayna was dead. A fist closed around his heart and squeezed.

"I'll go with you," he heard himself offer, aware of the possibility he'd just been played. "That way at least you'll have someone there to make sure you don't get hurt."

At his words, she went absolutely motionless. So still, he wondered if she was breathing.

"Look, I—" he began.

Shooting him a sharp glance, she interrupted. "Thanks, but no. Even though I asked you before, I've reconsidered. Shayna went there to…" Flushing bright red, she seemed to suddenly realize to whom she was speaking.

"To pick up men," he finished, an answering spark of anger blooming inside him. "I get it."

"Then you'll understand having you with me will kind of defeat the purpose."

He thought fast. "Not necessarily. We're a couple, looking for some fun to spice up our relationship."

If anything, her blush deepened. Desire uncoiled inside him, raking him with sharp claws.

"I don't think so," she said faintly. "Look, I appreciate you offering, but I think it's best if I go alone."

Imagining all the things that could happen to a single female in that part of town made his skin crawl. Though she wasn't his responsibility, wasn't his anything, he didn't think he could live with himself if something happened to her. Shayna's disappearance was bad enough.

Certainly he didn't want to analyze that.

"Look, Zoe. I'm going. You have no choice. I'll be with you, at your back."

"Fine," she said finally, her tone an enticing combination of grumpy and pleased. "You can come with me, at least one time. If it doesn't work out, I'll ask Cristine."

Satisfied that she'd seen sense and he wouldn't have to fight her to keep her safe, he nodded. "When?" he asked.

"Tonight. I'll tell people you're my cousin from out of town."

"What time should I pick you up?" he asked, his insides churning as if he and Zoe were going out on a real date. More proof that he was a fool.

"After dinner," she said. "Nine?"

He must have looked surprised, because she smiled.

"Don't you remember when we used to go out dancing? Things never got going until around ten."

Oh, he remembered. All too well. Just like that, images of them intertwined on the dance floor, sweat-slickened limbs so close, so intimate, they might as well have been making love.

Christ.

He looked away, just in case she saw something in his eyes. "All right," he managed. "I'll pick you up then."

She couldn't decide on a dress. Tossing her fifth pick of the night—a basic black sheath—she cursed under her breath. This was more than bad, it was awful. Since moving to New York, she'd become very decisive and she wasn't the type to dither over outfits.

But all of her dresses screamed *New York chic* rather than small-town biker bar. What the heck should she wear?

What would Shayna have worn? Pacing in front of the closet, Zoe realized she actually had no idea.

Before she could talk herself out of it, she retrieved her phone and pulled up Cristine's number. "Hey, Cristine. Quick question," she said, hoping to cut off any curiosity from the other woman. "What kind of outfits did Shayna wear when the two of you went out partying?"

Slow in responding, Cristine sounded as if she'd just gotten out of bed. Knowing what she now knew, Zoe considered that a very real possibility.

"I… Why?" Cristine asked. "Did you find something of hers?"

"No. I was just curious," Zoe lied. "Did she wear jeans and heels or something more dressy?"

"It depends. If we were just out for a good time, not trying to pick anyone up, we wore Miss Me jeans and high-heeled boots. But if we had an itch, you know, and really wanted to get laid, we'd slut it up."

"Slut it up," Zoe repeated, inwardly cringing.

"Yeah." Cristine giggled. "Low cut, short shirt, as sexy as we could make it. Shayna loved to wear corsets with a tiny, black leather mini."

"Ok, thanks." Zoe hung up. She glanced at her watch. She had time to drive to Mesquite to go shopping. One of the shops in Town East Mall used to sell things like corsets and leather miniskirts.

It wasn't until a few hours later, as she viewed herself in the full-length mirror, that she realized she'd have to face Brock dressed like she had sex for sale.

Her entire body flushed at the thought. Ever since he'd picked her up at the airport, she'd been trying like heck to ignore the sparks that had always arced between them. Foolishly, she'd imagined the passage of time might have erased this pure and powerful desire.

Not so. Briefly, she allowed herself to entertain the fantasy of giving in, letting the passion carry her away. They were both adults, both able to give and receive pleasure.

But no. Regretfully, she knew this would never be possible. She didn't believe he'd ever be able to forgive her. So how to deal with this? Again she surveyed her mirror image. Outwardly, she appeared cool and calm, but inside the buzzing of her nerves made her feel faint and dizzy.

He'd offered to accompany her. Nothing more, nothing less. And he was right—it wouldn't be smart to go alone.

But with Brock, of all people? Pressing her palms to her overheated cheeks, she moaned.

She hadn't expected to still want him. But every time they were together, she positively ached to touch him, to feel his corded muscles under her hands. She longed to press herself against him, body to body, and match the heat of his arousal with her own.

In the five years since she'd left him, she'd made many changes to her life, as had he. But this desire that arced between them had remained, like coals glowing from a banked fire, just waiting for the right moment to burst into flame. If she allowed it to, she had no doubt she'd be the one badly burned this time.

Shayna. She'd come here for Shayna, not to go stirring up ghosts from her past.

Finally, arriving home with barely ten minutes before Brock was supposed to pick her up, Zoe got dressed.

The little black minidress did exactly what she'd needed it to do.

She chose a pair of dangling silver earrings and a matching cuff bracelet, as well as her tallest pair of stiletto heels. Surveying herself one final time in the mirror, she shied away from picturing Brock's reaction.

She halfway wanted to wrap up in a blanket to shield herself from his gaze, but she shook off that feeling and straightened her shoulders. Zoe Onella had never been a quitter and she wasn't about to start now.

He knew better. Brock shook his head, completely disgusted with himself. Yet he couldn't keep from imagining what she'd wear—or what she *wouldn't wear*. He wondered if she knew what kind of dive they were going to. The place had been bad enough fifteen years ago. Now, it was worse. He'd actually visited the Hitching Post a time or two in his falling-down-drunk days.

He was pretty sure enough time had gone by that no one would recognize him. And so what if they did? It might actually work out to their advantage if he fit in.

Pulling up in front of the Bells' at nine sharp, he sat for a moment in the parked car, willing his pulse to slow. He wasn't sure he was up for a lengthy conversation with Mama Bell.

To his relief, just as he was about to get out, the front door opened and Zoe emerged.

His first impression was one of reprieve. She wore a long, gingham dress that appeared to be three sizes too big, held around her by a large and ugly belt. Then, as she approached the truck and he realized she'd put on the outfit *over* something else, he laughed out loud.

"What?" She gave him a cross look as she gathered

the long skirt in one hand and climbed in. "You don't like my clothes?"

Instead of answering, he simply shook his head.

"I had to put something on to cover up my mini-dress," she explained with a sheepish smile. "Mama Bell would've had a fit if she saw me go out dressed like a...tramp, to use her words."

He couldn't help but laugh. "Well, you're certainly not, dressed like that."

"Oh, but I am." Smiling, she lowered one elastic shoulder to reveal something sleeveless, black and extremely tight underneath.

Just like that, his pulse sped up. "Oh" was all he could think to say.

While he drove, she began the arduous process of removing her granny dress, wiggling and squirming with her seat belt still in place. Trying not to sneak glimpses of her was as hopeless as attempting not to breathe. He could no more manage it than he could control his growing arousal.

He tried like hell to think of something else, anything else, but the rustling fabric and her soft murmurs of frustration didn't help things. If she turned her head and glanced at him, she couldn't help but notice.

Gripping the steering wheel, he cursed under his breath. They'd be at the bar in twenty minutes. He had to get himself back to normal by then or he wouldn't be able to get out of the truck.

Somehow, by the time they pulled into the parking lot across the street from the Hitching Post, he'd managed to regain control of his libido.

The area surprised him. As he parked in the well-lit lot, he saw that part of town had apparently been undergoing a renovation. Gone were the boarded-up windows and prostitutes lingering under dirty streetlights.

Even the Hitching Post looked totally different. The formerly faded storefront had been redone with new lumber and fresh paint. Rows of gleaming motorcycles were parked in a well-lit lot off to the side.

"Wow." Zoe echoed his thoughts. "It actually looks like a respectable bar."

He nodded. They walked up to the front door side by side.

It turned out the interior didn't match the exterior. Once they crossed the threshold, they might have been stepping back into the previous version of the place.

The air inside the dimly lit bar was heavy with cigarette smoke, mingled with the acrid scents of sweat and alcohol. In the back, men leaned over pool tables, intent on their games. Country music wailed on the jukebox.

Just like that, he was back in another time and place. Where he'd found solace in the bottom of a bottle.

His mouth went dry. Damn, he wanted a drink. But this was an old and familiar battle, one he faced on a regular basis. He could handle this.

Looking around, he took a deep breath. Staying close behind Zoe, Brock couldn't help noticing that every single man in the place watched with avid interest as Zoe sauntered up to the bar. She might as well have been naked, the way they undressed her with their eyes.

The hair on the back of his neck rose as he worked to stifle the low growl that rose in his throat.

Clenching his fists, he slid onto the stool next to her. It took a major effort of willpower not to throw his arm across her shoulders, thereby claiming her as his.

As it was, several of the men continued to leer at her, their calculating looks as intimate as if she was alone.

"Stop looking at them like you want to kill them," she murmured, and leaned close enough that her warm breath tickled his ear. "I'm here for one reason only."

He nodded, the buzzing in his ears subsiding somewhat as he remembered. Shayna. They'd come here for clues about Shayna.

And Zoe wasn't his. She hadn't been, not for a long time.

At that moment, the strength of the temptation to order a drink made him sway.

"What'll it be?" the bartender asked, gazing only at Zoe.

"Two beers," she said, smiling flirtatiously at the bearded man. "Bud Lights."

"Club soda for me," Brock said, but the bartender had already turned away to fetch the drinks.

"No beer?" Zoe asked, surprised.

"No." Trying to appear casual, he shrugged. "I don't drink."

"Since when?"

He shrugged again, giving her a look to try to tell her not to make a big deal out of it.

"Here you go." The bartender set two cold bottles in front of them.

Brock stared at his. He reached out and traced the sweat running down the brown bottle with a shaky finger, before sliding it over to Zoe. "You can have this."

She stared, her gaze searching his face. He broke the look first, signaling to the bartender and asking for a club soda. It was a good thing he'd stopped in at TJ's the other night. It had been his first time in a bar atmosphere in a long time and had proved to him that he could handle it.

Which meant he could also handle this.

His club soda appeared in front of him. He gave a grateful nod and took a fortifying sip.

Zoe continued to watch him, the compassionate look in her soft brown eyes not doing him any good at all.

"Go ahead," he told her, working to unclench his teeth. "Work the room. I'll keep an eye on you from here. Let me know if you have any trouble."

"I'm going to the restroom." She flashed him a reluctant grin. "You sound like you're my pimp or something."

Before he could respond, she slid off the stool and headed to the ladies' room. Brock couldn't tear his gaze away from her cute little backside, along with most of the other patrons.

After she'd disappeared inside, he pulled up a picture of Shayna on his phone and motioned the bartender over. "Have you seen her?"

The other man laughed. "Oh yeah, though she hasn't been around in a while. That's Shayna. She's a regular here."

"When was the last time you saw her?" Brock asked.

"I don't know." The bartender thought for a second. "It's maybe been a couple of days, maybe a week." He squinted down the length of the long bar. "She left with Mike there."

Brock looked in the direction he'd pointed. Several men occupied bar stools, all of them appearing to be alone. "Which one?"

"Third from the end. Big guy with the ponytail and the beard."

Right after he pointed Mike out, someone called for another beer, and the bartender left.

Zoe returned. Brock relayed the information to her.

"All right then. Well, he's certainly muscular at least." She dusted her hands on the front of her miniskirt, drawing Brock's gaze like a magnet did to metal. He swallowed, a wave of heat suffusing him.

Zoe didn't appear to notice. "Come on," she said. "Stay a few steps behind me, okay?" She moved off without waiting for an answer.

"Hey there." Sidling up to Mike, she smiled. "Are you alone?"

He brightened. Of course he did, Brock thought darkly. He was male, after all.

"Sure am, pretty lady." Patting the empty stool next to him, he grinned. "How 'bout I buy you a beer?"

"First, I need to know something. I'm wondering if you know my friend. She's tall and blonde. Her name is Shayna."

"Shayna?" Slurring his words, the bearded man took another long pull on his beer. He blinked, clearly trying to focus. "The name sounds familiar, but I don't know…"

Zoe whipped out her cell phone, scrolling until she found a picture of Shayna. "Here. Does she look familiar?"

His eyes widened. "Oh, *her*." He licked his lips. "She and I, uh…got together a while back. But I haven't seen her since then." Scratching the tattoo of a shotgun that covered his entire arm, he grimaced. "Does she owe you money, too?"

Chapter 7

Too? Zoe glanced at Brock, one eyebrow raised, before turning her attention back to the man. "She's my best friend," she said, her voice saccharine. "Did she borrow money from you?"

He tilted his head, looking from her to Brock while he considered. "What is this really about?" he asked, his voice suspicious. "Who are you?"

"I'm Zoe," she said. "And you are?"

"Mike."

Zoe leaned in closer, giving Mike a good close-up of her plunging neckline. Every muscle in his body tensed, and Brock had to force himself to look away.

"Let me buy you another beer," Zoe crooned, sliding up on the bar stool next to Mike with the shotgun tattoo. She flashed a smile full of mystery and sex, a smile that no man with red blood could hope to resist, Brock thought grimly.

"Okay."

Now that Mike had agreed, Zoe motioned behind his back that Brock should move away. Begrudgingly, he stepped back, moving behind a pillar, out of Mike's direct line of sight but close enough that he could still hear the rest of the conversation.

Zoe ordered two more beers, even though she'd barely touched her first one. "So, Mike, did my friend owe you a lot of money?"

He shook his head, mumbling something under his breath, too low for Brock to make out the words.

"I'm sorry." Practically purring, Zoe patted Mike's muscular arm. "She does like to party."

"Yeah." Taking another swig of his drink, Mike brightened. "How about you?"

Zoe looked blank. "I'm sorry, what?"

He leaned in, close enough to kiss her, no doubt giving her a shot of his alcohol-laden breath. "Do you like to party?"

"Oh." Zoe laughed, flipping her hair over her shoulder. "Sometimes. I haven't nearly had enough to drink tonight. So, when was the last time you saw Shayna again?"

Subtle, she was not. But captivated by her sensual beauty and with his senses dulled by beer, Mike didn't seem to notice.

Considering her question, he dragged his hands through his longish graying hair, then scratched his salt-and-pepper beard. "A week or so ago, I think. We hooked up here and, after last call, we headed out to the lake to keep partying."

"The lake?" Zoe froze. Even though she couldn't hear him, Brock silently urged her to act normal. He figured Mike would clam up the instant he sensed the importance of her questions.

"Yeah." Draining his beer, Mike set the bottle on the counter, hard. "Thanks for the brew." He half stood, swaying slightly. "But I gotta run."

Damn. Cursing, Brock thought about moving forward to intercept the other man but decided to wait and give Zoe a chance to handle it.

"Aw, don't go." Zoe clutched at his arm, pouting prettily. She slid the untouched beer over to him. "Have one more beer, on me."

Mike glanced from her to the sweating brown bottle. He hesitated, just enough. "All right." He grinned at Zoe, his calculating expression telling Brock he wasn't as drunk as he was pretending.

Which brought up the question of why?

Zoe and Mike put their heads together. She laughed at something the other man had said, leaning in so close to him they looked like they could start making out at any moment.

Or maybe, Brock thought as his blood started to boil, that was only his imagination. He took a sip of the club soda, then a deep breath. While he'd known he wouldn't be comfortable watching Zoe work her wiles on other men, he hadn't expected to teeter this close to the edge of losing control.

Which proved he was more of an idiot than he'd realized.

Through a haze of smoke and rage, he realized Zoe was motioning him over. Moving stiffly, he went.

"Hey, Brock," she said. "Quick question. What time

was it that Cristine said Shayna called you the night she disappeared?"

Next to her, Mike stiffened.

"Eleven," Brock answered, carefully setting his drink on the bar as he balanced on the balls of his feet.

"Well, that's just about the time that Mike here claims he and she were partying out at the lake," she said brightly. "Isn't that right, Mike?"

Swiveling to face Brock, Mike crossed his arms. "Maybe a little before that, but yeah. So?"

This time Brock answered. "Shayna hasn't been seen since."

Mike looked from Brock to Zoe, then back again. "What's your point? Me and Shayna partied, had us some fun and then went our separate ways. I haven't seen her since then."

Taking a step closer, Brock kept his arms by his sides, hoping the nonthreatening posture wouldn't provoke the other man.

"Why don't you tell us exactly what happened?" he asked, his voice calm.

"Sure. I don't have anything to hide." Mike drained the last of his beer. "Though I might need another drink first."

"No problem," Zoe said coolly. She signaled the bartender and, after another bottle of beer had been placed in front of him, she smiled. "So you and Shayna were at the lake. Where, exactly?"

"In a wooded area by one of the public boat ramps," he replied. "Right off FM 3033. I brought a blanket. We had some primo weed and a bottle of wine. We smoked a bowl, and then…" Mike's leering grin grated on Brock's nerves. He suspected Zoe felt the same, judging from her narrowed eyes.

"And then?" Zoe prompted.

"That girl was hot to trot," Mike said. "If you know what I mean. We fooled around, and after that, she took off."

"Why?"

Mike shrugged. "Who the hell knows? Maybe she's crazy."

"She's not."

He took one look at Zoe's closed expression and shrugged again. "Whatever you say."

"How'd she get home?" Zoe asked.

"Beats me. I offered her a ride home, but she said she wanted to go for a walk and maybe a swim. She was pretty loaded, so I told her I didn't think that was a good idea. She just laughed at me and told me to take myself off."

"Did you?"

"Yeah." He grimaced. "I went home. Got there a few minutes after eleven. My roommate was there. He can vouch for me."

"You said earlier she owed you money?"

Mike's expression darkened. "Yeah. She wanted to buy the rest of my stash. I had about two fingers of good Colombian in that baggie. She promised to pay me the next night. We were supposed to meet up here. She never showed."

Before Zoe could say anything else, Mike stood. "I'm going to take off."

Zoe grabbed his arm. "Can I get your number, just in case I have any more questions?"

He stared down at her, his expression hard. "I don't

think so," he finally said. Inclining his chin at Brock, he turned to go. "You two have a good night, now."

Silently, they watched him make his way through the crowd to the door.

"We need to have the police search the lake," Zoe said, her expression glum. "What if Shayna went swimming drunk and drowned?"

"What if she didn't?" Brock countered. "We don't have any proof."

"Did you not hear what Mike said?" Zoe's voice rose. "He left her there!"

Taking her arm, Brock steered her gently toward the door. She didn't resist, for which he was grateful. They were still drawing attention as they made their way through the bar.

Outside, she shook her arm free. "Come on, Brock!" Rounding on him, she stood toe to toe. "You heard the man. He *left* her there, all by herself. Who knows what could have happened? Someone could have followed them, or he could have gone back and…"

Though her close proximity inflamed his already overheated senses, he managed to respond in a reasonable tone of voice. "Zoe, I understand, but Mike already got what he wanted from her. He had no reason to go back. And don't you think if he did something to harm Shayna, he would have kept quiet about even going to the lake with her?"

Hands on shapely hips, she lifted her chin. He almost smiled. He should have known she wouldn't back down.

"This is the best lead we've gotten," she argued. "And we got it on our first try out."

Damn, he wanted to yank her up against him and kiss her. Battling back that impulse was as difficult as willing his heartbeat to slow, but he managed. Good thing, too, because when he glanced up, he realized a crowd had gathered.

Not smart, especially in a place like this.

"Is that guy bothering you, honey?" One of the men in the group watching them called out.

Zoe blinked, letting Brock know she hadn't even realized they had an audience. He would have felt flattered if he didn't know how much trouble the wrong move could put them in.

"Zoe," he murmured, his voice a quiet rumble. Luckily, she caught on immediately.

"Oh, he's not botherin' me at all," she purred, wrapping her arms around his neck and pressing her body close.

Instantly, he lost all control over his lower body. She had to feel it, as close as she was. The little hitch in her breathing told him she did.

But it was what she did next that floored him. While the small group around them watched, she grabbed Brock's head, pulled him down to her and kissed him.

No closed-mouth, chaste, this-is-for-show kiss, either. Mouth open, this was the kind of heat-generating mating of tongues that led to much, much more.

When she finally lifted her head, he felt as if he was coming up for air after diving to the bottom of the lake. Vision blurred by a red haze of lust, he couldn't think, couldn't speak, or move.

"Come on, darlin'," she whispered, taking his hand and tugging him toward the parking lot as the men hooted and called ribald comments. "There's a lot more where that came from."

Though his arousal made walking difficult, he managed.

Only when they were safely inside his truck and driving away did Brock allow himself to take a deep breath. "What the hell was that?" The words exploded from him. He dragged his hand through his hair and fought for control.

"Acting." She grinned at him, apparently having no idea of her effect on him. "I'm pretty good at it, aren't I?"

Jaw set, he struggled to find the right words. Finally, he thought the hell with it. "Do that again and you'll find yourself backed up against the wall with me buried deep inside you."

She gasped. "Brock—"

"If that offends you, too damn bad. You felt what you did to me."

"But—" She tried again.

"Just give me a minute," he interrupted through clenched teeth. "Please."

Shifting in her seat, she complied. But she didn't turn away. Instead, she watched as he tried to get himself under control.

"I'm sorry," she said after a few minutes had passed.

"I am, too," he admitted.

Dipping her head, she considered him. "Let's forget about it, okay?"

"There's nothing I'd like better," he replied, well aware he was lying.

Taking his words at face value, she nodded her head, one corner of her shapely mouth tilting up. "I don't think those men back there would have bothered us," she said, her tone light. "But I had to make sure. That's why I kissed you."

He decided not to argue the point.

"I didn't mean anything by it," she continued, clearly not knowing when to stop. "Nothing at all."

And therein lay the problem. Yet again, he simply clenched his teeth and then nodded.

She stretched, drawing his attention to where the stretchy material of her dress pulled across her breasts. Almost immediately, he again felt desire stir, nearly making him groan out loud. He needed a distraction and, damn it, there was none to be found.

"Can I ask you something?" She looked directly at him.

"As long as it has nothing to do with that kiss."

"It doesn't."

He sighed. "Sure."

"Why weren't you drinking back there?"

Crap. "I told you, I quit."

"Why?" Her voice was soft but persistent.

A flash of pain worked like a dash of ice water to extinguish the lingering embers of his desire. He'd wanted a distraction and, by God, he'd gotten it. Zoe had succeeded in reminding him exactly why he shouldn't want her, couldn't want her. She hadn't been there to help him out of the deep, dark hole he'd dug. Though the decision to begin drinking heavily had been his and his alone, even now he still considered her disappearance as the underlying reason.

Or maybe that was a massive oversimplification. Her vanishing had begun a chain of events, culminating in his father's death and the end of Brock's dreams.

There'd been more than one reason he'd tried to drown himself in alcohol.

"That's really none of your business," he told her, his voice stiff.

"Sorry." Lifting her palms toward him, she made a strangled sound. "I forget we're not friends."

Friends. If there was one thing he knew for certain, it was that she was not his friend.

Opening his mouth to concur, he closed it, instead. He was drained, tired of fighting his attraction to her, worn-out from the constant, self-protective need to stay one step ahead of her. So he let the comment go. No way was he up for a long, drawn-out, female kind of talk about defining their relationship. As far as he was concerned, they didn't have one.

Nor would they ever.

"I'll talk to the police," he said, aware that would distract her and keep her from asking any more probing, personal questions. "Roger Giles might listen to me."

"Thank you," she said softly. "The quicker we find out if Shayna is in that lake, the sooner Mama and Mr. Bell can get closure."

He heard the pain in her voice but refused to acknowledge it. If she needed comfort, he wasn't the one to provide it.

"I'll let you know what he says."

"I really appreciate that." She sighed. "Before we get to Mama Bell's, can we stop at one of the fast-food places on Main Street so I can change back into my other dress?"

He'd managed to completely forget about that. "Sure." And then, in that night's apparent tradition of failing to keep his mouth shut when he should have, he asked her if she wanted to get something to eat while they were there.

Turning to eye him, she frowned in apparent confusion. "Sure, I guess. A burger would taste really great right now."

This despite the fact that it was nearly eleven at night.

What harm could there be in sharing a quick meal? None. He turned into the parking lot of Abe's Fast Burgers. A neon sign flashing in the window advertised they were open twenty-four hours a day. Zoe hurried to the restroom to change.

The only other customers inside were a tired-looking woman and her two small children. Emerging from the restroom, the instant she saw them, Zoe stopped. Brock narrowly avoided crashing into her.

When he glanced at her, a look of gut-wrenching pain flashed across her face so quickly he might have imagined it.

"What's wrong?" he asked, against his better judgment.

She blinked. "Nothing." She cleared her throat and hurried over to the counter. "Dinner's on me."

So he wasn't the only one with secrets. Interesting. Or it would be, if he actually cared.

The sun beamed hot from a cloudless blue sky, reflecting sharply off the still, smooth lake. A perfect spring day, one made for picnics and hiking, cheerful things. Not the kind of weather Zoe would have ordered up for what they'd come here to do. Gray, overcast skies and the soft mist of a chilly rain would have been much better suited for the task at hand.

Zoe had risen early and updated her blog. The night

before, she'd been a bundle of nerves, unable to sleep, so she'd come up with a slightly humorous take on the difference between men in Texas and those in the Northeast. An hour after posting it, she'd gotten close to five hundred comments, which meant the topic was a success.

None of that helped her mood, considering today they were looking for Shayna's body.

Brock had persuaded Roger Giles to order a search of this part of the lake. The sheriff had done so grudgingly, according to Brock, and only because he owed Brock a favor.

Wearing black wetsuits, the dive team waded into the murky water near the shore. There were three of them, two on loan from Dallas. Zoe had listened silently while they were given instructions. The lake had been divided into quadrants. For now, they were sticking to the area near the western shore, where Mike had claimed to picnic with Shayna. They'd also done some sort of calculation with wind currents and the water, and were also searching an area where debris was most likely to wash up. Lastly, they had a few others searching the remainder of the lake, just in case the currents might have moved something.

Though they didn't use the word, Zoe knew they meant *body*.

"Hey." Brock came up behind her, his expression distant but civil.

She inclined her head in a halfhearted greeting.

"I'm going to put my boat in." His blue-eyed gaze searched her face. "Do you want to come with me?"

Her heart leaped, though she kept her expression impassive. "Did you clear it with the police?"

"As long as I stay away from the area where the divers are searching, I'm fine. One of the guys mentioned they might be able to use my assistance."

Temptation warred with the desire to have nothing to do with him. "I'm thinking you can see what's going on a lot better from the water."

He nodded and held out his hand. "Come on. You know you want to, if only to distract yourself from thinking the worst."

That last remark alone should have been enough to make her decline. But she hated being reduced to pacing the uneven shore, unable to see, unable to participate, just waiting helplessly to see if they found her friend's lifeless body.

Even considering such a thing nearly had her doubling over in pain and grief. Shayna couldn't be dead. But all evidence suggested they'd find her here, somewhere in the water, badly decomposed.

Argh. Swallowing back the bile that rose in her throat, Zoe raised her head to see Brock still waiting, watching her.

She pushed away her doubts and slipped her hand into his. She ignored the immediate jolt of heat, aware he no doubt did the same.

He led her up a grassy hill. When they crested it, she saw his truck parked in the paved area leading to the public boat ramp. He had a newish bass boat, a sleek, slender thing with a huge outboard motor.

He caught her staring and flashed a brief smile. "It's fast on the water. Get in the truck and after I back the boat in, do you mind pulling the truck and trailer out and parking it? I'll swing the boat over to the dock there and pick you up."

The wooden dock ran along one side of the boat ramp.

Taking a deep breath, she nodded. "I should warn you that I've never driven a truck pulling a trailer before."

"No problem." He squeezed her shoulder, a casual gesture that she felt all the way to her bones. "All you have to do is drive straight ahead and park in the little area over there."

Again she nodded, moving away from him toward his truck.

Once he'd backed up enough so that the boat trailer was in the water, he put the truck in Park, applied the brake and jumped out. Wading to the boat, he climbed up the front and uncranked a cable that kept the front of the boat tethered to the trailer. Then he sat at the driver's seat and started the engine. It roared to life on the first try.

Zoe watched over her shoulder as Brock backed his bass boat off the trailer and into the water. He made it look spectacularly easy, though she suspected a certain level of skill must be involved.

After the boat was in the water, he signaled her to pull the truck forward. She disengaged the parking brake and pulled forward, driving the truck and lightweight trailer to the area he'd indicated.

When she'd finished, she headed over to the wooden dock. He'd pulled his boat alongside and tied it loosely to the pier. After hurrying down the length of the pier, she carefully got on board, waving away his outstretched hand. Once she'd taken a seat, he untied them and they backed away from the dock.

She gripped the side of the seat tightly, taking a deep breath before looking around. She hadn't been out on the water since high school. She'd forgotten how much she'd liked it.

And, thinking that, she wondered if she'd always from this day forward, associate boating with finding Shayna's body.

No. Positive thinking. She lifted her head, letting the wind sift through her ponytail, glad she'd had the foresight to wear it.

Keeping their speed low, Brock took them out to the center of the search operation and killed the engine. He dropped the anchor, his blond hair shining golden in the perfect sun, his tanned skin gleaming, his muscular arms flexing.

Even without touching him, she once again felt that familiar, intoxicating pull low in her belly.

Damn.

She stood, shading her eyes with her hand. The divers had gone under, and the nervous anticipation made her feel ill.

"Mama Bell doesn't know about this?" Brock asked, breaking her concentration on the flat surface of the water.

"No. I didn't want her to worry."

He nodded. "Probably a good idea."

"Yeah." Her attention drifted back to the water. "I really hope they don't find anything."

"They won't." He sounded awfully certain. Too certain, which made her wonder again if he knew something he hadn't mentioned.

Several hours later, it appeared Brock was right. All three of the divers had resurfaced, made their way to shore and were removing their equipment. Brock motored over as close to shore as he could. "Find anything?"

One of the men shook his head. "Nothing, and we've done a thorough search of the entire lake. We're calling it a day. Since we don't have actual evidence that she went in the water, I don't think we'll be back."

Brock nodded, then looked at Zoe. She wasn't sure if she was disappointed or relieved. He put the boat in gear and slowly motored away, heading in the direction of the boat ramp.

"Do we have to go back right away?" she asked.

"No." Watching her closely, he seemed wary. "Why?"

Her shrug deliberately casual, she glanced from him to the open water. "I haven't been on a boat ride in years. I wouldn't mind a bit of distraction right now."

Still, he eyed her the way a man does when he's not sure how he's supposed to react. Finally, he shrugged. "Ok, fine. Fast or slow?"

"Fast," she instantly responded, as he'd no doubt hoped she would. Any man who owned a bass boat with a 250-hp outboard motor would no doubt welcome the chance to use it.

And so he did. When they'd traveled a decent distance from the area the divers had been searching, he opened the throttle and they took off, the water parting before them to plume up after.

Moisture sprayed her, making her smile, her first genuine smile in ages. She sat up straight, the wind whipping her ponytail, and let the thrill of speeding across the lake drive all other thoughts from her mind.

But, as with everything else, her temporary respite didn't last. After making a sharp turn near the dam,

Brock slowed and finally cut the motor. Since there was no wind, they wouldn't drift far.

"Are you okay?" he asked.

She nodded. "Thank you for that. I needed it. It's the first time since I've been back in Anniversary that I didn't worry about Shayna. It's hard to stop.

"I don't know if someone grabbed her and hurt her or what. All I can do is pray she isn't dead. Or, worse, that she's not some crazy man's prisoner."

Closing her eyes, she shuddered at the thought. "We've got to find her, Brock. We have to."

"I know," he said quietly, crossing over to her and smoothing her hair with one hand. "And I have to admit, I'm finding it more and more difficult to believe Shayna took off on her own."

Relieved, she nodded, moving away even though all she wanted to do was lean into him. "Thank you. I know she didn't. Her credit cards haven't been used, and she has no cash. Plus, she'd never have left without her phone."

He stood a moment longer and then returned to his spot behind the driver's console. "Devils advocate, but she could have had a secret stash of money. Maybe, like you, she wanted to leave all trace of her old life behind. She could have gotten one of those prepaid, untraceable phones."

Ignoring the slight dig, she sighed. "Shayna and Mama Bell always knew I was okay, though they didn't know where I was for a long time."

"Why didn't you go to the police?"

"I couldn't take that chance. The only person I told was Shayna. She helped me get out of town that night."

"And you didn't think to come to me?" The pain in

his face nearly shattered her. "I would have helped you, kept you safe."

"I couldn't risk it," she whispered, aware he'd hate her now. She couldn't blame him. He'd never understand what she'd given up—her home, her friends, her family, and her fiancé—out of love. She'd left in order to keep them safe.

"And then they caught the guy," Brock said, letting her know she'd spoken out loud. "He was convicted, when another eyewitness came forward, and sent away to prison, where he remains to this day."

"Yes. I check compulsively to make sure he hasn't been paroled."

"And still you didn't see fit to clue me in."

She glanced up in time to catch the flash of pain in his eyes. "Brock, I couldn't tell you for your own safety."

"Right. Because that would have put me in danger." The cold edge of irony in his voice told her he didn't think much of that explanation.

"And you would have come after me," she finished. "Or, failing that, you'd have wanted to wait for me. It was better if you didn't know. That way you could move on with your life."

"Move on with my life? Is that what you thought I wanted?"

The violence in his tone spoke of old wounds not entirely healed. She swallowed, digging deep for her reserve of strength. "Yes," she answered.

"Once you felt you were safe, after he was put away for good, why didn't you return? Why didn't you come back?"

To Anniversary. To the Bells, who were the only

family she'd ever known. To him. The man she'd been engaged to marry.

Hands clenched into fists, Zoe tried like hell not to cry. She'd naively hoped that this time, she and Brock could part as friends. She should have known she could never wipe out the pain her actions had caused him. Until now, she'd managed to convince herself that her own pain had been buried away so deeply it would never return.

Lies, all around. And still more to come, because Brock must never know the true reason she'd stayed away long after it was safe to return. No matter how much it hurt. She couldn't let him get attached to her, or she to him, because when all this was over, she would return to New York without a backward glance.

A painful truth. No matter what he might think he wanted, they could never be together. At first, she'd figured she'd stay in New York a couple of years, explore her freedom and then maybe go back home. That possibility had been erased, mostly because of the baby she'd carried and lost. The baby—his baby—that he'd never known about.

Chapter 8

No one, not even Shayna, knew that Zoe had been pregnant when she'd left town. No one knew about Zoe's miscarriage in the first trimester. Or her subsequent diagnosis of severe endometriosis. Her fallopian tubes had been irretrievably damaged. She'd been told in no uncertain terms that it was extremely unlikely she would ever be able to have children.

Brock deserved a woman who could have his children. More than anything, he wanted to be a father. Before everything had gone to hell in a handbasket, they'd discussed the family they wanted to make together. Brock had wanted six kids, she two, and they'd compromised at three. They'd been so starry-eyed, so young, so full of anticipation for their future together.

Her eyes teared up, damn it. Fiercely, she swiped at them, keeping her face averted. He must never know the truth. There was no way she could have gone back to him after that. Not then and not now. He shouldn't have to settle. She couldn't ask that of him, or of anyone.

So she'd embraced her new life, formed a new persona and tried to live. If she occasionally felt empty, well, that was the price she had to pay.

He grabbed her arm, spinning her around to face him. "Aren't you going to answer me?" His gruff voice hinted at the depths of his emotion. "Why didn't you come back to Anniversary? Why didn't you come back to me?"

Staring at him, she summoned up the necessary strength for giving him only a partial truth. "Because I made a new life, Brock," she said firmly. "I was happy in New York. The city had something that I didn't even know I was missing here. I didn't want to give it up."

"New York." He spoke the words as if they were a curse. "You chose a place over all you had here? Over us?"

Desperate, she tried one last time to get back on solid ground. "I think we need to redirect the focus to where it needs to be. On Shayna."

"Hiding again?" he asked.

"No." She met his gaze head-on to show him what she meant. "We can't change the past. But we can try to influence the future. I don't think Shayna ran away. If that was the case, she would have let her mother know, at least. Shayna wouldn't have wanted the woman to worry."

As he stared out at the peaceful lake, a muscle worked in his jaw. "Zoe, honestly. What do you think happened to her? Why do you find it so impossible to believe she might have done the exact same thing you did five years ago." Harsh voiced, it was more of a statement than a question.

Suddenly she couldn't do it anymore. She didn't have the strength to keep piling lie upon lie.

"Take me back to the dock," she ordered in a toneless voice, gripping the boat railing so tightly her knuckles showed white.

"With pleasure," he snarled, sounding the opposite of toneless. He turned the key and the motor roared to life.

They took off. This time she found no pleasure in the speed. Tight-lipped, she stared straight ahead, the spray stinging her eyes, the sun blinding her.

He slowed their speed as they approached the pier. "I'll leave you off here," he said. "I can load the boat by myself."

Aching, she nodded. She couldn't explain, because she couldn't stand the hurt of wanting him again. The pain of being noble had nearly killed her once. She wasn't sure she could survive it again.

Having him despise her was better. Safer. So she did the only thing she could. She had to save herself, after all, and, in doing so, save him too.

Without another word, she turned and walked away, leaving him for the final time.

Brock felt savage. The urge to drown his pain in the comforting numbness of alcohol reared up so strongly he cursed.

No. He was sober and he would stay sober.

He got the boat loaded and drove home. Somehow, someway, he needed to put Zoe Onella from his mind and get back to his real life. He'd thought time had healed him. Clearly it had not.

Rubbing the back of his neck, he grimaced. One thing for sure, something crazy had been going on with Shayna. So many lies. He couldn't help wondering how much of what she'd told him was the truth, especially where it concerned Zoe.

Disgusted with himself, he shook his head. None of this was his concern. He squelched the annoying desire to go grab a beer, driving instead to the local A&W for a root beer float.

Then he went home to his empty apartment, turned on the television and tried to lose himself in a true-crime drama.

The next morning, Cristine showed up at the feed store. Since she didn't have livestock or even own a pet, she hadn't come to make a purchase. What now?

"I need to talk to you," she said, her expression troubled.

"About Shayna?" he asked, hoping it wasn't about Zoe.

"Yes." She took a deep breath. "It's been bothering me ever since she disappeared. I know you and Shayna had troubles and—"

"Troubles?" What the hell? Trying not to show his annoyance, he crossed his arms. "I have no idea what you're talking about."

Coloring, she looked down. "Come on, Brock. Shayna and I were best friends. You have to know she told me everything."

"There was nothing to tell."

Anger flared in her hazel eyes. "Cut the crap, Brock. I know you hit her. I saw her bruises."

He couldn't have been more stunned if she'd hauled

off and punched him in the stomach. "Hit her?" he repeated, feeling sick. "I didn't…wouldn't. I've never hit a woman in my life. Shayna or anyone."

Frowning in confusion, she stared. "You're telling the truth."

"Of course, I'm telling the truth," he exploded. "What the hell is wrong with you?"

She began backing away from him, the sick look of fear on her face telling him she thought he might slug her.

"You're a-angry," she stammered. "I didn't mean to bother you. I'll go."

He felt as if he'd kicked a dog. "Cristine, wait. Please."

She'd already turned to go and almost tripped over her own feet when he called her back. For a moment, she appeared torn between fleeing and staying.

"Come on, Cristine. You know I'm not a monster."

Slowly, she walked back over to him. "Brock, like everyone else around here, I'm just trying to get answers."

"I know." Unable to keep the weariness from his voice, he indicated the chair again. "Please, sit."

"I'd rather stand." Hovering near the door, clearly so she could flee if he made the slightest move, she eyed him.

Stunned, shocked and uncomfortable, he stared back. Had everyone in this town lost their minds?

"I just came here for one reason," Cristine said, nerves showing in her trembling voice. "I want to know if you did something to Shayna."

That did it. He pushed to his feet. "Get out. Right now. Turn and walk away and don't say another word."

He expected her to scurry away, as she'd done earlier. Instead, she lifted her chin and met his gaze, a half smile hovering around the edge of her mouth. "Or what, Brock?" she asked softly. "Will you make me disappear, too?"

Then, while he was standing speechless, Cristine turned on her heel and marched away.

After the front door closed, Brock put his head in his hands. Had Cristine completely gone off the deep end? Surely no one else believed he'd hurt Shayna, did they? Folks here knew him. He'd grown up in this town, with these people.

"Are you all right?" Eve asked.

He looked up to see his baby sister eyeing him, her blue eyes full of concern. Since his mission in life was to shield her from worry, he opened his mouth to tell her he was fine but then reconsidered. Eve had her own set of friends in town. He wanted to know what they were saying about Shayna. And about him.

"Not really."

She lounged in the doorway, leaning on the frame. "I figured. I saw Cristine leaving. What's going on with her?"

Leaning back in his chair, he put his hands behind his head and sighed. "You're not going to believe it, but she came to ask me if I'd done something to Shayna."

"Why would Cristine think that?" Eve asked, frowning. "That doesn't make sense."

"I know. I tried to tell her that, but she acted like I was about to attack her."

Eve shook her head. "She's fried her brain," she said, her voice echoing with authority. "Too much alcohol, too many drugs. After a while, it's got to affect your thinking."

With difficulty, he kept from smiling and tried to appear stern. "Where'd you hear something like that?"

She shrugged, clearly not bothered. "I'm in college, Brock. I'm not a child any longer."

When he laughed, she did, too.

"Thanks for that," he told her. "So Miss Woman-of-the-World, what's the word on the street about Shayna?"

"Most people think she ran off with one of those biker guys she was always hanging around."

He wished like hell that Eve's thoughts would prove true.

"Why don't you go get us lunch?" Eve smiled winningly at him. "I'm craving a fajita taco."

Digging a twenty out of his pocket, he handed it to her. "How about you do that? I've got a few things I need to tend to here."

Her grin widened as she snatched the money. "Will do."

After Eve had left, Brock prowled the empty store. Cristine's unfounded—and crazy—accusation had shaken him, especially since he figured she'd go to Zoe next with her insanity.

He actually picked up the phone and dialed the Bells' number, then reconsidered and disconnected the call.

Why he cared what Zoe thought, he couldn't say. But one thing he did know for sure was that if Zoe bought into Cristine's nonsense, then she truly had become someone he didn't know at all.

Following lunch, Brock dealt with a steady stream of customers.

Mama Bell sailed into the feed store shortly before closing time. She'd dressed as if she was going to church—dress, hose, heels, even a matching hat. The instant she spotted him, she made a beeline toward him, wearing a determined look.

"Good afternoon, Brock," she said, clutching her square black purse tightly. "I'd like a word with you, if you have time."

"Of course," he said, offering her a pleasant smile even though a chill of foreboding snaked up his spine. Things both good and bad came in groups of three, after all.

Steadying himself, he glanced around at the nearly empty store. Eve was tidying up in preparation for closing.

"Follow me." He led the way to his office. As she settled in the chair, he closed the door. "Is everything all right, Mrs. Bell?"

"Not really," she answered crossly. "But I didn't come here to talk about me. I came here to discuss you."

Great. "Have you been talking to Cristine?"

A look of distaste crossed her face. "Lord, no. I can't stand that girl. Shayna didn't start acting crazy until the two of them began hanging around together. Let me guess, she's trying to blame you for Shayna's disappearance."

He nodded, the tightness in his chest easing somewhat.

Shaking her head, Mama Bell patted his hand. "Pay no attention to her. She's a lunatic. If there's one thing I know, it's people. You would no more have hurt my daughter than you would that little girl out there." She indicated Eve.

"Thank you." Gratitude filled him. "What did you want to discuss with me?"

A determined glint in her eyes, she met his gaze.

"Zoe. I need you two to try and get along, so you can work together. No matter what Miss Cristine thinks, Shayna loved the two of you best. If anyone can find my daughter, I believe you and Zoe can."

Brock swallowed. Because he knew she was right.

Though Zoe hadn't really wanted to, when Cristine called and asked to meet for dinner and a drink, she agreed, just in case the other woman might have thought of something new. She was pleasantly surprised when Cristine suggested Papa's Pasta, a family-owned Italian place in one of the smaller shopping strips. Zoe'd eaten there once with Brock, right after he'd proposed. She vaguely remembered the food being good. At least she thought so—her mind had been on other things.

Brock. Again. It seemed she couldn't get away from thoughts about him as long as she was here in Anniversary. All the more reason she needed to find Shayna and head back home. At least in New York, she managed to go days without him crossing her mind. It had taken every bit of five years for her to get to that point in her life and now, with her return to the place where it had all begun, she was back to square one.

Longing for something that could never be.

Frustrated, she drove to the restaurant and parked. As she walked inside, she saw Cristine had already arrived and was seated at a small table near the front window. Lifting her hand in a short wave, Zoe made her way through the crowded dining area.

She pulled out a chair and had barely taken a seat when Cristine started talking. "I think I might have made a breakthrough toward finding Shayna."

Cristine had a definite flair for the dramatic, and

Zoe knew anything she said had to be taken with a grain of salt.

"What's going on?" Zoe kept her tone and expression mild. The waitress came over and took her drink order, returning a moment later with a tall glass of iced tea.

The special of the day was homemade lasagna. Both Zoe and Cristine ordered that. The waitress had barely left when Cristine began squirming in her seat.

"I confronted Brock today," Cristine said, her voice ringing with self-satisfaction.

Zoe stirred a packet of artificial sweetener in her iced tea. "About what?"

Leaning forward, Cristine looked around, as though she wanted to make sure no one else could hear. "Shayna told me he hit her a few times."

"Brock?" Zoe's voice rose. "No way."

"Yeah, that's what he said." Cristine sat back, frowning. "I have to say, he seemed sincere in his denial. But so was Shayna, when I asked her how she'd gotten some bruises and a black eye."

Stunned, Zoe wasn't sure how to respond. She needed to be tactful with this woman. But still… "Is it possible Shayna might have had a bit of a problem with telling the truth?"

Cristine opened her mouth and then closed it. "Maybe," she finally said. "I don't know."

Zoe persisted. "You must have some idea. You knew her better than most."

Cristine shrugged. "Well, that's true. But I didn't exactly fact-check what she told me. I mean, why would she lie?"

"My thoughts exactly." Zoe took a long drink of her

iced tea. "But she also told me that she and Brock were engaged."

"What?" Cristine appeared startled. "She never said anything to me about that."

"It wasn't true," Zoe said gently. "At least, not according to Brock or her mother. The worst part is, Shayna dragged it out for a long time. I can't tell you how many phone calls we had about that subject. From stories about her and Brock picking out the ring, to her search for the perfect dress, and wanting me to save the date. It was a hell of an elaborate lie."

When Cristine looked up, the misery in her eyes made Zoe lightly touch the back of her hand. "You didn't know, did you?"

"No." So much unhappiness in that single word. "And I just accused Brock of being abusive to her this morning."

Zoe winced. "Ouch. How'd that go?"

"Not well," Cristine said glumly. "He called me a liar. He was upset, and probably understandably so. I'm thinking I might owe him an apology."

"I think you almost certainly do," Zoe said gently.

Cristine sighed. "Yeah, maybe. But he still hurt her. He might not have hit her, but he hurt her just the same."

"How so?"

"Though she didn't want anyone to know it, Shayna was in love with Brock."

"That's what she told me, too." Zoe bit her lip, considering. "But in the end Brock says they were just roommates. Separate bedrooms and all. They were lovers for a while, but he said Shayna wanted more."

Cristine nodded. "She might have, in the beginning. But in the end, when she decided she was through being serious and wanted to have fun, they were still close. Though they did sleep in different rooms then, they stayed lovers, too. Shayna made a video. I've seen it."

Zoe's first reaction was disgust. Her second was consternation. Now who was lying? Brock or Cristine? "She really showed you this video?"

At least Cristine had the grace to flush with embarrassment. "Not, not exactly. You know how I got her phone back after she left it at the Hitching Post? I was going through it and found the video."

Ok, at least that was an improvement over the thought of Shayna going around showing people an intimate video. Not much better, but slightly. "Please tell me you don't still have it. Why haven't you turned the phone over to the police?"

"I'm going to." Cristine frowned. "I wanted to get your opinion whether or not to delete the video."

Damn. On the one hand, it might be considered evidence. On the other, it could be very damaging to Brock if news of a sex tape got around. The very idea of Brock... Zoe shut down the thought immediately. "Cristine, I don't know. It might be considered evidence. Or not. I'm not sure. Maybe I should talk to Brock."

Cristine frowned, then slowly nodded. "I think it's still on her phone. I can show it to you if you'd like."

"No!" Zoe blurted. The last thing she wanted to see was Brock making love to her best friend. "Absolutely not. I have no interest in viewing something like that. You probably need to delete it, but don't do anything until I find out."

Face still crimson, Cristine looked down. "I guess I could wait."

"Cristine!" Rapidly losing patience, Zoe took a deep

breath. "Do you know if someone else saw it? Like when Shayna left her phone in the Hitching Post? The bartender or some of the waitresses could have seen it. That's private between Shayna and Brock."

"Maybe." Cristine didn't sound too sure.

Stomach churning, Zoe realized Shayna's mess got more and more convoluted the longer she stayed in Anniversary. What was truth and what was a lie? If Shayna had taken off like half the town thought, Zoe was beginning to understand why.

She took a deep breath. "Does Brock know about this video?"

"I don't know." Swallowing hard, Cristine suddenly grinned. "Are you sure you don't want to see it?"

"No! Good Lord, of course not."

Cristine shrugged. "He's pretty hot. I had no idea the man worked out. He has a nice six-pack."

Revolted to the point of nausea, Zoe ignored that, focusing instead on Cristine's revelation, trying to figure out the best way to deal with the news.

Even at the end, after Brock had said things were strictly platonic, Shayna and he had continued to be lovers. Ignoring the stab of jealousy in her gut, Zoe tried to get past the idea of the video and think objectively.

Bottom line, Brock had not told the truth. Ick factor aside, she had to wonder why he'd do such a thing. If he'd lied about this, who knew what else he might have falsified?

"I'm going to go find out," she said, putting down her menu and sliding out of the booth.

Cristine looked up. "Find out what?"

"I need to talk to Brock."

"But you haven't had your lunch yet." Cristine sounded bewildered. "Aren't you at least going to eat?"

"No. Sorry. I've lost my appetite." Dropping a twenty onto the tabletop, Zoe inhaled. "Have a nice meal on me. I'm sorry if this inconveniences you. I'll let you know what to do with that video."

With that, she left. While she'd never really warmed up to Cristine, at this point she wished she never had to hear another word of filth from this twisted woman's mouth. She'd more than mixed herself into Shayna's drama—she'd encouraged and participated in it.

Now Zoe needed to go find Brock. The lies had to end. Right now.

Since the feed store was closed, she went to his apartment. Though she wasn't sure exactly which unit he lived in, she'd call him when she got there and see if he'd invite her up.

Parking, she did exactly that. Brock answered on the second ring. She told him she was in the parking lot and needed to talk to him. He gave her directions to his unit, exactly as she'd hoped.

Though furious with him, she had a brief misgiving about the wisdom of allowing herself to be alone with him in his home. Since she had no right to feel that way since she left him, she ignored it. They were both adults. Surely she had enough self-discipline to keep herself under control. This was too important to wait.

Brock had just finished heating a TV dinner and popping open a can of cola when Zoe called. The instant he heard her silvery voice, his heart rate doubled. Worse than that, he had instant visions of all the erotic things he'd like to do with her on his unmade bed.

Realistically he knew she hadn't come to his apartment looking for a hookup, but his craving for her went into high alert as soon as he opened the door.

Zoe stood on his threshold, the sun turning her dark hair to copper, wearing a pair of faded jeans that clung low to her hips and a tight, black T-shirt that outlined every lush curve.

Staring at her, he temporarily lost the ability to speak. She had no right to be so damn beautiful and sexy. From somewhere, he gathered his fragmented thoughts. "Hi," he said, internally wincing at how eager he sounded.

"May I come in?" she asked, since he continued to block the doorway.

"Sure." Immediately, he stepped aside, unable to keep from glancing at her perfect behind as she brushed past him. "What's up?" he asked. Not only was she not smiling or relaxed, but she looked downright angry.

"Why didn't you tell me you and Shayna were lovers all along? You flat out stated at the end that you two were nothing more than roommates."

Lovers? He stared at her as if she'd grown two heads. Really, had the entire town gone insane?

Eyes dark, expression furious, Zoe looked spitting mad, on the edge of losing control. As if she had the right.

Just what he didn't need. This was going the opposite of what he'd hoped, he thought ruefully.

"Calm down," he told her, giving her a carefully blank look. "After we broke up, even though we still lived together, Shayna and I were no longer lovers. I wouldn't do that to her. Come on, Zoe. I think I've already told you in no uncertain terms that even though we tried, it didn't work out. In the end, we were only roommates."

"Roommates with benefits?" Crossing her arms, her voice rang with sarcasm. Stunned, he realized she really believed this nonsense.

"No. Just roommates." Speaking slowly, he took a step toward her, stopping when she jerked her entire body back. "Zoe, what's wrong with you? What's going on?"

"I just met with Cristine. She told me that Shayna had a video of the two of you."

Cristine. He should have known she was somehow involved with this craziness. He refused to get alarmed. After all, he had no reason to worry. "A video of what?"

Her porcelain skin flushed, she pushed on. "Of the two of you, making love, having sex, whatever you want to call it."

For a moment he couldn't even respond. "She's lying." Voice strong and certain, he didn't even hesitate to refute her claim. "There's no video, I assure you. I don't even own a camcorder and my cell phone doesn't take video. I'm not into that sort of thing. End of story."

Chapter 9

Zoe shook her head, her beautiful mouth twisting. Brock realized not only was she trembling, she appeared to be on the verge of tears. "Cristine says one thing, you say another. One of you is lying. But why?"

Damn it, he shouldn't have felt so disappointed. "You don't believe me," he said.

"I don't know what to think. Cristine sounded absolutely certain about this video. She even offered to show it to me."

"Perfect." Pulling his cell phone from his pocket, he held it out to her. "Call her. Tell her to bring it over here. I want to see it. We'll put an end to this once and for all."

"Cristine's probably still at Papa's Pasta." Slowly she dialed the number. Cristine answered on the third ring.

"The video? I just deleted it," she said, in response to Zoe's request. "I was going to take it to the police, but

I thought about what you said. It was private. Shayna wouldn't have wanted anyone to see it, right?"

Defeated, Zoe agreed. Telling Cristine she had to go, she hung up. "She says she deleted it," she said.

"Of course she did. And I'll bet she would have accidently deleted it or something if you'd asked her to see it earlier."

Zoe cursed. "This is getting ridiculous. I mean, it's become clear that Shayna had issues with being truthful. Apparently Cristine does, too."

He despised the gratitude that flooded him. To cover, he moved restlessly. "Thanks for that, at least."

"For what?" Looking confused, she met his gaze.

"For accepting me at my word and not assuming I'm the one that's the liar."

"I know you, Brock," she said quietly. "Whatever else I don't know, at least there's that."

He lowered his chin, waiting for the sudden lump in his throat to disappear. "Yeah, well. Just this morning Cristine accused me of hitting Shayna."

"I heard about that." Zoe looked down, making him realize she was twisting her hands as if she was nervous. "Look, I know you don't like me, and I can't say I blame you, but I need your help. It seems there's a lot of deception going on around here, and I don't understand why."

"You mean Cristine."

"Not only her. Roger and Mike. Especially Mike. And Shayna, too. I told you what she'd said about the two of you getting married. Brock, she carried on about that for months! In elaborate detail. I would have sworn on a stack of Bibles that she was telling me the truth."

He dragged his hand through his hair. For once, Zoe

sounded vulnerable. Which made him ache to pull her into his arms and comfort her, which was the opposite of what he wanted. It was too raw, too personal, too dangerous with the potential to get hurt again. He almost wished she'd get back to her high-handed, superior New Yorker attitude. He'd always been a sucker for being needed.

"I'm all alone here," she said, her voice doing that peculiar little hitch it always did when she was trying not to cry.

Damn. His stomach did a corresponding lurch.

"You're not alone," he heard himself say. "I'll do whatever I can to help."

"Really?" She raised eyes the color of melting caramel to him. "Even if it means you'll have to put up with my company a bit longer?"

"Yes." A dawning sense of rightness made him feel slightly better. "It's time we straightened this out and found out the truth once and for all."

She gave a short, bitter laugh. "The truth seems mighty hard to come by around here these days. Even Mama Bell is in denial."

"What do you mean?" That had to hurt, coming from her. He knew how much Mama Bell meant to her. *Had,* he reminded himself. He didn't know what Zoe Onella considered precious these days.

Obviously, her loyalty to Shayna ranked up there. Grudgingly, he had to admit he admired her for that. At least she was loyal about *something.*

"From everything I've been hearing, Shayna was out of control," Zoe continued. "But Mama Bell didn't act, even after noticing something wasn't right. She commented that Shayna had started avoiding her, but that was about it."

"Blinded by love," he said gently. "Kind of like when you disappeared."

He knew he'd said the wrong thing. Her expression shut down, became guarded.

"You always have to come right back to that, don't you? It's not the same," she said.

He didn't contradict her, even though she had to know, in a way, it was.

"Since we're being so blindingly honest, I should tell you that Mrs. Bell was at the feed store today also," he said.

Her brows rose. "First Cristine, and then Mama Bell?"

"What can I say?" He spoke casually, hoping to mask the fact that he had to fight not to kiss her. "I'm a popular guy."

"I guess you are." That faraway look clouded her eyes, letting him know she was lost in thought. He gave her a minute.

"What did Mama Bell want?"

"I'm surprised she didn't tell you. She wants us to put our differences aside and work together to find Shayna."

Though she nodded thoughtfully, she didn't comment.

"Zoe, sit down." He indicated the chair across from his desk. Grabbing a yellow legal pad and a pen, he began to make notes. "Let's write down what we have so far, okay?"

Clearly relieved, she blinked and pulled the chair closer to the desk to sit.

"I think we should focus on the last two people to see Shayna."

"That Mike guy from the bar?" She frowned.

"And…"

"Cristine," she said softly. "Do you think she knows something she's not telling us?"

"It's possible." He grimaced. "Five years ago, Shayna pretended not to know anything when you disappeared. No matter how many times I asked her, the answer was always the same."

It always came back to that, somehow. Her leaving without a word of goodbye.

But this time, Zoe refused to comment on the past. "Shayna did that because I asked her to," she said. "It was important, for reasons you didn't understand at the time."

He wanted to tell her he still didn't understand. They'd been inseparable back then. He'd believed they were a team. For her to think he couldn't protect her when she'd been the only thing that had made his life worth living…

Swallowing, he forced himself to focus only on the present.

"My point is, when you ran off, Shayna was the only one who knew why. It's entirely possible we have the same situation, only this time Shayna asked Cristine to keep quiet."

Zoe sat up straight. "If so, she needs to quit playing games." Her expression was animated, reminding him so much of the woman who'd once agreed to become his wife. It took every bit of willpower he possessed not to go to her and claim her. Life *was* too damn short to let what he wanted, needed and craved slip through his fingers a second time.

He felt a rush of heat and, moving without conscious thought, crossed to her, pulling her into a rough embrace. He held her, only that, but it was enough. It was everything.

She'd always been able to rock his world, without even trying.

Pulling back so he could look at her, he gazed down at her upturned face and caramel eyes. Zoe's wide-eyed stare and dilated pupils told him she battled the same demons as he.

"Brock…" She opened her mouth, as if to protest.

"What the hell," he muttered, before claiming her lips in a hard kiss. A river of heat blazed between them, a tidal wave of fever. Searing him. Them.

"This," he growled against her mouth, "We always got this right at least."

Clutching him to her, she made a sound, a wordless protest, perhaps, or urging him on.

To what? The realization was like a dash of ice water. He could fantasize, he could crave her, but if they connected intimately on any level, one of them was bound to get hurt.

Most likely him.

Yet his body, so aroused he hurt, urged him otherwise.

Then, as he struggled with his conscience and his desire, she raised her face to his and murmured his name. The single syllable was pure invitation.

And just like that, he was lost.

He wanted to be gentle, he wanted to go slow. But as they shed their clothes, both breathing hard, he wondered if he could. And when they rushed together, skin to slick skin, he abandoned all attempts to rein himself in.

There was nothing tentative in this, the first intimate touch in far too many years.

Tongue to tongue, fingers to skin, sinew and muscle and bone, he wanted it all, everything, all of her. Equally hungry, she explored him and claimed him, her touch inflaming him. He couldn't catch his breath, inhaling her scent, though he desperately wanted to slow things down and make this last.

"Now," she said, pulling him with her down onto the couch. She writhed beneath him, urging him with her body. "I want you inside me now."

Passion had turned his blood to fire and for a moment, he couldn't think. He throbbed with need, the size of his arousal a hard testament.

As she closed her hand over him, she moaned, the erotic sound stripping him of the last shredded vestiges of his control.

Need filling him, desire pure and explosive, he let go of the last remnants of his shredded self-control. Finally. Pinning her beneath him, he nudged apart her thighs and pushed himself into her. Again she cried out, even as her wet warmth welcomed him.

He began to move, trying to go slow and knowing with each thrust that he was fighting a losing battle. She gasped and her body clenched around him. Shivers of heat radiated from her as she gave herself over to her release.

Damn. Clenching his teeth, he held himself perfectly still as he rode the wave of passion. His only movements were the rise and fall of his chest with his harsh breathing, and involuntary tremors, the kind that would be his undoing if he let them.

And then…she kissed him. Claimed him, mouth to mouth, tongue dancing with his, teasing him as though he wasn't already buried deep inside her. Along with the tingling sense of knowing he was now complete, a wave of heat hit him so strongly he was helpless to do anything except move again.

Heat. Raw and primal. As the ache inside him intensified, his thoughts shattered and he gave himself over to the hot tide.

She rode along with him, her movements consuming and fueling him. He felt her give in to the burning sweetness of release one more time, and he rode to the peak along with her. And then, drowning in sensation, he let himself join her.

After, as they lay quietly, arms and legs and bodies still entwined, he still longed for something he knew he could never possess. Her. The heights they'd reached made him want to weep, because he'd tried so hard to forget. This was how lovemaking was supposed to be. He hadn't experienced such depths since Zoe had left him. And he knew once she left again, he never would.

Only with Zoe.

Even as he struggled to articulate his thoughts, she stirred and stretched. Her gaze touched on his, unsettled. "I'd better be going," she said, her tone light.

Climbing out of his embrace, she picked up her discarded clothing from the floor and disappeared into the bathroom. As he watched her go, he realized yet again, he'd been a complete fool.

When she returned, fully dressed, he was waiting for her, also having put his clothing back on.

"We can't do this again," Brock said, his voice blessedly emotionless.

"Don't tell me you didn't enjoy yourself, because I know differently." Eyebrows raised, her attempt to sound flippant vanished when she caught a glimpse of his expression.

He could only imagine what that looked like. Tortured? Anguished? Or just plain pissed off?

"Brock, I…"

"Don't." He closed his eyes, the craving for her ten times worse than any he'd ever felt for alcohol. Even now. Still. Always.

"No, I completely understand." Now her normally vibrant tone sounded as colorless as his. "How about we focus on finding Shayna, without all this personal stuff?"

Hearing her reduce his feelings to the generic *personal stuff* seriously pissed him off. But hearing her say it only reinforced his desire to put these feelings, this *stuff* behind him. Maybe now, he could finally get on with his life.

"Agreed," he told her, and walked her to the door.

Almost there, she stopped and put her hand on his arm. "I'm sorry," she began.

"Don't. When you go home tonight, why don't you write down any ideas you have toward locating Shayna and I'll do the same. We'll get together tomorrow and see what we've come up with."

Driving home, her body pleasantly sore, Zoe refused to think too much about what had just occurred. Mama Bell was right. Zoe and Brock needed to focus and work together to find Shayna.

Sniffling, she wondered why her chest felt so tight. She had to work harder to convince herself. Just because their bodies had joined together as though they'd been ripped apart since birth shouldn't make her want more. Right?

What was wrong with her? Why did she have the compulsion to turn fantastic sex into something else? She knew better than anyone that there could never be anything between her and Brock. No matter how much she might want him in her life, he deserved so much more than she could offer.

Amazing. She'd known her fate for years, but the knowledge still hurt like hell.

Tears streamed down her face. At least she hadn't started crying around Brock. Best that he think her a cold, unfeeling bitch. No emotions involved, no sir.

Though she'd had to get out of there before she said the wrong thing, she felt reasonably confident that she'd convinced him that they'd used each other to release some tension, with a touch of nostalgia thrown in for old times' sake. Nothing more, nothing less. When in fact, nothing could be further from the truth.

She loved him. She always had and always would.

After all this time, Brock was long past being hurt by anything that happened between them. As was she.

Then why did her throat feel so tight and why did her eyes sting as the tears continued to flow? She sniffed, wiping at her eyes with the back of her hand. She'd already pieced together her broken heart once. She couldn't risk tearing it apart again. That was just too much pain to survive.

She had to be careful, remember the reason she couldn't stay. Brock deserved everything he'd always wanted, especially children. He should have a woman who could give them to him.

So no matter what, she had to make sure Brock believed she didn't care. One thing she'd learned from Shayna's disappearance was how easily a house made of cards could blow apart.

As she turned the corner onto the Bells' street, she realized Mr. Bell's truck was parked in the driveway. Her heart skipped a beat. She felt an odd flash of guilt as she pulled up and parked. She'd been in town nearly a week and hadn't seen hide nor hair of the man she considered an adoptive father of sorts. Every time she'd asked Mama Bell about him, she'd said he was working. Apparently after that, he was sleeping somewhere else.

Not wanting to be intrusive, she hadn't pressed Mama Bell for details, aware the older woman would open up about potential marital problems when she was ready.

Still, Zoe had missed Mr. Bell. He was a bighearted man who'd taken in a scared and forgotten little girl and acted like a father to her. Now he'd finally come home from wherever he'd been.

Jumping out of the car, she hurried toward the open garage and went in through the door, which would put her directly at the kitchen.

She spotted him immediately, his hair still thick and dark, cut in the same military haircut he'd favored forever. He stood facing the table, with his back to her.

"It's about time you put in an appearance," she said, wrapping her arms around him in a quick hug.

Using only one arm, he hugged her back, but the motion seemed automatic rather than heartfelt. About to try to search his face for a hint of what might be going on, she happened to glance at Mama Bell first.

The older woman was seated at the kitchen table, hands over her face, crying so hard her shoulders were shaking.

Looking from one to the other, Zoe realized she'd walked right into the middle of something personal.

"I'm sorry," she said, aching to go to Mama Bell and comfort her. "I'll just go into town. I'll be back later."

"No." The fierceness in Mama Bell's voice contrasted with the despair in her tear-ravaged face. "Stay. Mr. Bell has something to say to you."

Mr. Bell shook his head. Pain, horror and guilt shone in his eyes. "Eunice, please…"

"She has a right to know," Mama Bell hissed. "Tell her, you—" Biting back whatever word she'd been about to say, she pushed to her feet and hurried from the kitchen to the bathroom, slamming the door hard behind her.

More than anything, Zoe wished she hadn't come home at that precise moment. Mr. Bell wouldn't look at her, and she couldn't exactly blame him.

"I'll go," she said again. "The last thing I want to do is get in the middle of a fight between the two of you."

She'd turned to do exactly that when Mr. Bell reached out and stopped her. "No," he said, his voice as heavy as his expression. "You should probably know this, since it might have some bearing on where Shayna is."

Turning slowly, she tried to ignore the dread coiling in her chest. "All right."

His face still wore the grim look of a man about to bare the darkest part of his soul. Suddenly, acutely, Zoe wished for Brock. How she would have welcomed his steady strength right now.

"You'd better take a seat." Mr. Bell indicated the closest chair.

Zoe didn't move. "No thanks, I'll stand."

"I think—" Instead of protesting, he sighed. "Fine. Suit yourself."

He walked to the sink and stood with his back to her, pretending an avid interest in something in the yard. Whatever he had to say must be bad. Eyeing him, she fought the urge to flee.

"I had an affair," he began, his voice rough. "Biggest mistake of my life."

An affair? Whatever she'd expected him to say, it hadn't been that. And what did that have to do with Shayna?

"I didn't mean for it to happen. It just did." Now he turned to face her, his face a study in misery. "I thought it was an innocent flirtation, harmless, clean fun. But she was so persistent."

"I'm sorry," Zoe said, as gently as she could manage, considering she now understood the depths of Mama Bell's pain. "But this all seems very personal, something that should be between you and your wife. What does this have to do with Shayna?"

Even as she asked the question, she suddenly realized she knew. His next words confirmed her guess.

"Shayna walked in on us."

Her heart sank. She felt sick. "Who?" she croaked. "Who was it?"

Eyes bleak, he spoke the name she never thought she'd hear. "Cristine."

Zoe blinked, unable and unwilling to hide her shock. "What?"

"It's true. I slept with Shayna's best friend. A girl the same age as my own daughter. Shayna was furious."

"At you or at Cristine?"

"Both, I'd guess. Mainly me." He let his shoulders sag in defeat. "Cristine rushed out of the room. Shayna didn't follow. Instead, she had a few choice words for me. I deserved them, but still."

"But still?" Zoe wasn't sure what to say, how to react. One thing she did know for sure, the second Mr. Bell had finished confessing, she was going over to Cristine's. She had to believe she and Shayna had hashed this out. How on earth were they still friends?

But Mr. Bell was still talking. "Shayna looked at me with hatred in her eyes. My baby girl told me she'd never forgive me. Do you have any idea how much that hurt?"

Zoe closed her eyes. "I'm sure she was stunned and hurt herself. When exactly did this happen?"

"About three weeks before she disappeared." He dragged his hand across his mouth, his eyes watery. "I tried to contact her for weeks after that, but she'd have nothing to do with me."

"She probably needed time," Zoe said, not sure why she was even trying to soothe him.

"Well, she got time," he replied. "Cristine refused to see me again after that. And it appeared Shayna and Cristine were still thick as thieves, so I don't know what Cristine told her. But whatever it was, it was enough to make my own daughter despise me."

"And don't forget your wife." Mama Bell reappeared in the doorway, her gaze shooting daggers of anger at her husband. "Marshall, I want you to leave." She pointed at the front door with a shaking finger, her eyes red and swollen from crying. "You've already left this family. This time, you should know you're not welcome back."

Both she and Zoe watched as he complied. After the door closed behind him, Mama Bell turned the dead bolt. "I'm calling a locksmith tomorrow and having all the locks changed. I'll make sure and give you a set of new keys."

Zoe nodded. "Mama Bell," she began, moving toward the other woman with the intention of offering a hug.

"Hush." Mama waved off her clumsy attempt. "I want you to go and talk to that horrible woman and see what else Cristine might have forgotten to tell us."

"Good point." Then, before Mama Bell could stop her, Zoe rushed over and hugged her, planting a kiss on her plump cheek. "I love you."

"I love you, too." Flashing a watery smile, Mama Bell pushed Zoe in the direction of the door. "Now get going. Find my Shayna. I need her more than ever."

Zoe nodded. "I'm on my way." Where, she had no idea. Anywhere but there.

She hopped into the car, taking deep breaths as she tried to control her anger. Since coming home to Anniversary, she'd constantly felt as if she was starring in a soap opera or a crazy reality show.

Now this.

Turning on the radio, she located the classic rock station and cranked the volume up.

A gust of wind hit her car, nearly making her swerve into the next lane. Glancing around her, she realized the weather had changed. The green cast to the gray sky made her shiver. Off to the west, a solid line of darker clouds created a wall. Though it'd been five years since she'd lived there, any native Texan knew what a sky like this meant.

Slowing, she rolled down her window and swore softly. Even the air felt charged. The birds had gone silent, and the unnatural stillness warned of an ominous storm.

Sure enough, a familiar tone beeped on the radio. Severe thunderstorm warning for Henderson County. Worse, there was also a tornado warning. The announcer warned that the radar clearly showed the storm taking the awful bow-shaped arch that was never a good thing. All residents should take immediate cover.

Zoe glanced behind her, wondering if it would be quicker to head back to the Bells' or try to take shelter in town. She was actually closer to Brock's apartment. Even though they hadn't parted on the best of terms, she knew his building would have safe shelter.

Driving to Brock's, Zoe took a deep breath, striving for calm. Though the weather forecasters were, as usual, panicked, all around her everyone continued to go about their normal activities. There were numerous other cars on the road, and people were at the filling stations buying gas. During spring tornado season in Texas, if people went and hid every time a tornado threat loomed, nothing would ever get done. As long as the sirens weren't sounding, everyone took a business-as-usual attitude.

The rain started, a sudden drenching as if someone had taken a sharp knife and ripped a hole in a cloud.

She turned her wipers on high and continued creeping along the street toward Brock's.

In the past, weather like this had energized her. These days, she had a healthy respect for it. Scary stuff.

Little by little, hands on the steering wheel in a death grip, she tried to relax. She counted down the minutes to Brock's place. Better to be safe than sorry.

The pouring rain made it difficult to see. She drove slower than normal, headlights on and her wipers going overtime. She was almost there. She only hoped it didn't hail, at least until she reached Brock's place. If she was fortunate, she'd snag a spot under the covered parking.

She lucked out and parked, glad of the shelter. Opening her umbrella, she took off at a run, relieved when she made it to the stairwell only slightly drenched. Closing her umbrella, she shook it out and headed up to Brock's apartment.

As she hit the first set of stairs, hail started to pummel the ground. Worse, as if on cue, the tornado sirens began to wail.

Which meant a tornado had been sighted in the vicinity.

Crud. With her heart pounding, she ran the last set of stairs, reaching the landing just as he threw open the door.

He looked stunned to see her, but with the imminent threat, neither of them had time for social niceties.

"Come on." He grabbed her arm, herding her back the way she'd come. "There's a storm shelter inside the clubhouse. It's right around the corner."

The tiny hairs on her arms were electrified, her pulse skipping as they took off.

The wind picked up, turning the rain and hail into

miniature bullets. An audible roar, like the much talked about train sound, made talking difficult.

Heart in her throat, she ran, not even bothering with her umbrella. Though he could have easily outrun her, Brock stayed with her, steering her in the right direction since they could barely see three feet in front of them.

"Come on," he shouted, glancing over his shoulder. "It's close."

She knew better than to look. Instead, she put on a burst of speed, nearly screaming with relief when the clubhouse door materialized.

Outside the sky had turned black.

They got inside somehow, barely able to close the door.

"Come on," Brock urged. "Over here." He began tugging on a solid metal door marked Safe Room. For use in Tornado. "Come on, come on."

The roar grew louder, drowning out the nonstop wailing of the siren. A transformer exploded, plunging them into darkness.

He tugged again. Miraculously, the thick metal door opened. "In here," he said, and grabbed Zoe's hand, yanking her into the room with him. He slammed the door behind them. Suddenly, all was silent.

Chapter 10

Instant panic flooded Zoe. She was claustrophobic, though she'd believed she'd managed to overcome that phobia by riding in numerous elevators in NYC. This felt different. There were no windows in this small, dark room. Truly a confined space, from which there was no escape. For her, sheer terror.

She began practicing her breathing exercises exactly as her therapist had told her. They'd always worked before. She really needed them to work now.

"Do you have your phone?"

Standing frozen in place, she fumbled, trying to locate her purse. "I can't find my purse. What is this place?" She forced the words out, wrapping her arms around her soaked self and clenching her jaw to keep her teeth from chattering.

"A tornado shelter. It's made of reinforced concrete. Supposed to be able to weather a direct hit by an EF-4."

From the sound of his voice, he was turning. Or moving.

A wave of nausea rolled over her. Tiny, cramped blackness. No. Don't think of that.

"If you keep hyperventilating, you're going to pass out." Brock's deep voice soothed. She jumped as he reached her and wrapped his arms around her from behind. "It's okay, Zoe. We're safe."

Just then, the building shuddered. But the walls of their little room held. She turned until she faced him, so she could burrow her face in his muscular chest. His body heat, despite the fact that he'd gotten as soaked as she, warmed her. In fact, snuggled up against him like this made it easier for her to breathe.

"You're still afraid of small spaces?"

She nodded. "But I'm more afraid of tornadoes."

He chuckled, smoothing her hair. "We're damn lucky we made it here in time. That was a close call."

Breathe in. Breathe out. Don't give in to panic. This was Brock. Rock solid. Here for her. He wouldn't let anything happen to her. If anyone could, he would chase the demons of her fears away.

"Is this the only tornado shelter in the complex?"

"Yep." The deep rumble of his voice made her feel safe.

"That's weird. I don't understand. Where is everyone else? I assume the apartment-leasing office knows about this place."

"And the other tenants." His warm breath tickled her ear. "I can only assume they either didn't take the sirens seriously, or they weren't home. A lot of people are still at work."

Despite his positive tone, Zoe couldn't help but hear the words he didn't say. It was entirely possible the others hadn't made it.

No. Forcing her dark thoughts away, she felt the steady thudding of his strong heart under her ear. Here in the blackness, so close they could have been one body, she could breathe in his scent and pretend things had never changed between them.

Temptation. For the space of a breath, she felt that this was where she belonged. In this town, with this man.

He shifted, and she realized he was fully aroused. A wave of answering lust washed over her, making her knees weak.

"Do you think we took a direct hit?" she asked, her voice wavering.

He didn't answer for a moment. Having put his hand to the small of her back, he began making circles. Each one pressed her closer and then again released her, the action mimicking something much more intimate.

She swallowed hard, the sound loud in the silence.

"It must be the eye," he said, apparently detecting the change in the quiet. "If it was, then that is one big tornado."

Just like that, the mood was broken. She went to move back, but he held her in place. "Not yet."

"Brock—" she began.

His lips brushed hers, effectively silencing her. Despite herself, she leaned into him, wanting more. But, instead, she felt the incredibly erotic sensation of his mouth, kissing the hollow of her throat.

A sound broke the darkness. With a sense of shock, she realized it had been a moan, escaping her.

"Brock," she tried again, not even sure what she wanted to say. She could beg him to make love to her, right here, right now, or she could ask him to stop.

A horrible crash, the sound of something slamming against the door, decided for her.

They both jumped.

"It's okay," he said, but she knew his response was automatic.

Immediately, a hundred thoughts raced through her mind. First and foremost, she couldn't shake the idea that they were now trapped there, locked inside a tiny concrete tomb. Whatever had hit the door sounded huge, and who knew how long it would be before rescuers came.

Again she began to hyperventilate. Which was bad, because they could run out of air.

"Zoe?" As if he somehow sensed her rising panic, Brock gathered her close again. Though she still felt his arousal pressed against her, this time his touch was soothing rather than meant to stimulate.

"Make me forget where we are. Help me think of living, rather than dying," she muttered against his chest, before pulling him down to her and claiming his mouth in a hard, deep kiss. If she was going to perish in this place, she was going to go out right, damn it.

With the man she...

No. That was the one place she couldn't, wouldn't allow her thoughts to go.

Instead, she touched him like she'd been aching to do. The complete and total darkness made her other senses more acute. Overwhelming. His skin felt like molten silk. She felt his harsh intake of breath as she slid her hands across his flat stomach.

At the edge of his jeans, she hesitated. This was wrong. They'd already agreed. But why did it feel so right?

Just then, the door was yanked open. Brilliant light blinded her as she stumbled, away from Brock. Even so, he steadied her, putting his arm around her waist.

"Are you folks okay?" a masculine voice asked.

Shading her eyes with her hands, Zoe realized their rescuer was a firefighter, wearing a yellow, protective suit.

And then she smelled smoke.

"The tornado tore up this place pretty badly," the firefighter said. "The structure is on fire. Someone said they saw people run in here. Come on." He held out his hand. "We've got to get you out before the entire building goes."

Zoe let herself be led from the room, still blinking as her eyes adjusted to the light. As they did, she realized the apartment clubhouse was now wreckage, as were many of the surrounding apartment buildings.

She turned to look at Brock. "Your place?"

Cursing, he ran.

As he rounded the corner, he saw his building. The roof was missing, and most of the windows were shattered, but the structure itself was still standing. When he headed toward it, one of the firefighters moved to block his path. He wore the insignia of a neighboring town, which was why Brock didn't recognize him.

"I'm sorry, sir, but I can't let you in there."

Brock glared at him. "What do you mean? I live there. That's my home."

"The structure isn't safe, sir. It's likely going to be condemned."

Striving to sound reasonable, Brock nodded. "I can understand that. I just need to get inside and grab a few of my things."

With that, he went to move around the guy, only to run into a harried-looking deputy named Frank. "Is there a problem here?"

"This man is trying to go inside a dangerous building."

"Come on, Frank. I live there."

Expression apologetic, Frank took Brock's arm and turned him away from the entrance to his building. "I'm sorry, man. But it's not safe. After it's inspected, I'm sure you can run in and get your things."

"When will that be?" Brock shouldn't have been surprised, but he needed to get a change of clothes and some toiletries.

"I have no idea." Frank shrugged. "Hopefully soon."

"How bad is the rest of town?"

Wincing, the other man looked down. "We've called in the National Guard. The State Police are on their way, too. The twister went right down Main Street. So far, we haven't found any casualties, but that could change at any time."

Brock clapped Frank on the back. "Go on, then. You've got worse things to worry about."

Muttering his thanks, Frank hurried off.

When Brock returned to where he'd left Zoe, she was sitting on the back tailgate of the ambulance, wrapped in a blanket and sipping something from a plastic cup. She looked so forlorn in the moment before she noticed him that his chest ached.

More than anything, he wanted to wrap her in his arms.

He didn't. He couldn't. But the storm had made him realize something. Nature had ripped away his old life. He now needed to start anew.

First up, he had to find another place to live. After he got the basics in order, he and Zoe would have a heart-to-heart.

After receiving a text from his sister letting him know she was all right, Brock drove Zoe home. She appeared slightly shell-shocked. Mama Bell's car, while undamaged, had been pinned in under the carport by fallen trees. The fire department had promised to notify her as soon as it was safe to pick it up. Right now, they had more urgent demands.

Driving back to the Bells' was difficult due to fallen trees and downed power lines and police barricades announcing various road closures. The sheriff's office was spread thin, yet they were doing what they could to keep the citizens of Anniversary safe.

When they reached the Bell home, Zoe invited Brock inside. Shaken, and glad to see them, Mama hugged them both before motioning toward the TV. She had the news report on. Both Zoe and Brock watched, still standing side by side, at the coverage of the damage. The Dallas stations had all sent reporters and camera crews and were broadcasting views of damaged buildings and uprooted trees.

At this point, the report announced, no one even knew if anyone had been wounded or—heaven forbid—killed.

The damage had been confined to the downtown

area. The tornado had cut a swath through many businesses and apartments in the center of town. As far as they could tell from preliminary reports, the northern part of downtown—the area that had been recently renovated and restored—had been hit directly. Some of the roads leading to the lake were blocked with downed trees. The older parts of Anniversary, including the area near the Hitching Post, appeared untouched.

"I didn't see Sue's Catfish Hut," Mama Bell said. "Or TJ's or Joe's." She named all the mainstay town favorites.

"Maybe they're okay." Crossing to the older woman, Brock placed his hand on her shoulder, offering comfort.

Zoe found herself tearing up at the sight.

Telling herself it was only because she'd been through a lot, she went into the kitchen and got the pitcher of iced tea Mama always kept on hand. She suddenly felt parched. "Would anyone like some tea?"

Mama jumped up and hurried over, taking the pitcher out of Zoe's hands. "Go sit down," she said, reaching for three glasses. "I'll fix this, along with some of those cookies I baked earlier. You need to rest."

The phone rang. "Would you get that?" Mama asked, her hands full. Zoe answered, exhaling as Mr. Bell's worried voice asked her if everyone was all right. After assuring him they were, she asked him if he wanted to talk to his wife. As she expected, he muttered something about having to get back to work, and he hung up.

Returning to the living room, she found Brock trying to use his cell phone. "Nothing will go through," he said. "I keep getting that annoying fast beep."

She pointed toward the old-fashioned wall phone.

"Landlines are working. I'm sure Mama Bell won't mind if you use that."

He nodded, his expression remote. "I've got to find a place to live. I can't stay with Eve, because she lives with two other women in a too-small apartment."

Hearing this, Mama Bell glanced from Brock to Zoe and then back again. "You can stay here," she said. "You can have Shayna's old room."

Horrified, Zoe hoped he'd decline. She and Brock both had enough difficulty resisting temptation as it was. With him in the bedroom next door, she wondered how they'd be able to keep their hands off each other.

Apparently, the same thing had occurred to him. He didn't even look at Zoe, keeping his gaze on Mama. "Thank you so much, Mrs. Bell," he said. "I'll keep that offer in mind."

Which meant he'd try all other options first. Attempting not to feel too guilty, Zoe nodded.

Mama Bell handed them each a tall glass of iced tea. When she went back to the kitchen to retrieve her own, she returned with a plate of her famous chocolate-chip cookies.

Zoe's mouth began to water when she saw them. Growing up, she and Shayna had joked Mama could make a fortune if she'd sell them. They were beautiful and so delicious they were addictive.

Good for an extra pound or two, Zoe thought, even as she reached for three.

After a few minutes—and several cookies—Brock left. He again thanked Mama Bell for her kind offer and promised to let them both know where he ended up.

Though she wanted to hug him, Zoe stayed where she was and waved goodbye.

The instant the door closed behind him, Mama Bell rounded on her. "What the tarnation was that?"

Briefly debating pleading innocence, Zoe closed her eyes instead. "Please, Mama. I'm exhausted. I just survived a direct hit from a tornado."

"What were you doing with Brock? I thought you were going to go talk to the sheriff?"

Briefly, Zoe explained what had happened.

A breaking alert on the news caught her eye. A body had been recovered from a building on the southeast side of downtown. No identity had yet been established.

Sobering. "At least one fatality," Mama Bell said, her voice sad. "You and Brock were very lucky."

Just like that, exhaustion swept through her. "I know," Zoe said, rising and finding her legs unsteady. "If you don't mind, I'm going to go lie down for a while."

She made it to her room before collapsing on her bed. Not entirely sure why, she began to cry, turning her face into her pillow so Mama wouldn't hear. She felt as if she was in mourning, as if the destruction caused by the twister was symbolic of her life.

She wanted what she couldn't have. And now she had to wonder if she could ever be happy again with the hand fate had dealt her.

Though initially the idea of staying at the Bells' had horrified him, by the time he'd made seven phone calls looking for a place to live without success, the idea was beginning to grow on him.

Hell, all that instant access to Zoe would probably drive him insane.

She hadn't been thrilled with the idea, either. He

wasn't sure whether to take that as a compliment or an insult. He decided her reluctance was due to the fact that she knew they'd be unable to keep their hands off each other if they were so close.

He'd have to try harder to find an alternative. After all, he'd just told her they had to stop giving in to their sexual attraction. He knew better than she how much letting go when she returned to New York would hurt. He'd done it before.

Despite that, he couldn't find anyone in town able to take him. So many people had been displaced because of the tornado, it seemed everyone already had a temporary guest.

Out of desperation, he checked Anniversary's lone motel. As he'd guessed, they were already booked up. Finally, he gave up. Looked like he'd be staying with the Bells.

He made the call before he could reconsider. Mrs. Bell seemed genuinely happy to have him. After letting her know he had to see if he would be allowed back into his apartment long enough to get his things, he promised to be there for dinner.

He decided to let her tell Zoe.

Watching the Dallas news station report on the ongoing cleanup after the devastation left by the tornado in Anniversary, Zoe was shocked again by the amount of the damage. When the camera showed a shot of Brock's apartment complex, she realized exactly how lucky they had been.

Several others hadn't been so fortunate. The death toll currently sat at five, with a dozen more injured.

Refusing to endure any more of the television sensationalism, Mama Bell had been busy in the kitchen for the past hour, humming under her breath and seeming genuinely happy for the first time since Zoe had been home. Maybe she didn't miss her husband as much as Zoe'd thought she would.

When the doorbell rang, Zoe got up to answer. As she pulled the door open and saw Brock, her heart foolishly skipped a beat. When she realized he carried a duffel bag, she understood why Mama had been cooking up a storm.

"Can I come in?" he asked, a smile in his voice.

"Sure." She swallowed and stepped aside, eyeing his bag. "I take it you're going to be staying awhile?"

"Didn't Mama Bell tell you? I took her up on her offer to let me stay until I can get back in to my apartment."

Her stomach did a slow roll.

As he moved past her, he lifted his head, inhaling. "That smells unbelievable."

His happiness was contagious, though she had no idea why. She found herself smiling back at him. "She's making chicken enchiladas."

"That's fantastic." He hefted his duffel.

"Hi, Brock!" Mama Bell chirped, appearing in the kitchen entrance. "Go ahead and get settled. You'll be staying in the middle bedroom. I changed the linens earlier today. You and Zoe will have to share a bathroom, but I guess you two can make that work."

Glad her back was to Brock, Zoe swallowed. The words *sharing a bathroom* conjured up the steamy showers she and Brock had shared in years past. Her entire body heated at the thought.

"I'll show you the way," she said, moving away and

hoping he didn't notice the huskiness in her voice. He followed her down the hallway, too close, she thought, even as she fought the urge to turn and wrap her arms around him.

Great. She hoped this wasn't a foreshadowing of how difficult it was going to be, sleeping in the room next to him.

Opening the door, she flicked on the light and stepped carefully inside. Since Shayna had moved out, Mama Bell had updated the room with a queen-size bed that had formerly been in the guest room, and some flowery framed prints.

"I'll let you get situated," she said, careful not to look at Brock. And then she rushed away, wishing she had somewhere else to go.

Dinner that night was an odd combination of pleasure and pain. Brock and Mama Bell chatted quietly, comfortable with each other, while Zoe sat silently eating her food. The growing ache in her throat made swallowing difficult. She couldn't help but realize that this could have been her life. If she hadn't had to run away to keep herself and everyone she loved from being killed, she and Brock would have been comfortably married. If she hadn't miscarried or had scar tissue, they might even have had a couple of kids by now. The might-have-been images wounded her more than she could bear.

Afraid she'd burst into tears, she pasted a pleasant expression on her face and let the conversation swirl around her.

Mr. Bell's conspicuous absence bothered her, too. As far as Zoe knew, since dropping the bomb on his wife and being asked to leave, he'd made no attempt to reconcile. Until today, he'd never even called. This seemed to bother Zoe more than it did Mama Bell, which maybe said something.

Despite that, sitting around the dinner table with the woman she considered her mother and the man she'd almost married, Zoe felt more like part of a family than she had since she'd gone to New York. More than she ever would again.

After dinner, Brock insisted on doing the dishes, overriding the older woman's protests. With her heart pounding in her chest, Zoe excused herself to go read in her room, leaving Brock and Mama Bell chatting amiably.

She barely closed her door before her eyes filled with tears. Not only did this hurt—she hadn't expected to have to continue the charade of not caring 24/7—but it also made her furious. It was like fate or whoever pulled the strings up there in the cosmos wasn't done torturing her.

Taking deep breaths, she got herself under control. She managed to concentrate on her book, tuning out the sounds of their voices mingled with the television. She got ready for bed as soon as humanly possible, washing quickly in what was now her and Brock's shared bathroom before rushing back to her room. At least sleep would keep her from hurting, from wanting things she couldn't have.

She knew she was hiding, knew too that she had no alternative. Gradually, she managed to fall into a troubled sleep.

Of course, she dreamed of him. She'd known she would, and if she was honest with herself, she'd been looking forward to the dreams before she even put her head on her pillow.

The dreams weren't the worst of it. The temptation—oh, the temptation made her burn. She actually got up and had her hand on her doorknob, before she made herself go back to her own bed and stay there. How she was going to make it through night after night of this, she didn't know.

She must have finally fallen into a deep sleep. When she woke and stretched, she felt better. As if she'd wrestled all her worst demons to the ground. She could handle this. She *would* handle this.

Dragging a brush through her hair, she listened to see if anyone else was up and heard the sound of the shower running. Apparently Brock had also risen and was getting ready for work.

Taking a deep breath, she pulled on a pair of jeans and T-shirt and wished she'd been able get in there first and brush her teeth. She tried not to picture him there, completely naked, though even the thought made her body buzz.

No. She wasn't going to begin her day thinking like this. Today she had work to do as well as trying to come up with some sort of a plan to speed up the search for Shayna. She refused to let anything bother her on this bright and sunny morning.

In the kitchen, she snagged a cup of coffee and, after doctoring it with half-and-half, took a seat at the table and checked out the morning paper.

When the bathroom door opened, she deliberately turned her back, rising to get coffee for Brock. She even remembered how he liked it. Black.

The act of pouring him his morning drink made her feel distinctly wifely. Warmth flooded her. Though the feeling was from one of last night's dreams, she decided not to care. Just this once. She even smiled at him when he strolled into the kitchen. The intimacy of the two of them, alone in the morning, wasn't lost on her. Pushing away the pain, she inhaled and again reminded herself that she could handle this.

But he looked so good. Well-worn jeans hung low on his narrow hips, and his T-shirt did little to disguise his muscular chest. Even his dusty black work boots looked…manly. Her mouth went dry and she felt her face color as she thought of the incredibly erotic dreams she'd had the night before.

"Mornin'," he drawled, accepting the cup from her. Something in the way he looked at her—maybe the decidedly wicked glint in his eye—had her wondering if somehow he *knew* what she'd dreamt.

Or how close she'd come to sneaking into his room. Damn.

Turning away to try, too late, to hide her blush, she busied herself with scrambling eggs. "Do you want some eggs?" she asked, trying to sound casual. "I was just about to eat."

"No, thanks. I'm headed over to Joe's before going in to the feed store. Eve's opening this morning."

Lifting her chin, she nodded, hating that she'd even offered. Blinking back sudden—and stupid—tears, she tried as hard as she could to come up with a smile. Her words got caught in her throat.

"Hey." With his voice turning gentle, he took a step toward her. Then, reconsidering, he drained his coffee and placed the cup on the counter near the sink. "Thanks for the coffee. We'll talk later about what we should do next to locate Shayna."

She nodded, pretending to focus on keeping her eggs

from burning. "Have a good day." To her surprise, she managed to sound normal. Maybe she was getting good at pretending to feel something she really didn't.

"You, too," he said softly.

She didn't turn around to watch him go. Only when she heard the sound of the front door opening and closing did she relax.

Turning off the burner, she transferred her eggs to a plate and carried them to the table. What the hell was wrong with her? Was she so deluded that she was willing to pretend there was something between her and Brock when, in fact, there wasn't. Nor would there ever be. No matter how badly she wanted it.

After she ate, she carried her dishes to the sink, rinsed them and loaded them in the dishwasher. Then she opened her laptop, checked her email and wrote a short blog on the power of happy memories. As usual, she held nothing back, finding comfort in putting her soul into words that could hurt no one. Such was the power of anonymity.

When she finished this, it was barely ten o'clock. She wanted to go talk to Roger Giles but knew Shayna's case had most likely been put on the back burner due to the tornado. Instead, she thought she'd take a drive into town and see the damage for herself. While she was there, she could talk to a few people about Shayna and see if anything new turned up.

Mama Bell finally got up. Though Zoe remembered her as an early riser before, these days she slept in, often not rising until ten or later. As she poured herself a cup of coffee, Zoe offered to fix the older woman something to eat, but Mama waved her away.

"Thanks, but I'm just going to have some oatmeal."

Zoe was struck by how much Shayna's mother had aged. Despite the cheerful facade she'd put on for Brock the night before, in private she carried her sadness like a weight. Where before she'd always walked with her shoulders back and her head held high, now she seemed to shuffle, her shoulders rounded and her posture defeated.

"I'm going to head into town and take a look at the tornado damage," Zoe said. "Do you want to come with me?"

Again Mama shook her head. "No, thanks. I want to be here in case anyone calls about Shayna. Plus, my stories will be on soon, and I don't want to miss them."

This made Zoe smile. As long as she could remember, Mama Bell had refused to miss her soap operas. When she had to, she'd record them, but she preferred to watch them as soon as they came on.

So Zoe would be going into town by herself.

About to back from the driveway, she waited for a truck to go by so she could pull out into the street. Before she had the chance, a police car pulled into the driveway, effectively blocking her in.

Dread, immediate and heavy, filled her. Putting the car in Park, Zoe killed the ignition and got out. Roger Giles and one of his officers, both in uniform, got out of the squad car slowly.

One look at the solemn expression on the sheriff's rigid face and Zoe knew. Shayna. This was about Shayna.

"What is it?" she asked, stepping in between them and the house, her voice trembling despite her best efforts.

He wouldn't meet her gaze as he brushed past her. "I need to speak to Mr. and Mrs. Bell."

"Please." She hurried after him, ignoring the pitying looks the deputy gave her. "Is this about Shayna?"

When she tugged at the chief's arm, the deputy—someone she didn't know—intervened. "Ma'am, I'm sorry, but I'm going to have to ask you to step aside. If you know the victim's family, perhaps you could be of assistance to them, but—"

"The victim?" Zoe cried out, her throat closing up. "Oh Lord, it *is* Shayna. You found her, didn't you?"

Before anyone could answer, the front door swung open. Mama Bell filled the entrance, her red-rimmed eyes taking in the scene. She looked from one man to the other and, instantly, she seemed to understand why they were there.

Backbone stiff, head high, she stepped onto the front stoop. "Sheriff?"

Roger Giles swallowed and removed his hat. "Mrs. Bell, I'm sorry to inform you that we recovered the body of your daughter this morning."

Hearing this, Mama Bell reacted as if he'd pulled out his service revolver and shot her point-blank in the chest. "No," she cried, crumpling to her knees, still holding the door frame with one hand. "Not my baby girl. Not Shayna." She began sobbing, the sounds of her grief terrible and heart wrenching.

Zoe's heart broke. Shayna was dead. The sheriff and the deputy exchanged a quick glance. Neither man moved.

Chapter 11

Heedless of her own tears, Zoe rushed over to her adoptive mother and wrapped her arms around her. "Shh, Mama Bell. Come on, let's get you inside."

With the sheriff's help, they got the older woman up and inside the house. First she'd lost her husband. And now she had to learn her beloved daughter was also gone.

Once Zoe had the still-sobbing Mama settled on the couch with a box of tissue, Zoe turned to face the sheriff. "Tell us what happened. Where did you find her? How did she die?"

Clearing his throat, Roger took a deep breath. Visibly shaken, he walked over to the front window and peered out for a moment before turning to face them.

"The tornado knocked some trees down on Old Fort

Road, near the lake. We used a backhoe to clear the road."

Zoe nodded.

"While doing that, we found her. She'd been buried in a shallow grave about thirty feet from the road." He swallowed hard, his face pale. "Long story short, the tornado unearthed what was left of her remains. We found positive ID on the body, though we'll be confirming with dental records."

This town, Zoe shuddered. Now, not only would every dark corner replay the moment her mother had been murdered, but Shayna, too. Yet again, someone she loved had been murdered.

"What happened?" Zoe choked out. "How did she die?"

"We don't know at this point, Zoe. Right now, it looks like it's a homicide investigation."

Homicide. Murder.

From the rigid way Mama Bell straightened, Zoe knew she'd caught the word, too. Shayna had been murdered. Yet another act of senseless violence in a town where people had believed it had once been so safe that no one locked their doors. Once Zoe's mother had been killed, Zoe had known better.

"Where is she?" Wiping at her eyes, Mama Bell spoke up, her mouth trembling. "I want to see my baby's body."

Clearly uncomfortable, the sheriff tugged at his collar. "Her remains were sent to the Henderson County Coroner's Office. Mrs. Bell, I should warn you the remains are in no kind of shape to be viewed. In addition to scavengers, the backhoe—"

"Enough." Zoe cut him off. "We understand. Thank

you so much for coming." She shepherded them to the door, practically pushing them outside. "I'll notify the rest of the family."

Sheriff Giles nodded. He and his deputy climbed into the squad car without another word and drove away.

Only when they were gone, did the enormity of what had happened truly sink in. Shayna was dead. She hadn't taken off—she'd been murdered. Someone had killed her.

Wiping her eyes, Zoe went back inside the house. There were phone calls to make, first among them to Mr. Bell. No matter their differences, he needed to come back home and help his wife in this time of loss.

Luckily, Mama Bell kept a printed list of numbers taped to the inside of a notebook that sat near the phone. Heart breaking, Zoe dialed Mr. Bell's cell phone. As soon as he answered, she told him what the sheriff had said.

"I'm on my way," he told her, and ended the call.

Though there were a dozen more people she needed to notify, Zoe called Brock next. As soon as she heard his deep voice, she broke down, crying so hard he could barely make out what she was trying to say.

Eventually, when he understood, he said he'd be right there. Relieved, she thanked him and then sat staring at the phone, too drained to move.

Shayna's death—or murder, Zoe reminded herself— changed everything. All along, everyone—including Zoe—had been going on the supposition that Shayna had taken off. Now they had to find out who had killed her and why. And judging from the craziness of the life Shayna had been living, there were way too many people with motive.

Marshall Bell walked in a few minutes after Zoe's call. He went straight to his wife and wrapped her in his arms. The two of them huddled in the den. Mama wept while her husband murmured what sounded like soothing words. Watching the two of them locked together in their mutual grief and sorrow broke another chunk off Zoe's already shredded heart.

Brock arrived ten minutes later, which meant he'd broken every speed limit on the way over. Zoe'd been pacing by the front picture window, watching and waiting for him. As soon as he pulled up in the driveway, she opened the front door, wiping at her streaming eyes.

She filled him in again, aware she'd been barely intelligible when they'd talked over the phone.

"A homicide investigation?" Pacing, Brock sounded angry. "So now the sheriff's office is taking this seriously? When it's too damn late. All along, every time I tried to talk to him, Roger Giles acted as if he was absolutely positive Shayna had simply left town. He had me convinced, as well."

"A lot of people thought that," Zoe felt compelled to point out, when both of the Bells didn't react. They sat together on the couch, arms around each other, huddling close. Mr. Bell handed his wife tissue as she continued to intermittently sob and blow her nose.

"True. But who would kill her?" Brock's closed expression and the fury in his eyes made him look as if he wanted to take a swing at someone. Zoe had the strongest urge to go to him and offer comfort, as if by leaning on each other, like the Bells, they could manage to get through the pain of this awful time.

As if they were a couple. Which they most definitely

were not. Though she ached for comfort, she stayed where she was.

"We can discuss this another time," Zoe gently pointed out, motioning with her head toward the Bells. "Right now we've got funeral arrangements to work out."

"Not yet." Mama Bell spoke up, her voice both broken and fierce. "I want to see her body first. I need to make sure this isn't some sort of mistake."

Mr. Bell raised a face wet with tears, his jaw tight. "I agree. But I'll do it, Eunice. You heard what the sheriff said. I don't want you to see her that way."

Mama Bell gave him a mutinous look but didn't argue.

"We need to notify the rest of the family," Zoe said, keeping her voice mellow.

"Not until we know for sure." Mama Bell's angry whisper spoke of deep emotion. She seemed about to say something more, but instead she folded over on herself, sobbing.

At that, the iron control Zoe had imposed on herself gave way. Tears filling her eyes, she got up and ran from the room.

A moment later, Brock followed. Waving him away, she went into her old bedroom, closed the door and locked it.

The next day, Zoe called him and let him know she was going with the Bells to identify the remains. Immediately, Brock asked if he could accompany them. After a moment's hesitation, Zoe agreed.

Brock had talked to the sheriff immediately after leaving the Bells the afternoon before. From what Roger had reiterated, the remains were so badly damaged and decomposed, they weren't even recognizable. Only Shayna's jewelry and the driver's license she'd tucked in her pocket enabled them to identify her. The Henderson County Coroner's Office had custody, and they'd have to drive to the county seat and visit the morgue there.

He couldn't think of anything he'd dreaded more, though sitting in the Bells' living room, tangible grief swirling all around him, ranked right up there.

While they stood side by side, the Bells weren't touching or speaking. After insisting she be allowed to accompany them, Mrs. Bell appeared to have turned in on herself. Meanwhile, Mr. Bell also seemed to have checked out.

And, through it all, Zoe was…their rock.

Though he had to admire the brave front Zoe presented to the world, Brock knew how close to the surface her raw emotions ran. He kept his arm around her slender shoulders, both to offer his support and also because he wanted to keep her close. He could feel the way she was shivering, which made him wish she could draw on his warmth. Though they hadn't settled anything between them, if he knew Zoe—and he did—she'd be catching the first flight back to her beloved New York City as soon as this was all over. He hoped he'd get a chance to change her mind.

Before they made the drive out to Henderson, they were headed to the sheriff's office. Roger had promised a police escort to make things easier. The Bells waited in the car while Brock and Zoe went in. Brock had never seen the place so busy.

"Hey, Brock." One of the uniformed officers glanced up and nodded.

"Is Roger around?" Brock asked, keeping his tone deliberately casual.

"No, he's out on a call." The man cleared his throat. "But I've been assigned as your escort. Are you ready to go?"

"We are," Zoe said, only the dark sunglasses over her eyes to show she'd been crying. "Lead the way."

Though their guide nodded, he shot Brock another curious glance, evidently wondering about his silence.

On the drive, Brock had replayed a hundred scenarios in his mind. If at all possible, they had to keep Mrs. Bell away from the remains. Her insistence to be present was, while understandable, bad enough. No way did anyone want her to see what was left of her daughter. Marshall Bell had taken Brock aside and emphatically stated he needed Brock's help.

But once they got there, Mrs. Bell ignored both men and Zoe and demanded she be taken back to the morgue. The county coroner led them into his office, where he informed them that a positive ID had been made using dental records.

Rather than breaking down at his words, the normally stoic Mrs. Bell became combative and irate. With her husband on one side and Brock on the other, she was led from the office, muttering under her breath and using swearwords Brock hadn't even been aware she knew.

On the way home, she huddled in the corner, crying into her hands and ignoring them all.

Finally, they got her home. She and Mr. Bell disappeared into the bedroom. When Zoe suggested that they give the Bells some privacy, he agreed.

"I know we're both shell-shocked, and I'm sort of

embarrassed that I'm thinking of things like eating, but are you hungry?" he asked her, as they walked to his truck. He wanted to be around her longer, and this was the only way he could think of extending their time together. Well, that and…not going there.

Cautiously eyeing him, she considered. "Grief is a strange thing," she mused. "Part of me wants to curl up and die, but I could eat, I guess. What did you have in mind?"

He remembered what had been her favorite meal. Stupid, the kind of weird stuff he remembered. It hit him when he least expected it, like a surprise punch to the gut.

So he said the one thing he knew she couldn't resist. "How about some catfish?"

Immediately her expression brightened. Not quite a smile but better than tears. "Sue's? I haven't been there in ages."

Sue's Catfish Hut was one of the most popular eateries in Anniversary and Zoe had always loved it. At one point, she'd wanted to have the wedding rehearsal dinner there.

Again, more unwanted and unnecessary thoughts. He shoved them away.

"Let's go," he said, resisting the urge to hold out his hand for her to take.

The instant they stepped into Sue's, Brock felt they'd traveled back into the past. He'd stopped in for catfish a time or two since Zoe had left, but by and large he tended to avoid the place. Too many unwanted memories.

"Hey!" Tina, one of the waitresses, rushed over and gave Zoe a big hug. "Zoe Onella. I heard you were back in town and I was wondering if you were going to stop in."

"I couldn't resist." Zoe tried to smile but failed miserably.

"I'm sorry." Tina hugged her again. "I heard about Shayna. I was hoping she'd just moved away or something."

Zoe nodded. "Me, too."

Tina led them to a booth. Luckily, one of the back corner ones was available, which would give them some privacy. They both ordered iced tea and the catfish basket, handing back the menus unopened.

After Tina had brought their drinks and hurried away, Brock decided he might as well get this over with. "About the other night," he began.

Zoe's eyes widened. "Now, Brock?" she asked, her voice rising. "You want to discuss this right now?"

"Why not?" Keeping his tone deliberately casual, Brock leaned his elbows on the table.

"Because it seems pointless." She exhaled, looking anywhere but at him. "You know as well as I do that what happened was a mistake."

"Was it?" He didn't know why he felt compelled to push her buttons, but he did. As she'd said, grief did strange things. "How so?"

Instead of answering immediately, she looked down at her hands. "We took a trip down memory lane."

"I see." But he didn't, not by a long shot. Still, if that's how she was going to play it, damned if he'd try to dissuade her. She hadn't cared enough about him to come back at all when she knew she was out of danger. Had he really thought anything had changed?

"How about mutual comfort? Comfort sex might help

us forget," he said, leaning back in his chair and hoping like hell he looked calm. Actually, anything except the way he really felt. Hurt and stupid. And through it all, the sharp pain of grief.

Sipping her tea, she lifted one shoulder, making him frown. Was she actually *agreeing* with him?

A buzz, desire again, thrummed through him.

"Maybe it's the heartache talking, but that might not be a bad idea."

Suddenly, he felt as if he'd walked to the middle of what he'd thought was solid ground, only to learn he was on cracking ice. Cursing himself, he said the one thing guaranteed to stop whatever this was before it started. "Though once Shayna has been laid to rest, I guess you'll head back home."

At this, Zoe stared at him as if he'd suggested she run down Main Street naked. "I'm not going anywhere until I find whoever did this to her."

Yet again, she'd succeeded in surprising him. Careful not to show any emotion, he crossed his arms. "I'm sure the sheriff's office is running an investigation."

She snorted. "That idiot you call Sheriff couldn't find his own car in a mall parking lot. I sure miss Renee."

"We all do, but we've got to let due process take its course."

"Due process? Come on, Brock. The sheriff was one of Shayna's lovers," she pointed out.

He shrugged. "He's single, so there's no reason why he shouldn't have been."

"Don't you think that's a conflict of interest?"

Narrow eyed, he studied her. "Surely you don't think the sheriff had something to do with her death."

"Anything is possible. I want to make sure he's investigating everyone. Every man Shayna dated and even those she didn't. It could be—"

"Zoe." He reached across the table and took her hand. "Despite his misguided call on what happened to Shayna, Roger knows how to do his job. Now that there's been a crime, he'll be on the ball. And he's got some of the best officers working for him. Remember Mac Riordan, the guy I talked earlier? He used to work for the Albany, New York, police department. He's got years of experience."

She let herself relax the tiniest bit. Still she persisted. "He needs to talk to Cristine immediately."

"I'm sure he will." Suddenly, he realized what he was doing and let go of her fingers. Anyone who'd seen them across the crowded restaurant would have thought they were intimate. While they had been, he wasn't sure he wanted news of that hitting the gossip rounds in town. The last thing he needed was pity when Zoe left this time. Once had already been bad enough.

Zoe's words finally registered. He frowned. "I agree he needs to talk to Cristine, but why immediately? Roger has enough on his plate between the tornado and Shayna's murder."

Gently she moved her hand from the tabletop to her lap. "With all the drama that's been going on, I'd forgotten you didn't know."

"Know what?"

Glancing left and then right, she leaned forward. "Marshall Bell had an affair with Cristine."

He let his mouth drop open. "What? No way. Are you sure?"

"He confessed to Mama Bell shortly before the sheriff arrived to give us the news. And worse, Shayna walked in on them."

"When?" He dragged a hand through his hair.

"Right before she disappeared. Mr. Bell said Shayna wouldn't have anything to do with him after that. Neither would Cristine. I'm guessing she was embarrassed, though with her, you never know."

He grimaced. "As she should be. And now Mrs. Bell knows what her husband was up to?"

"I think they were on the verge of splitting up permanently before Shayna's…" Her voice broke. Collecting herself, she swallowed hard and continued. "Before Shayna's body was discovered."

Before Shayna's sudden disappearance, he'd thought life in Anniversary was pretty routine, almost boring. Now he wondered how he'd missed all the undercurrents.

"That's sad. I feel bad for everyone involved."

"I do, too. Shayna must have been devastated. I have to think she discussed this with Cristine. Yet Cristine never even mentioned it."

Straightening, Brock watched her closely. "In light of Shayna's murder, I agree. We need to see what Cristine has to say about all this."

"Immediately." The firm set of her mouth told him she'd made up her mind. "Before the funeral, if possible."

Though, if Zoe had been in charge of the weather, she would have ordered up a solid gray cloud cover and a sharp, northern wind, the day of the funeral dawned bright and sunny. The cloudless blue sky seemed in direct opposition to the atmosphere inside the Bells' house.

In this time of grief, Mr. Bell had moved back in. Despite the unspoken agreement that this would only be temporary, just to get them through this, he'd returned to sleeping in the master bedroom with his wife. Zoe heard the sounds of them arguing late into the night.

There was blame, recrimination and bitterness to go along with the unrelenting grief.

Gazing out the window at the perfect early summer morning, she pushed the thought away as a product of insecurity. There was nothing she could do now to save Shayna. But she could still do something for the Bells and for herself. She could, and would, help find Shayna's killer. If only she knew how.

Zoe still found it difficult to believe her best friend and the woman she considered her sister was gone forever. Guilt filled her. She should have visited or had Shayna come see her. She should have done something, anything, and maybe her best friend would still be alive.

Even though she knew she wasn't responsible, guilt lodged like a rock inside her heart and wouldn't go away.

Cristine had been beside herself when she got the news. Sheriff Giles had paid a visit to the law office where she worked as a paralegal. According to the gossip that ran rampart around town, Cristine had nearly fainted at her desk when the sheriff told her Shayna was dead. Word was he'd also asked her to come in for questioning.

Which meant he was doing his job. Maybe Brock was right about him. From what Zoe had heard when she went to Sue's Catfish Hut, Sheriff Giles had asked nearly a dozen people to come in and talk to him about Shayna. Zoe couldn't help but wonder who was going to interrogate the sheriff. He'd dated Shayna, after all. He should be just as much a person of interest as anyone else.

Out of curiousity, Zoe had tried to call Cristine a few times, but Cristine let the calls go to voice mail and never returned them. No doubt, she knew Marshall Bell had come clean to his wife. Zoe tried to forgive her, aware the other woman was grieving deeply. Still, at some point, Cristine had to take responsibility for her actions.

Mama Bell and Mr. Bell were locked into some sort of grief-stricken battle. Neither had time or energy to expend dealing with anyone's sorrow but their own. In time, they'd emerge from whatever dark place they'd walled themselves into, but for now, she was on her own.

Or would have been, if not for Brock. Through it all, he had been by her side. A rock. Asking no questions and making no demands aside from hinting about the ways they could comfort each other. She hadn't taken him up on that. Zoe knew she had to set things straight with him, but at the moment she was so numbed by grief, she hadn't been able to summon the willpower. She was just grateful that he was willing to help her get through this despite the fact that he must have been grieving as well.

The funeral was held on a Sunday afternoon, so most of the town turned out to honor Shayna's memory. The Bells had elected to have the memorial service in the funeral home's chapel rather than the Baptist church they'd attended for most of their lives. Though Zoe didn't know all the details, apparently Shayna had had a falling-out with the congregation a few years ago.

Keenly aware of Brock's supportive presence at her side, flanked on the other side by the Bells, Zoe barely made it through without breaking down. Only the burning desire to be here in town when they found out who had done this kept her going.

Glancing at the broad-shouldered man who stood, steadfast and strong, close enough for her to touch, she figured he most likely felt the same way. His rugged profile somber, he surveyed the crowded chapel as though watching for something.

After the funeral, the church threw a huge potluck supper. This was everyone in town's chance to get together, talk about Shayna and try to begin the healing process. The Bells had argued about this. Mama Bell had insisted they go, while Mr. Bell had wanted to bow out, saying he needed to grieve alone. In the end, it appeared Mama had won, as Mr. Bell drove to the church. Zoe and Brock followed in his truck.

Though Zoe had been part of the church family for most of her life, at least since the Bells had taken her in, she had no desire to go, either. While she understood and appreciated the tradition, it seemed like a waste of valuable hours, time she could spend searching for clues as to who had taken Shayna away from them. She needed to go back to the Hitching Post and start talking one by one to the people who might have been Shayna's party friends.

No doubt the sheriff's office was already doing this. She hoped so. Though right now there seemed to be nothing evident, Zoe knew the killer had to have made a mistake. Everyone slipped up and, as far as she knew, there was no such thing as a perfect crime.

With that in mind, she traveled to the church with the family and as they were walking toward the meeting room, she excused herself and headed to the bathroom. Brock followed, as she'd known he would.

"I'd like to go talk to the sheriff," she said, when they were alone in the hallway. "I didn't see him at the funeral."

"He's here." Brock gestured back to the rapidly filling room. "He knew Shayna, too. Plus he never could pass up a chance for a free meal."

"That's my point," she said, trying to keep her voice down. "Not the free-food part, but the fact that he dated Shayna. I heard he's finally questioning everyone who could even remotely be considered a suspect. I want to know who's going to question him."

Brock stared, then nodded. "I don't think Roger would have hurt Shayna, but I see the necessity of considering all possibilities."

"He had as much motive as anyone else. From what I've heard, Shayna liked to, er, love 'em and leave 'em."

Looking off into the distance, his chiseled features remote, Brock finally nodded. "I see your point. I'll keep an eye on him, maybe talk to him myself."

"Good."

Brock nodded. "Now, how about we go back in there and have some of that great-smelling buffet they're laying out. I don't know about you, but I'm starving."

Since he'd been more than kind to her, she agreed. Only a man could think about food in the middle of something like this. But then her own stomach growled, and she realized she hadn't had anything to eat all day.

For some reason, this realization helped lift the heavy mantle of grief and anger that had been dogging her all day.

Cristine found them as they were digging into their plates. Carrying a cup of coffee, she took the empty chair next to Zoe. She wore huge dark sunglasses, even inside. "I don't know how I'm going to make it," she wailed. Zoe nearly recoiled at the wave of alcohol on her breath. Already? It was barely noon.

"Cristine, have you been drinking?" Brock asked, the fumes apparently having reached him, too.

"Of course." Giving them both a watery smile, Cristine pulled a silver flask from her purse and poured a liberal dose into her coffee. "How else do you expect me to get through this?"

She sounded serious.

Brock frowned. "You know that might mean you have a problem?" he asked, his voice compassionate but stern. "I speak from experience."

Cristine waved him away. "Hush, Brock McCauley. You haven't been any fun ever since you became sober. Don't you dare start preaching to me. Not now. We all gotta cope the best way we can. This is mine."

Jaw tight, Brock nodded. "My apologies," he said, not sounding the least bit apologetic. "Please, excuse me." Carrying his plate, he went back to the end of the buffet line, apparently to get seconds.

"Oh, good." Cristine leaned in close, treating Zoe to another dose of liquor-scented breath. "I'm glad he's gone. I wanted to talk to you about him, anyway."

"Cristine," Zoe said. "Maybe this should wait until you're...you know...sober?"

"No." Cristine gave her a lopsided grin. "Now is the perfect time. I think Brock did it."

Chapter 12

At first, Zoe didn't understand. Then, when Cristine's meaning sank in, she wasn't sure how to respond.

Cristine didn't seem to notice. "If anyone can get him to confess, you can." She turned to make sure Brock was still up at the buffet. Then she continued. "But if you ask him about it, be careful. I'd hate for you to become his next victim."

Reminding herself that the woman was drunk, Zoe considered her words carefully. "Cristine, I know you cared about Shayna, but—"

"I did, I did," Cristine interrupted, starting to cry.

"But Brock would never—"

Again Cristine cut in. "Shh. He's almost here. You don't want him to hear you." Plastering a wobbly smile on her lip-glossed mouth, she took another giant swig of her doctored coffee.

"What's going on?" Carrying his second loaded plate, Brock looked from one to the other.

"Oh, I was just telling Cristine here that you and I are helping the sheriff try to find out who killed Shayna."

"You are?" Cristine's mouth fell open. "How's that work?"

"Well," Brock said, looking from one to the other before he sat, "I wouldn't exactly call it that."

"Oh, stop being so modest." Zoe waved his comments away, wishing she could text him or something to let him know what Cristine had just accused him of. "Brock and I have been hanging around the Hitching Post, talking to a lot of the regulars. We're close to learning who was the last person to see Shayna the night she was murdered."

"Close?" Cristine leaned close, one hand still clutching her coffee cup, sloshing it onto the table. "How close exactly? I think it might have been that Mike guy who went down to the lake with her."

Both Brock and Zoe stared. "How do you know about that?" Zoe asked.

Cristine shrugged. "Everyone in the bar is talking about it. What about him? Do you think he did it?"

"He's got an alibi and has pretty much been ruled out as a suspect."

At this, Cristine frowned. "So do you have someone else in mind?"

"Maybe." Zoe made her smile deliberately mysterious. "But I'm not at liberty to discuss it yet. Not until we have stronger evidence."

Catching Zoe's eye, Brock looked at her as if she'd lost her mind. When she only stared back, hoping he realized she wanted him to just go along with her, he finally shrugged and resumed eating.

"Maybe I could help," Cristine said, her words slightly slurred. "I'm a regular there, you know. People like me. They'll talk to me before they'd talk to you."

"I'll keep that in mind." Noncommittal, Zoe stretched and made a show of eyeing the dessert table. "I hear a piece of cheesecake calling my name. Do either of you want anything?"

"No, thanks." Brock pointed to a large slice of chocolate cake. "I'm good."

"I'm not hungry." Draining the last of her coffee, Cristine stood, none too steady. "I've got to get going."

In silence, they watched her walk away.

"I'm trying not to judge her too harshly," Brock said, his voice full of regret. "We all have our own ways of grieving."

Though she knew he wouldn't speak so kindly if he knew what Cristine had just accused him of, she didn't say anything. Not yet. Not here. If Cristine was saying things like that to Zoe, no doubt she'd been talking to the sheriff, too.

This wasn't good. Especially since Zoe didn't for one second believe Brock had harmed even one hair on Shayna's head. She wouldn't let him be a scapegoat. More than anything, she wanted Shayna's killer brought to justice. The *real* killer.

She'd tell Brock later. Not at Shayna's funeral. After, when they were alone in his truck.

After he'd cleaned his second plate and then polished off dessert, Brock sat back in his chair and surveyed the gathering. Mr. and Mrs. Bell occupied a round table near the front of the room. They were surrounded by so many well-wishers, poor Marshall could hardly eat. Mrs. Bell simply sat stoically, moving food around on her plate, her eyes unfocused and shiny with tears.

"Brock?" Zoe tugged at his sleeve. "Can we go? I need to talk to you."

"Sure." Though he managed to sound relaxed, inwardly he winced. What now?

She waited until they were in his truck, seat belts fastened. "Cristine told me she thinks you killed Shayna," she said, not mincing words.

Though he should have been expecting something weird like this, the bald statement hit him like a slap in the face, temporarily knocking the wind from him.

"Damn," he muttered. "You know, she's been hinting, but I really didn't think she was serious. I can't believe…"

"I'm worried." Zoe put her hand on his arm, the heat of her fingers searing him.

Gently, he eased away from her, under the pretense of fitting the key in the ignition. "I'm not. I have no reason to be."

"But if she came to me with her crazy accusations, who else is she talking to?"

Putting the truck into Drive, he pulled out of the parking lot. "It doesn't matter. I grew up in this town. People know me. No one will take her seriously."

She shifted restlessly. It took every ounce of his willpower to keep his eyes on the road. What the hell was wrong with him? Five seconds alone with her and he ached to touch her. Touch her? Who was he kidding? He wanted to pull the truck over and rip her clothes off and bury himself deep inside her.

Taking a deep, shuddering breath, he worked hard to get himself under control.

"Where are we going?" she asked, as though they were spending the rest of the day together.

"I'm going to drop you off," he said, still careful not to look at her. "I've got some errands to run. But I'll be back soon and we'll talk about what else we can do to help the police find Shayna's killer."

"Oh, okay." She sounded disappointed. He told himself he didn't care. Even though he really had nothing planned for the afternoon, he needed time to himself to think.

As he pulled up in the Bells' driveway, she turned to look at him before getting out. "Thank you," she said softly, her brown eyes shining with sincerity.

His heart lurched. "For what?" he managed.

Then, to his horror, she leaned over and kissed him on the cheek. "For being my rock. I don't think I could have made it through this day without you."

And then, while he was still reeling, she got out of his truck and walked away without a backward glance.

Driving away, he rubbed at the spot where her lips had touched and resisted the urge to turn around and go back. This was torture. Gut-wrenching, pointless torture. And he had never been big on suffering. The longer Zoe stayed, the worse he wanted their lives to become intertwined. Not in a let's-hang-out-at-the-bowling-alley kind of way, but more of a back-against-the wall-and-have-hot-sex way. And more. So much more. Hell, he even wanted to cuddle under the covers with her, hold her close and make plans for a new life together.

Because he still wanted Zoe. Always and only Zoe.

After what she'd done to him, he should have despised her. They grown up together, been a couple since middle school. He'd thought they were tight, friends of a different type than she and Shayna had been. Close. Especially once passion had struck them like lightning. Fire and heat, they hadn't been able to get enough of each other. She was the other half of his whole and they completed each other.

And then, without warning, she was gone. His world had been destroyed, not with a nuclear blast, but with a quiet rustle of air in the night.

Life without Zoe. He'd been bereft, looking to drown his sorrows in the bottom of a bottle.

After he'd climbed out of the deep hole of grief, he'd grown angry. So he and Zoe had managed to spark some passion. Fine. He'd have it again, with someone else. But no matter how many women he'd dated, it was never the same.

No one compared to Zoe. He'd begun to realize no one ever would. And he wondered if it was the same for her.

Probably not. She'd made no attempt to contact him in the five years since she'd broken their engagement, not even once to explain or apologize after leaving his ring with Shayna to give to him.

He'd been broken, after that, a little crazed. He wanted to hate her, but couldn't. Failing that, he tried like hell to school himself to indifference. But all she had to do was smile at him and every emotion, even the ones he'd thought long dead and buried, came rushing back.

If she wasn't going to stay, Zoe needed to leave. Since

she said she didn't plan to go until the police solved Shayna's murder, he could only hope that was soon.

He was on his way to the sheriff's office when his cell phone rang. Roger Giles. Wondering if the sheriff had ESP, he answered.

"You got a minute to come in and talk to me?" The sheriff didn't waste time on small talk. "We can do it here at the station or at TJ's over a beer."

Obviously, Roger had forgotten that Brock didn't drink.

"I'm on my way to the station right now," Brock said. "I can be there in five minutes."

Roger agreed to wait for him.

On the way down in his truck, Brock's phone rang again. This time, the caller was Zoe. His traitorous heart skipped a beat when he heard her voice. "Evidently, Cristine's been spreading her poison. I just heard the most disturbing gossip," she said. "It's all over town. People are seriously talking as if you really might have killed Shayna."

He reeled. This was his town, his people, and the idea that they could even think this about him felt like a knife in the heart. "I wouldn't pay any attention to idle gossip," he said.

"I'm not. Unless the rumors hamper law enforcement in doing their job and searching for the real killer."

He liked her response. "Speaking of whom, I'm on my way to the sheriff's office to talk to Roger."

"An interrogation?" She sounded horrified, which was gratifying. "Do they honestly think you could have—?"

"I don't know. Truth be told, I doubt I'm even a viable suspect. Roger is either clutching at straws or just trying to put those crazy, rampant rumors to rest."

"I still don't like this." Horror had been replaced with indignation. "Do you want me to meet you there as a show of support?"

Tempting. Pulling up to a stop sign, he briefly closed his eyes. "No need, thanks. This should only take a few minutes. But I appreciate the offer."

Her voice clearly unhappy, she made him promise to call her the instant he was finished. He refused to let her concern touch him. That was the last thing he needed, to let his emotions about Zoe get the better of him any more than they already had.

He had enough on his plate as it was.

The sheriff and one of his deputies waited in the empty reception area, along with Agnes, who stared at him with reproachful eyes. Everyone else had already gone home for the night.

"Sorry about this, Brock," Roger said, punching him lightly on the arm. "Come on back to my office."

Following, Brock noticed the deputy stayed right behind him, as if he thought Brock might flee.

"Have a seat." Pointing to a folding metal chair across from his gunmetal-gray desk, Roger sat. "I called you in here today to talk about Shayna Bell."

Brock nodded, waiting for the other man to continue.

"Cristine Haywood was in here earlier. She told me some things I have to say I find mighty disturbing."

Brock could only imagine. Considering that Cristine had already tried to insinuate that he'd not only slept with Shayna, but been physically abusive as well, he had to wonder what she'd told the sheriff.

"And?" he prodded, when Roger didn't finish.

As expected, Cristine had trotted out the same old lies, though this time she'd gone too far. Cristine was trying to implicate Brock in Shayna's murder.

The question was why? Did she really believe her own lies? And now, the sheriff had no choice but to question him.

"First off, I've never hurt Shayna," Brock said, his tone even. "And secondly, though we'd broken up and she was moving out, I was cool with that. When she went missing, we were roommates, nothing more. Friends, maybe. You dated her. You should know that."

Though the sheriff gave him an apologetic smile, the look in his eyes was still hard and considering. With a sinking feeling, Brock realized the other man truly did consider him a suspect.

Damn and double damn. He felt like a bear caught in a trap. For the first time he realized he could actually be arrested for a crime he hadn't committed.

And whoever had really killed Shayna would go scot-free.

Though Brock had sounded certain he didn't want her to go to the sheriff's office, there was no way Zoe could let him be questioned without her support. She wanted Shayna's killer found as much as anyone. Probably more. But trying to pin this on Brock was not only wrong, it also meant the real murderer would get away with murder. Shayna deserved justice, not a mockery of it.

So she jumped in the car and headed into town, even though she had no idea what she would say when she arrived.

As she pulled into the parking lot, she saw Brock's truck was still there. Good.

Hurrying inside, she ignored a sputtering Agnes, and rushed past the reception counter, continuing down the hall to the sheriff's office, Agnes hot on her heels.

The door was closed.

"You can't go in there," Agnes sputtered.

"Watch me." Hesitating, Zoe took a deep breath, knocked sharply twice and then pushed the door open.

Both Roger and Brock looked up, the sheriff's face registering his surprise. Brock, however, appeared resigned.

"Uh, Zoe." Roger stood. "This is not a good time. I'm in the middle of something."

"I can see that." She glanced from one man to the other. "I came to speak to Brock. Don't let him railroad you. Calling an attorney would be the wisest choice."

Unsmiling, Brock spoke. "Not necessary, Zoe. I told you not to come."

Now the sheriff appeared confused. "I'm just asking Brock a few questions. There's really no need for you to—"

"You're looking in the wrong direction," Zoe interrupted. Again she looked at Brock, who sat stone-faced, his arms crossed. From the looks of things, he wasn't at all happy to have her come barging in like this.

Tough.

Sitting down, the sheriff leaned back in his chair, one eyebrow cocked. "And now you're going to tell me how to run my murder investigation?"

"Why not?" she shot back. "You weren't exactly trying too hard to find Shayna to begin with. If you'd searched more diligently, you might have been able to save her."

At her words, Roger's expression hardened. "We did everything we could. We put her name into NaMus—the National Missing and Unidentified Persons System. We interviewed friends and relatives. Beyond that, we had no indication of foul play. Our hands were tied."

Zoe swallowed. He had a point. But still… "Okay, I get that. I really do. But how can you even consider Brock McCauley a suspect? If you know him at all, you'd be positive he could never do something like that."

"Zoe," Brock warned. "I think you've said enough."

"That's all right." Roger waved Brock's protest away, focusing his bright blue eyes on Zoe. "It's my job to investigate all angles, you know that." He gave her a half smile, making her realize he was only pretending to be angry. That struck her as so odd she froze, letting him continue.

"As to my questioning Brock, I have to. Anyone with a motive, no matter how slight, has to be checked out. I'd think you'd want that, too."

"I do." Feeling slightly abashed, she took a deep breath. "I'd like to help."

Brock made a sound of frustration. She ignored him, keeping her gaze locked on Roger Giles.

Crossing his arms, Roger stared back at her. "Help how?"

"I don't know. But there must be something I can do."

As he considered her, a hint of a smile played around his mouth. "How about go out to dinner with me?"

"What?" Stunned, she wasn't sure she'd heard him right.

"I'm serious. Cops have to eat, too."

"I…" Enraged, she wasn't sure how to respond. No way in hell did she want to go out with him, but if he was the killer, he might give something away.

Instinctively, she looked at Brock. Anger had flared in his eyes, but he didn't protest, though he watched her closely.

Roger eyed her like a hawk contemplating prey.

"I don't know," she began.

"There's no reason not to," Roger said. "Unless of course, you and Brock are back together."

Now she understood. He was fishing, trying to see if there was more to the story than what Brock had told him. Did he seriously believe Brock would have abused Shayna and eventually killed her in the hope of getting back together with Zoe should she ever come home?

"No, we are not," she said, her voice cool. She had to battle the urge to find out who was his superior and call and make a complaint. "And I'd love to have dinner with you sometime, as long as you promise to keep me updated about whatever you find."

"Agreed." His smile made her realize exactly how handsome he was. And how slimy. Again, she wondered about him and Shayna. How perfect for him if Brock were arrested for a crime Roger himself had committed.

"How about tonight?" he asked.

Careful not to reveal the flash of panic that went through her, she swallowed, careful not to look at Brock. "I wasn't…um, sure. What time?"

"I'll pick you up at seven."

When he held out his hand for her to shake, she took it, praying she could hide her revulsion.

Brock stood, also. "Are we about finished here?"

he asked the sheriff, sounding as if he spoke through clenched teeth.

Looking thoughtful, Roger nodded. "I think so. I'll give you a call if I think of anything else."

Brock escorted Zoe out, anger positively radiating from his body. The instant they cleared the door, she turned to him, sensing that he was upset and trying to head things off before they started.

"Look, I didn't know what else to do," she began.

Coldly, he contemplated her. "How you act and what you do is clearly none of my business."

With that, he strode away from her, got in his truck and drove off.

Though he knew Zoe stood staring after him, her beautiful expression shocked, Brock refused to look in his rearview mirror.

She and Roger Giles were going out on a date. Why? She claimed not even to like the man.

The jealousy that coiled in his gut infuriated him. Zoe didn't belong to him. He shouldn't care if she had dinner or drinks with any man in town. Beautiful women like her had no trouble attracting men and he didn't doubt she'd known plenty during her five years away.

After all, despite his certainty that their making love meant something, Zoe had made it clear she viewed it simply as a form of recreation. Her actions had hurt much more than he'd expected.

Now this. She couldn't have chosen a better action to drive her point home. He got it, he truly got it.

Yet fool that he was, he felt like doubling over in pain. He knew what he'd be doing come seven. He'd be sitting in his apartment, fighting both the urge to go to TJ's to have a beer and then to drive through town so he could see where Roger had taken Zoe for dinner. The hell with beer—he was craving shots of straight whiskey, the more rotgut, the better.

The awful thing was, he wanted a drink so badly he felt dizzy. Even thinking about it made him break out in a cold sweat. Shocked and furious, he gripped his steering wheel as if it were a life preserver. He had to get himself under control. This sort of thing hadn't happened to him very often, not since his early days of sobriety.

He'd fought this battle before and won. Inhaling slowly, he forced his mind blank, picturing a single candle with a perfect flame.

Only when he'd achieved the necessary calmness did he open his eyes. He no longer craved alcohol. The woman, however, was another story.

Since he wasn't a stalker, he knew he shouldn't go to town, but a little after seven he found himself with truck keys in hand, heading into town to grab a bite to eat. This time, he didn't dare go to TJ's or any place that served alcohol. He saw no reason to tempt fate.

He chose Sue's Catfish Hut again. A good meal of fried catfish, along with perfectly seasoned fries and hush puppies would go a long way toward filling the yawning emptiness inside him.

And he knew he wouldn't run into Roger and Zoe on their date. The sheriff wouldn't take her here, especially if he was hoping for a little romance. Just the thought had Brock clenching his teeth. He ordered iced tea and the Captain's Platter, sitting back in his booth and surveying the early-evening crowd.

Mostly families, a few older couples. He knew just about everyone, and watching the typical dinner outing in the town he'd always called home calmed him.

After Tina brought his tea and took his order, she hustled off to the kitchen, promising it'd be out soon. Brock nodded, reassuring her he was in no hurry.

Just then, Marshall Bell walked in. He was alone, which said something. Since Shayna's funeral, Brock had gotten the impression that he and Mrs. Bell were reconciling. Though Brock looked for her, Marshall appeared to be alone.

He spotted Brock sitting by himself and hurried over. "Mind if I join you?" he asked. Grief had made new lines in his weathered face.

"Of course not."

Marshall had barely taken a seat when Tina appeared with a menu. "No need, honey. I already know what I want." He ordered the same thing Brock had.

After Tina hurried off, Marshall heaved a weary sigh and sat back in the booth.

"How are you holding up?" Brock asked.

"It's been a long week." Passing his hand across his eyes, Marshal grimaced, his eyes conspicuously shiny and red. "How are you doing?"

Brock shrugged. "Okay." If he didn't count the number Zoe was doing on his equilibrium. He glanced out the window, again wondering why she had agreed to go out with Roger.

When he looked back, he realized Marshall was studying him.

"I'm not much on talking about feelings," Marshall said, and took a sip of his tea. "So I won't. Damned if I want to break down in the middle of Sue's."

Brock nodded. "I don't know what to say."

"Then don't." Clearing his throat, Marshall hesitated, as if not sure what he wanted to say. "Zoe has a blog, you know. Shayna told her mother about it. Apparently the two of them read it frequently, though I don't think Zoe knows."

A blog? Brock didn't get on the internet much other than to order supplies or check his email. He frowned, wondering what exactly Marshall was trying to tell him.

"From what my wife says, it's pretty popular. I took a look at it myself the other day. Not only did Zoe write an obituary for Shayna, but she writes plenty of other interesting articles. I didn't read too much of it—that kind of stuff isn't my thing. But from what I can tell, it's personal, pretty revealing, if you know what I mean."

Again, Brock had no idea what Marshall meant.

"Here." Pulling a pen from his shirt pocket, the older man scribbled on a napkin, then slid it across the table to Brock. He'd written an URL. "That's the web address. You might check it out sometime. Funny how you think you know someone, and then you don't."

Their meal arrived right after that, saving Brock from any further discussion.

Once she got home from her dinner with Roger Giles, Zoe felt dirty, like she needed a shower, and weary all the way to her soul.

"What are you doing going out on a date with that man?" Mama Bell, alone for the first time since Shayna's funeral.

"It wasn't really a date," Zoe felt obliged to clarify. "Though I think the sheriff had high hopes. I let him know romance wasn't even a remote possibility. He seemed to take it well. I really wanted to pump him for information on where he is in the murder investigation."

"Hmm." The older woman made a tsking sound. "Do you still plan to return to New York as soon as you can?"

"I'm not sure," she answered slowly. "I'm conflicted about both things. I love living up north, but I feel more at home here in Anniversary."

"And then there's Brock," Mama Bell pried none too gently.

Zoe sighed. "Brock. I'm not even sure how to respond to that."

"You still love him, don't you?" Rather than being judgmental, Mama Bell spoke in a soothing voice.

Zoe almost crumpled. "I don't know what I think." Though she managed to lift her chin and try for nonchalance, the telltale quiver in her voice gave her away. Especially to someone who knew her so well. "I have my life and he has his."

"Has he forgiven you?"

The question took Zoe by surprise. "I don't know," she answered. "But I don't think so. We haven't actually discussed it." She took a deep breath. "It was so long ago I was hoping maybe he'd forget."

Even as she said the words, she knew the foolishness of them. There were some things one never forgot, especially those things that had been meant to be, like her and Brock. Hell, she hadn't forgotten or even forgiven herself. If she couldn't, then neither could he.

"I've made such a mess of things," she said sadly.

"Everything doesn't have to be so serious, you know." Yet again Mama Bell surprised her. Zoe had been expecting something else—a solution maybe, or some of Mama's famous advice.

"Serious?" Drawing her knees up below her chin, Zoe sighed. "What do you mean?"

"You're acting like every kiss has to lead to something more. It doesn't, you know. You can still have fun, share some memories, maybe even part friends, if you try hard enough."

Good advice. For anyone but Zoe and Brock. "We seem to have a love/hate relationship. I don't see how we could ever be…just friends. And there really is no other alternative."

"Maybe not," Mama Bell said in a matter-of-fact tone. "Life is too short, believe me. I do have to confess, I always thought you and Brock would have been happy together. Shayna told me all about what happened with your mother. I figured once they locked that murderer up, you'd have come back to him."

The exact same words Brock had used. Suddenly, Zoe was just plain tired of carrying the burden of her awful secret. She hadn't even been able to tell Shayna that part of the past.

Maybe the time had come to finally reveal it.

Chapter 13

"There's something you don't know." Zoe took a deep breath. "After my mother was killed, I ran to escape the threats from her killer. But I also ran to escape the pressure from Brock. He pushed for us to get married. I knew I loved him, but we were so young. I wanted to wait. So I didn't come back. And then I learned I was pregnant with Brock's baby. I still planned to come back, to tell him, but I had to wait until the trial, until my mother's killer went to prison."

The older woman's expression remained the same. When Zoe didn't continue, she nodded encouragingly. "Go on."

"I had endometriosis. It caused scar tissue, and the baby wasn't able to attach properly to my uterus." Even now, five years later, she found herself blinking back tears. Some kinds of grief never vanished. "I lost her."

Compassion shone in Mama Bell's eyes, yet she seemed to sense that now wasn't the time to offer comfort. If Zoe was going to be able to finish the story, she needed to find her own composure.

"Her?" Mama asked.

Zoe lifted one shoulder in a half-apologetic shrug. "I just knew my baby was a girl. I have no proof, it was too early to tell."

"I'm so sorry."

Those simple words almost undid Zoe. Sniffing, she held herself together and managed a nod. "I am, too."

After giving Zoe a moment, Mama leaned forward. "You didn't come back home because you lost Brock's child? I don't understand. If there's one thing I know about Brock, it's that the man has had his share of tragedy in his life and emerged from it a stronger man. He could have helped you with this, and you both could have healed together."

Zoe nodded.

At that, Mama frowned. "And I suspect you already know this. So, you didn't think he could handle it, or what?"

Wincing, Zoe shook her head. "That wasn't the entire reason. I'd already decided to stay in New York. I couldn't get married. Not yet. But I figured I'd come back home someday. Then, when I lost the baby, I learned my insides are all messed up. My fallopian tubes have been damaged and my uterus is so full of scar tissue that…" Even saying the words made her insides ache, and she paused for a moment. "I can't have children, Mama Bell. Even through in vitro fertilization. My womb won't hold them."

Pushing up her substantial bulk, Mama crossed the

space between them and wrapped Zoe in her cookie-dough-scented arms. "I'm so sorry, sweetheart," she whispered, smoothing Zoe's hair as though she were still a terrified youngster rather than an adult woman in mourning. "I know how badly you wanted children."

"Not just me." The tears Zoe tried to keep back had begun escaping, stealthily making their way down her cheeks. "That's the reason I didn't come back to town after my mother's killer was sentenced to prison. Brock always wanted kids, even more than me. I couldn't take that away from him."

"So you stayed away." Releasing her, Mama Bell peered into Zoe's face. "You tried to save him from a childless life."

"Yes. Exactly." Giving the older woman a watery smile, Zoe sniffed. It felt good, a relief, to have finally told someone after all these years. And Mama Bell actually seemed to understand.

"He still doesn't have any young 'uns," Mama pointed out.

"I know." Misty-eyed, Zoe grimaced at her own foolishness. "I figured by now he'd already have two or three of them."

After a pause, no doubt to let this information sink in, Mama Bell continued. "Zoe, did you ever think of letting Brock make his own choice? Tell him the truth and let him say what it is that he wants to do."

"No. I can't." Chest tight, Zoe drew a shuddering breath. "Because Brock is an honorable man. He'd make the wrong decision to make sure he did the right thing."

"Aw, baby girl. I think you're mistaken."

Again Zoe's eyes filled. Mama Bell hadn't called her "baby girl" since she'd been nine or ten.

"Give the man a chance," the older woman continued. "At least then you won't have to always be wondering what if. At least then, no matter how painful,
you'll know."

The words rang with wisdom. Zoe nodded and promised to consider them, though even thinking about dis-
cussing such a thing with Brock filled her with terror.

It'd be safer and easier if she simply went back to
New York after this was all over. And cowardly, too,
her inner voice chided. Still, despite the prospect of her
empty life looming before her, she was pretty sure that
leaving was exactly what she was going to do.

Brock meant to, but he hadn't had a chance to check
out Zoe's blog. He'd tossed the napkin with the web address on his desk at work, telling himself he'd look at
it once he had time.

The truth of the matter was, he wasn't entirely sure
he wanted to. As far as he could tell, blogs were like online diaries. He had no doubt that anything New Yorker
Zoe had written there would only cause him hurt.

Even the name of the thing—*City Girl*—spoke of the
side of Zoe that Brock tried not to think about. As if by
leaving, she'd abandoned everything she'd used to love.

Yep, he was pretty damn sure he didn't want to read
anything City Girl had to say.

So he'd continued living his life, getting up every
morning and going to work, trying to ignore the yawning emptiness inside of him and wishing he could feel
normal once more.

At least people were talking to him again. At first,
the town hadn't been sure how to respond to the idea
that he could be a suspect in Shayna's murder. Everyone

knew Sheriff Giles had asked Brock in for questioning. Brock imagined some of the townspeople might even be convinced he'd done it.

There was nothing he could do about that.

At first they'd stopped talking to him, going out of their way to avoid him, even crossing to the other side of the street. He been stunned and hurt, wondering how he could have lived in a place his entire life and still people didn't know him.

And for two days, business dropped off at the feed store. But Brock tried not to worry. The ranchers and farmers would have to buy their grain and pellets and he doubted they'd want to drive forty-five minutes to Mesquite to get what they needed.

He was right. On this, the morning of the third day, the regular customers started drifting back in and making their usual purchases. To Brock's surprise, they all wanted to talk about the murder investigation.

Several of them clapped Brock on the back and let him know they knew he wasn't a murderer. A few, the Widow Jones and her friend Enid Bostler, cast sideways glances at him and made sure Eve rang them up.

Right before closing time, as Brock was tallying up the day's receipts, Zoe came strolling into the feed store. Brock froze, cursing under his breath. Eve promptly made herself scarce.

"Hey," Zoe said softly. "How have you been?"

"Fine," he lied, keeping his voice expressionless while recounting the register drawer he'd already counted and balanced.

"The other night, when I had dinner with the sheriff…" Zoe said, all the words tumbling out in a rush.

"After talking with him, I'm pretty sure you're not actually a suspect in Shayna's murder."

Easy, McCauley. Brock narrowed his eyes. He wanted to grab her, kiss her again and let her know exactly why she shouldn't be having dinner with any man but him.

Instead, because he shouldn't, hell, he couldn't, he simply pointed to the door. "Get out."

"Brock, I just wanted to…"

He began to sweat. She had to leave, or he wouldn't be accountable for his own actions. "Zoe, go. Now."

Instead, she came closer, hugging her arms close to her sides. "I don't understand. Please don't be like this."

"How am I supposed to be?" he growled, furious that even now he ached to touch her. "You waltz back into town and expect me to act like we parted friends? And now, you start dating the sheriff and expect me to be okay with it?"

Crap. He hadn't meant to say the last part.

"Dating?" Bottom lip between her teeth, she frowned. "I'm not… Is *that* what this is about?"

"Not really," he lied, feeling stupid, especially since anger still churned inside him. "I'm well aware we aren't in a relationship."

Something that looked an awful lot like pain flickered across her face. "Brock, I'd much prefer to be on friendly terms with you."

Friendly. He was coming to hate that word. He didn't want to be *friends* with her, dammit. And that, he realized yet again, made him even more of a fool.

Time to get back on familiar ground. "Did you really think it would be that easy to forget about what you did?"

A spark of anger fired in her brown eyes. He watched her in disbelief as she came closer still. "Everything I did was for a reason. I left to save my life and protect the Bells."

There was more, he sensed. Even now with the space of years between them, he could still look at this woman and know when she was hiding something. "Yeah, I know. So you already said. But there's more, isn't there? What is it you're not telling me?"

That stopped her in her tracks. He watched her anger disappear, replaced by a flash of what he could have sworn was fear. *Interesting.* What was she afraid he'd find out?

"You're right," she said, her voice shaky. "I should go."

He moved to block the doorway. "Zoe, don't you think you owe it to me to tell me the truth?"

She bowed her head. When she raised it again, her brown eyes were shiny with tears. "There's nothing to tell," she said. "What's past should stay in the past."

"Not if whatever you're keeping hidden will help me understand why you never came back." Refusing to let her tears move him, he did his best to sound unyielding and firm.

"No." Crying in earnest now, she pushed past him. This time, he didn't try to stop her or go after her. Instead, chest tight, he watched as she ran to her car, started the engine and drove away.

In that instant, he knew that no matter what it took, he would learn what Zoe was trying to keep secret from him. As soon as Shayna's killer was found, Zoe would bolt, but he'd be there to block her way. This time, he refused to let her get away with no real explanation. This time, if she was going to shred the rest of his heart to pieces, she would damn well tell him why.

After the humiliating encounter with Brock at the feed store, her emotions raw and hurting, Zoe tried to avoid running into Brock in the Bells' house. Each time his pickup pulled up, she hid in her room, declining dinner. She told Mama Bell she was working. And she was, writing posts and scheduling them in advance. That way, she wouldn't have to worry about neglecting the blog while she threw herself into searching for clues about who had killed Shayna.

No matter what Brock or Roger Giles or anyone said, she would make sure whoever had done this was brought to justice.

But first, she had to get her head in the right place. She needed to try to come to grips with Shayna's death. At first, the news hadn't seemed real. She'd gotten angry and kept moving as a way to avoid dealing with the staggering loss.

The funeral had truly hammered things home for her. Her best friend was gone. Forever.

So many things unresolved. Shayna's death, the Bells' marriage, and Zoe and Brock. Too many emotions, all battling for attention, swirling around inside her head. She felt sick.

So in order to keep her sanity, Zoe did what she'd learned to do best. Compartmentalize. She couldn't do anything about the Bells' marriage—that was for them to work out. As to her nonrelationship with Brock, well, she didn't really even want to think about it.

That left one thing. Shayna's death. She could try to help learn who'd killed her friend.

Suddenly she realized what she had to do. Go back to the Hitching Post and ask more questions. Shayna had been a regular there. And even if Mike was telling the truth, someone else might know something, something they'd be hesitant to tell the police.

Decision made, she instantly felt better. Since she didn't feel safe going alone, she had two choices. She could ask Cristine to go with her or she could ask Brock.

The last person Brock would have expected to find tapping at his bedroom door first thing in the morning was Zoe. After the way he'd practically thrown her out of the feed store, he noticed she avoided being around him as much as possible. Which was fine, for now.

He hated the fact that his heart leaped at the sight of her.

Taking a deep breath to steady himself, he opened the door.

"Brock," she began, her smile so endearingly serious he could scarcely breathe. "Good morning."

"Morning." Staring at her, he tried to sound as unwelcoming as possible. "What do you want, Zoe?"

"This is business, I swear." Without waiting for an answer or an invitation, she hurried inside his room.

Instantly, her gaze locked on his unmade bed.

Jamming his hands into his pockets—safer that way—he waited, burning to pull her with him onto that bed. Body throbbing, he simply stood, ready to hear her out so he could open the door and send her on her way.

"I'm going back to the Hitching Post," she said, lifting her chin as if daring him to contradict her. "I'd like you to go with me."

Though he hated the idea, he had to admire her tenacity. In reality, he didn't know what she thought she could find out that the police hadn't.

When he didn't answer, she shrugged. "If you won't, then I'll be going alone."

And there she had him. She knew good and well there was no way he'd let her put herself in danger like that.

Instead he tried to reason with her. "Come on, Zoe. You know the police have already been over that place."

"I know." She flashed him a wisp of her usual smile. "But sometimes people won't open up to the police."

She had a point. But still. "And you think they'll talk to you?"

"Something like that." And the strangest thing of all, the conviction in her voice almost had him believing her. Something passed between them, something not quite tangible. But he felt it and, if the way she suddenly shivered was any indication, she did too. The pull of it was compelling despite the fact that he kept a distance of several feet between them.

How the hell did she continue to have such a strong hold over him? Continuing to eye her, even while he pondered this, he couldn't help but remember the last time they'd been alone in his place.

Something must have flared in his eyes, because she took a step back, away from him.

Of course. One of them had to maintain a modicum of sense.

When he still didn't agree to accompany her, instead just standing like a lump, hands jammed into his pockets, she swallowed and turned to go. "Sorry to bother you," she said, reaching for the doorknob to let herself out.

"Wait." Then, against his better judgment, he nodded. "I'll go with you, Zoe. I might hate that I still want you, but even more I'd like to keep you from getting killed."

"Thank you," she said, her hand still on the door. "I really appreciate it. I'll see you tonight around seven."

He nodded. So much for his resolve to avoid Zoe as much as possible.

Leaving the Bells, he checked on the progress being made to repair his apartment building. He'd been lucky; his was one of the ones that wasn't immediately condemned and slated for demolition. Still, the tenants were not allowed to enter until the city finished making their assessment.

After that, he headed to the marina, got his boat and went out on the lake. Fishing always seemed to soothe away the stress. Every time he even thought about seeing Zoe later that night, he forced himself to think of something else.

When he returned to the Bells', he went straight to his room, then hopped into the shower before changing into a pair of Western jeans and a button-down shirt. Ready.

Steeling himself for whatever sexy outfit she might wear, he was completely surprised when he strolled into the living room to see Zoe waiting, wearing faded jeans, cowboy boots and a black, unadorned tank top.

"What, no minidress and high heels?" he asked, using humor to try to hide his disappointment. And relief, he told himself. Definitely relief. It would be much less difficult to have carnal thoughts when she wasn't dressed like sex incarnate.

"No need," she told him, businesslike. "I'm not trying to pretend to be anyone or pick someone up. I'm simply going in there and asking questions."

"Which the police have no doubt already asked."

She shrugged. "Maybe people will be more likely to talk to me."

Careful not to show his amusement, he cocked his head. "How so?"

"Because," she said softly, her eyes suspiciously shiny, as though she might cry. "Shayna was my friend."

He had no answer for that, so he simply nodded. "Well, come on then, let's go." Hesitating, he held out his arm.

When she took it, he felt that familiar pull, the urge to yank her up against him and kiss her senseless. It seriously pissed him off.

Once he'd started the truck, he turned up the radio, hoping she'd take it as a hint that he didn't want to make small talk.

To his relief, she stared out the window and listened to the music. When a George Strait song came on, she began making snuffling sounds and he realized she was trying to hold in tears.

Crap.

Scratching the back of his neck, he shot another glance at her. "Uh, Zoe? You all right?"

She nodded. "Yes. No." Sniffling, she wiped at her eyes. "I don't want to mess up my mascara. But this was Shayna's favorite song."

"Oh." He snapped off the radio. "Sorry." He didn't have the heart to tell her that Shayna had moved past old-school country and into hard rock.

"What are you planning to ask, exactly? The sheriff already interviewed that Mike guy. While he was the last person that we know of to see Shayna that day, we don't have proof that he did anything to hurt her. The field where she was found is close to the lake, true, but Mike's roommate vouches that Mike was home shortly after eleven. There's no evidence that he did it. The trail ends there."

"Not really," Zoe said. "We don't know if she called someone else to give her a ride. Obviously, she tried to call you. When you didn't pick up, she might have tried somebody else. I wonder if the sheriff got Shayna's phone from Cristine."

"He did, and he's subpoenaed the records from the phone company just to make sure. The phone showed there were no outgoing calls other than the one to me." He cleared his throat. "That was one of the reasons Roger was so interested in talking to me. He wanted to know if I went out there and picked her up."

She sniffed. "Someone must have. Does he still have the phone?"

"I believe so. You know, if Shayna was really drunk and couldn't get a hold of anyone, I wouldn't put it past her to have hitchhiked."

Zoe bit her lip. "I'd thought of that," she admitted.

They pulled up in front of the bar. Even though they were early, the parking lot was still packed. "They must have good happy hour specials," Brock said, as he drove slowly up and down the aisles looking for a space to park.

"I guess so." She shot him a sideways look. "Are you ever going to tell me why you don't drink?"

He took a deep breath, suddenly realizing he was tired of secrets. But to tell her this...

Swallowing, he met her gaze and began to speak.

"I developed a drinking problem." The words hung there, bald and unadorned. Damned if he'd explain the reason he'd started drinking in the first place. After all, Brock considered that to be glaringly evident. "When it got out of control, I joined AA, got sober, and that's that."

Though in his mind, that was a perfectly good explanation, he had a feeling she'd ask for details. Women always wanted more than just the bare facts.

To his immense gratitude, she pointed instead. "Over there. An empty spot."

After he'd parked, he couldn't get out of the truck fast enough. No way did he plan on going into details of his slow decline into drunkenness or how long he'd stayed there.

Hurrying around to her side, he opened the door for her and helped her out. The pulse of the music echoed off the surrounding brick walls.

Arm tucked firmly into his, Zoe took a deep breath. "Isn't this sort of thing difficult for you?" she asked. "Going inside bars, being around the atmosphere, the alcohol, all of it?"

"Yes." One word conveyed the truth.

Slowly she nodded. "I completely understand. If I'd known, I never would have asked you."

"Don't be like that." Though he knew he sounded curt, he couldn't help it. "I don't need or expect to be treated differently than anyone else."

"Why'd you keep it a secret from me?" she asked. An instant later, she colored, realizing what she'd just said.

"For the same reason you don't tell me everything," he said, feeling the need to be blunt. When she looked away, he sighed. While he'd love to know what she wasn't saying, now was not the time to try to find out.

They'd almost reached the front door of the bar. He held it open for her. Letting her precede him, he steeled himself and followed her into the dark, smoky room.

This time, since Zoe wasn't dressed like a woman looking for action, their arrival didn't cause a stir. Brock saw a few of the male patrons checking her out, but one hard look from him had them glancing away.

Spotting Mike sitting at the same place at the bar, Zoe made a beeline over to him.

The instant Mike saw her, he looked sick, as though he wished he were somewhere else. Brock found himself wondering if the guy actually knew more than he'd revealed.

Mike stood, downed the last of his beer and slapped a twenty on the bar. He shook his head at Zoe, and then tried to brush past her. When she grabbed his arm, he raised his hand as if he meant to hit her.

Brock moved fast, pinning the other man's arm at his side. "One more move like that," he growled, "and I'll deck you."

"Then tell your girlfriend not to touch me," Mike snarled, not backing down.

"I'm sorry," Zoe said. "I only wanted to have a word with you."

"I've said all I'm going to say." Voice definitely unfriendly, Mike took a step back. "Not only have I talked to the police several times, but my whole life has been messed up because of that woman."

"You mean Shayna?" Zoe's tone dripped ice. "The woman you had sex with right before she was killed? My best friend? *That* woman?"

Mike had the grace to look abashed. "Look, I'm sorry about your friend. But believe me, I didn't have anything to do with her death. The police have cleared me."

"I know," Zoe said. "I just wanted to ask you if you remembered anything else about that night?"

Looking from Zoe to Brock, Mike shook his head. "Like I said, I've already told the police everything I know."

"I'll buy you a beer," Brock offered. "Hell, man. Just humor us. Shayna was not only Zoe's best friend, but my roommate."

Brock couldn't tell if it was the offer of free alcohol or the fact that he'd been Shayna's roommate, but Mike finally nodded.

"One drink," Mike said. "Then I really have to go."

Two beers later, they left Mike happily sitting at the bar, nursing what remained of his brew.

"That was a complete waste of time," Brock said, taking Zoe's arm.

"Not really." Her brittle smile looked forced. "Did you notice he said Cristine was always with Shayna? Yet has anyone asked Cristine why she wasn't here that night?"

Brock nodded. "I'm sure Roger has. But I'd be interested to know also."

Zoe stiffened. "Well, I'll be," she drawled. "Look who just walked in."

Even before he turned to look, he knew. Cristine, wearing a skintight minidress and shiny black high-heeled shoes.

A quick glance at Zoe revealed her entire mood had

shifted. She noticed him watching her and grinned. "I guess you can see who we're going to talk to next."

Resigned, he nodded. "Let's go."

"Not yet." Grabbing his arm, she stopped him. "She hasn't noticed us yet. I want to see what she's going to do."

While they watched, Cristine strutted around the bar, frequently tossing her shoulder-length hair and laughing. She stopped to talk to several individuals, all of them male. When she spotted Mike, still planted on his regular stool, she waved and made a beeline for him.

As soon as Cristine reached Mike, she leaned in and kissed his cheek. Mike said something to her, then looked up and began searching the bar. When he'd located Brock and Zoe, he pointed.

Immediately, Cristine's formerly animated expression vanished. She pushed away from Mike and strode toward them, parting clusters of patrons with her body.

"What are you two doing here?" she demanded.

Brock spoke up, forestalling Zoe. "What do you mean, Cristine? Zoe and I wanted to get a drink, so we came here. Why?"

Looking from one to the other with narrowed eyes, Cristine appeared to consider her response. "No offense, you two. But the Hitching Post was mine and Shayna's hangout. Having you here crimps my style."

Out partying so soon after her best friend's funeral would have seemed wrong with anyone else, but for Cristine it was par for the course.

"How can we crimp your style?" Brock asked. "We weren't bothering you."

"Maybe not." Cristine pouted up at him. "But Mike says you two were bugging him."

Ignoring this, Zoe smiled. "We won't stay long. Hey, I need to ask you a quick question. Since you make it sound like the two of you always came here together, why was Shayna here alone the night she was killed?"

Chapter 14

Cristine reared back, acting as if Zoe had slapped her. "Look, Zoe. I know you don't have any idea of the kind of lifestyle Shayna and I live…er, lived. But if one of us hooked up with someone, the other often left alone. It was agreed and expected. After all, looking for a hookup was the primary reason we trolled the bars."

Zoe winced, but she didn't back down. "So what you're saying is that you'd met some guy and left with him, and Shayna was here by herself when she hooked up with Mike."

"That's exactly what I'm saying." Cristine tossed her hair. "Now, if you're done interrogating me, I've got people to see and places to go."

Without waiting for Zoe to answer, Cristine sashayed off, disappearing into the crowd.

They both watched her go.

"What now?" Brock asked.

"I want to find out who Cristine was with the night Shayna died."

"I do, too," Brock said. "With all the lying and trying to make me look like the killer, I think she knows more than she's saying about what really happened to Shayna."

"I agree. While I don't believe Cristine had anything to do with Shayna's death, I think she knows who did."

"It's possible." Taking her arm, he steered her toward the door. "Let's go."

But she pulled away. "Not yet. There's an empty table." She made a beeline for it, securing a seat with a triumphant look that made him smile.

Taking the chair next to her, he eyed her. "What now?"

"I want to have a drink and just watch the bar. You never know who might turn up."

She had a point. He signaled the waitress. He ordered tonic water with lime and Zoe ordered a glass of Shiraz.

Though they nursed their drinks a good forty-five minutes, Cristine never reappeared.

Despite telling himself repeatedly that he was a fool, sitting side by side with Zoe talking about mundane things like the feed store and the Bells, he again felt the strength of the connection between them. If he let himself, he might almost believe they were just another couple, out for a night on the town.

Finally, Zoe drank the last of her wine. "Are you ready to go?" she asked, leaning close, her breath tickling his ear.

Chest tight, too tongue-tied to speak, he nodded and stood, pulling back her chair and helping her up.

As they exited the bar, she nestled into his side, sending a bolt of heat straight to his groin. To the casual observer, they were a laid-back couple, leaving after enjoying a fun hour at a downtown bar. He had a sudden aching wish that life were that simple, that it could be so.

Making their way through the crowd, he continued to look for Cristine. Evidently, she'd felt they'd so invaded her space that she'd left. He glanced at the bar, noting Mike had apparently taken off, too.

While they walked, he kept watch for either of them, just in case. Judging from the way Zoe kept searching, she did, as well.

"I guess we scared Cristine away," Zoe said.

"Either that, or she and Mike had a rendezvous somewhere."

"Ew." Grimacing, Zoe glanced over her shoulder. "Do you really think she'd honestly sleep with the same guy her best friend did?"

"Who knows?" he answered. "The way she lives, probably."

She nodded, her expression pensive.

They'd nearly reached his truck when a movement to the left of them caught his eye. A man, moving furtively. He was slight, wearing a cowboy hat and a bulky jacket that was way too warm for the night. All in black, which was a warning in itself. Brock had a feeling they were about to be mugged.

"Zoe." His low tone contained a note of caution.

She froze. "What?" she whispered.

Practically pushing, he hustled her toward the truck. "Keep moving. Don't look back."

But then, in the instant before they were able to duck

safely between the rows of cars, the man Brock was watching stood up and pointed something at him. Something black. A gun.

Christ. Not mugged. Killed.

"Get down!" Brock shoved her to the ground, diving on top of her. The sharp report of gunfire echoed, and his passenger-side window shattered, sending shards of glass raining down on them.

"Are you okay?" he asked.

"I think so." She'd skinned her elbows. They were bleeding. Just as she tried to push back up, the man shot again.

And Brock's gun was in his truck. Even though he had a permit to carry a concealed handgun, since the Hitching Post had a sign up forbidding guns, the law forbade him bringing it inside. Right now it was in his glove box. Exactly where it was doing the least good.

"Stay down," he ordered. "We're trapped. If whoever that is wants to kill us, we're not going to make this any easier for him."

Eyes wide, she nodded. At his words, she'd begun trembling. "We must have hit a nerve in there," she said. "Did you recognize him?"

"No." Dragging her with him, he reached the driver's side of his truck. "I want you to climb in, but stay down on the floor. I'm going to try and start the engine and get us out of here. You got it?"

She nodded. "Yes."

"Good. One. Two. Three." Yanking open the door, he pushed her inside. Staying down himself, he leaned in and put the key in the ignition. The motor roared to life.

Now. He had to back them up and drive away without getting shot. He could only hope the shooter wasn't near enough to get them at close range.

Another vehicle pulled into the lot. As it cruised slowly past, he heard the chatter of several women, all excited. Coworkers, most likely. Here for happy hour. They'd probably saved his and Zoe's lives.

Praying he was right and that the shooter wouldn't risk being seen, he hunched over the steering wheel, slammed the truck into Reverse, then forward, tires screeching.

No more shots. No more sign of the shooter, either. The car full of women parked and they spilled out, still laughing and chattering happily.

"Get back inside your vehicle," he yelled. "Someone has a gun."

At his words, the women screamed, rushing back to their car. Brock waited until they'd started it and peeled off.

Praying they weren't in any more danger, he pulled into the street. "Call the sheriff," he ordered, tossing Zoe his phone. "He needs to get someone over to the Hitching Post to investigate."

She frowned. "Shouldn't we wait for him?"

"Not as long as some crazy is around taking potshots at us. I'm getting you out of here."

"Where to?" she asked, apparently agreeing with him.

"We'd better head down to the sheriff's office. They're going to want to take our statements."

Zoe guessed she must have been shell-shocked, because it wasn't until she was sitting in Brock's truck on the way to the sheriff's, that she began to shake. Not just shivers, either. No, these were bone-jarring, teeth-chattering, uncontrollable shudders.

A few seconds after she started losing it, Brock pulled over to the side of the road.

"You're in shock," he told her, his voice both soft and tough. "Come here," he said as he unbuckled and wrapped her in his arms.

He held her like that, in silence, until her shaking began to subside. A bone-deep weariness had taken hold of her and, with her head against his strong chest and the masculine scent of him filling her nose, the tension leached out of her.

Finally, she felt normal enough to lift her chin and thank him.

"Do you feel better now?" he asked.

She nodded. "Let's go give our statements."

After they reached the sheriff's office, the dispatcher on duty told them Roger had headed out to the Hitching Post after they'd called in the shooting. One of his other deputies, a man Zoe didn't recognize but Brock apparently knew, took their statements. The process took a little over an hour. When they'd finished answering his questions, Zoe could no longer hide her exhaustion.

On the way out, a clearly concerned Brock offered her his arm. Grateful, she took it, leaning heavily on him on the way to his truck.

When they reached the house, Zoe apologized and headed to her room. She curled up on her bed, fully clothed, and closed her eyes.

By the time she woke, it was after ten the next morning and the house was silent. Brock had already left for work and Mama Bell was ensconced inside her craft room with the door closed and her little television on.

Nothing had changed. Ever since Shayna's funeral, Mama Bell stayed shut up in her room. A grim-faced Mr. Bell came and went, barely sparing a word for Zoe as he bustled out the door on his way to his job.

The atmosphere inside the Bell house was so dark it felt suffocating. Grieving herself, Zoe endured it, certain that once Shayna's killer was caught, everyone would feel better.

The fact that someone had shot at her and Brock might mean the answer had something to do with the Hitching Post. If she didn't hear soon, she'd call the sheriff and find out what they'd learned. Meanwhile, she'd just have to keep at it and refuse to give up.

For now, she sat at the kitchen table with her laptop, working on her blog and keeping herself available in case Mama wanted to talk.

She also thought about Brock entirely too much, and several times she picked up her phone to call him. But, each time, she put the cell down without even pulling him up in her contact list.

The other person constantly in her thoughts was Roger Giles, the sheriff. She couldn't help wondering if he'd made any progress on the investigation.

She needed to find out. Again, she itched to call Brock. As she was attempting to talk herself out of it, her cell rang.

Caller ID showed her agent. Answering, she learned her book proposal had gone to auction.

"This is certainly news for celebration," her agent enthused. Apparently three publishers all wanted her book.

Any other time, Zoe would have been dancing with

glee. Now, she felt so mired in gloom and doom she only wanted to cry.

Which wouldn't do at all. Her agent would think she'd lost her mind. She was happy, she really was. She just couldn't show it.

"Zoe? Are you there, hon?"

"Sorry, I'm just rendered speechless by shock," Zoe said, trying to summon up some normalcy in her re-action. "That's absolutely fantastic," she continued. "I never expected this."

"I did," her agent said firmly. "Your blog is a huge success, so naturally they want the book. We'll have all the bids in within a few hours. The auction will be over later today. I'll keep you posted on the outcome."

With that, the call ended.

Staring at her phone, Zoe considered. Right now, she should feel electrified, ready to dance around the room. After all, this was what she wanted, what she'd worked so long and hard for. While the advertising she sold on her blog provided her with a decent income, this book would be the icing on the cake.

If she'd been in New York, she'd have called up some girlfriends to go out and celebrate. Or she and her agent would have met for drinks.

In Anniversary, with her best friend recently bur-ied, Brock was the only person she wanted to tell, and she couldn't. And while Mama Bell had always been interested in Zoe's life, Zoe didn't want to bother her in the middle of her grieving.

On the other hand, maybe this would be exactly the kind of distraction Mama Bell needed to help her get over the hump.

With that in mind, she crossed to the master bedroom

and tapped on the door. Mama Bell's halfhearted response only made Zoe more determined. Whatever quilt Mama was working on would have to wait. Zoe was going to drag her out for a subdued celebratory lunch.

But when she finally entered the craft room, instead of busily sewing on her latest quilt, Mama Bell sat in the corner, curled up in a ball on the floor. Apparently she hadn't bothered to change out of her pajamas—Zoe wondered how long she'd worn them. She barely lifted her head as Zoe approached. Her puffy eyes and red nose, as well as the pile of wadded-up tissues, showed she'd been crying.

Zoe nearly reconsidered her plan. Crouching down next to Mama, Zoe wrapped the older woman in her arms and simply held her.

"Come eat with me," Zoe said softly, smoothing Mama's gray hair back from her face.

"I'm not hungry."

"When was the last time you ate?"

Mama's tiny shrug was answer enough.

"I'm not taking no for an answer," Zoe insisted. "Now let's get you cleaned up so we can go out to eat. Your choice."

But Mama had already begun shaking her head. "Out?" she asked, her voice horrified. "I'm not leaving this house. Everyone in town will want to come and offer me their condolences, both for Shayna's death and the end of my marriage. I can't deal with that right now."

The end of her marriage? Zoe knew how fast gossip traveled around here—she supposed most small towns were like that. But as far as she knew, Marshall Bell had been sleeping here at night. She'd had high hopes the two Bells would be able to work things out.

Apparently not. And now was definitely not the time to comment on that.

"Okay, we won't go out," Zoe said. "I'll make us something. How about that?"

Wiping her eyes, Mama didn't bother to hide her horrified expression. "You, cook? Unless you went to chef school or something while you were gone, you couldn't boil water."

Zoe pretended to be offended. At least she'd gotten a reaction. "How about this?" she offered. "I'll go pick us something up. We can eat out on the back porch?"

After Mama Bell agreed, Zoe shut off her little television. She made the older woman promise to shower and get dressed, then snagged the car keys off the counter and headed to town, her mood better than it had been in days.

Whether she shared her news with Mama Bell or not, Zoe had reason to celebrate. Several times during the drive to town, she had to suppress the urge to call Brock. Even though he, more than anyone else, would be the one person she'd want to share such good fortune with, the news would also serve as a reminder that she had another, completely separate life. One where she stood a chance of finding happiness.

Maybe, she told herself, she'd celebrate alone, another time. Somewhere else.

Pacing the back storage rooms of the feed store and letting Eve take care of customers, Brock tried to come to terms with the depth of his rage. If Roger didn't catch the SOB pretty damn quickly, Brock planned to go hunting himself.

Whoever had shot at them could have killed Zoe. The

thought made his blood run cold. Even if she lived in some far-off, northern city, he couldn't imagine a world without Zoe in it. Add to that the possibility that this shooter might have been the one to murder Shayna, and it was all Brock could do to sit still.

So when Roger called and asked Brock to come down to the sheriff's office, Brock couldn't get there fast enough.

When he arrived, he was stunned to see Zoe pull up behind him.

"He called you, too?"

Zoe nodded. "Maybe he has good news."

"I hope so." Side by side, they walked into the building. Agnes immediately ushered them back to Roger's office.

"I think we got the guy." Once Brock and Zoe were seated, rather than sit behind his metal desk, Roger paced back and forth, hands shoved down in his pockets.

"You caught him?" Zoe sounded stunned, inadvertently revealing she'd had no faith in the sheriff's abilities regarding this case.

Roger exchanged a look with Brock, indicating he'd got that, too. "Yes." He didn't bother to hide his amusement at Zoe's reaction.

"What he have to say?" Brock asked.

"Not much. He's a messed-up meth head." Roger's voice rang with disgust. "Says he doesn't know why he did it. He claims he doesn't even know where he got the gun."

"Is it traceable?"

"We're working on it. The serial number was filed off it, but this particular manufacturer puts it in more than one location." He shrugged. "He's still being in-terrogated. We'll offer to reduce the charges if he rolls over on whoever hired him."

This surprised Brock. He glanced at Zoe, who also appeared shocked. "Hired him?"

"Yeah. It's clear this guy wasn't capable of acting alone. We checked his bank records and have proof. Confronted with that, he's already admitted he recently came into a large sum of money, which he promptly used to get high. Someone paid him to shoot at the two of you."

Zoe found her voice. "But why?"

Roger smiled at her and Brock found himself want-ing to deck the other man. "That, I don't know. Maybe your snooping around the Hitching Post is starting to bother someone."

"That's why I took Brock with me," she said. "If any-one can protect me, he can."

For that, Brock wanted to hug her.

"As well as that may be," Roger said, including both of them in his hard-eyed stare, "I want you to stop. Stay out of the Hitching Post. Let us do our job. We'll catch whoever killed Shayna, I assure you."

Zoe crossed her arms. "Now, do you really believe Brock and I were the actual targets?"

Roger nodded. "I do. Clearly it wasn't a random shooting. And even more incriminating, we found a piece of paper in his pocket with both your descrip-tions."

Brock cursed. A quick glance at Zoe revealed she seemed energized by this information rather than taken aback.

"It wasn't good news," Roger said drily. Evidently he, too, had noticed Zoe's reaction.

"In a way, it is," she said. "Because that proves we're getting too close. We're making the killer uncomfortable. Don't you see? We can't stop now. We have to go back."

Roger made an unintelligible sound. Brock couldn't tell if it was shock or surprise.

Brock looked down to hide his smile. If memory served, from now on out, Zoe would be like a dog with a bone. She wouldn't be able to leave this alone.

"Absolutely not," Roger barked. "I don't need two or three more murders on my hands." He lowered his voice, glancing from one to the other. "Please. As a favor to me, promise you'll stay away from the Hitching Post."

The silence stretched out. Though tempted to answer for her, Brock knew doing any such thing would guarantee that Zoe would do the opposite of whatever he said. She could be ornery like that. Truth was, he couldn't blame her. He too had a strong aversion to being told what to do.

"Zoe?" Roger prompted. "Come on, help me out here."

"Fine." Lifting her chin, Zoe looked the sheriff right in the eye. "Do your job. Find Shayna's killer."

With that, she sailed out the door.

"Doesn't she realize we're working on it?" Roger looked at Brock. "Is she serious?"

"I'm afraid so," Brock drawled. "I'd say you'd better get busy. You've got a killer to catch." Getting up, he followed Zoe out the door.

Outside, she stopped suddenly, causing Brock to run

into her. Instinctively, his arms went out, and somehow they were chest to chest. The rational part of him knew he should push her away. Instead, he tightened his arms around her. Damn, she felt good.

Her triumphant smile faded as she gazed up at him. He gave her a second to protest, and then he claimed her mouth in a kiss.

Mine, he thought fiercely. *All mine.*

It took several breathtaking seconds for Zoe to realize exactly what she was doing. Standing on the doorstep of the sheriff's office, kissing Brock for the entire world to see.

With a startled gasp, Zoe broke away.

He stood still, gaze riveted on her face. Despite his closed-off expression, she knew he was vulnerable. As was she. As was she.

Heart in her throat, she took a step backward.

"This isn't over, Zoe," Brock said. The sound of his voice stirred something inside her.

"I know," she answered, frozen in place despite knowing she needed to move. Anniversary was a small town. All it took was one person to notice them, one person to have seen them locking lips as though each never wanted to let the other go, and the rumors would start flying.

With a sense of shock, she realized she didn't really care. If she had a choice, she'd choose Brock. This realization brought such a deep, familiar pain it was enough impetus to start her moving.

She got in the car and, her hands shaking, fitted the key in the ignition. Luckily, Brock didn't follow. If he had, she wouldn't have had the willpower to send him away. She glanced toward where she'd left him and realized he must have gone back inside. Maybe to put more pressure on Roger to find the killer.

Some of the tension coiled inside her drained slightly.

Backing from her spot and pulling out into the street, she still had to head into town and grab food for Mama Bell. She went to the closest place, got some fried chicken in a bucket and drove home.

As she pulled up in the Bells' driveway, Zoe's cell rang. Caller ID showed Cristine. Great. For a heartbeat, Zoe debated pressing the decline call button. Instead, she took a deep breath and answered.

"Zoe?" Cristine's voice sounded muffled, as though she'd been crying.

Or drunk. Zoe glanced at her watch. She really didn't have time for this. Not right now.

"What's up?" Trying her best to sound breezy, Zoe jingled her car keys, aware the other woman would be able to hear them. "I'm on my way out the door," she lied.

"Oh, that's good." Cristine laughed, a bitter sound with way more pathos than humor. "Actually, it's kind of symbolic, since I'm on my way out, too."

At the words, a chill of alarm skittered up Zoe's spine. "On your way out where?" she asked.

"I'm finished. Done. I've decided to end it," Cristine said sadly. "I have no more reason to live."

Zoe's heart stopped. Struggling to find her voice, she hoped she sounded normal. "Where are you right now?"

"Home. I want to die at home."

Damn. "Listen, how about I come over there and we talk? Would that be okay?"

Silence.

"Cristine? Are you there?"

"Yes."

Though Zoe wouldn't have thought it possible, Cristine sounded even more lifeless. A horrible thought occurred to her. "Cristine, have you taken anything?"

"Like what?" She actually sounded puzzled. "Oh, wait. You mean like pills?"

"Yes. Exactly. Have you taken any pills?"

"No. I'm going to do this right." Cristine gave a hollow laugh. "Pills are too uncertain. I want to make sure I'm dead."

Zoe had just parked Mama Bell's car.

"Don't do anything yet. Promise me." She started the ignition.

Again, silence from the other end of the phone.

"Cristine." Tone sharp, Zoe gripped her cell so tightly she was surprised she hadn't cracked it. With her one free hand, she put the shifter in Reverse and backed into the street. If she remembered right, Cristine lived in the neighborhood behind the high school. "Promise me you won't do anything until I get there. We need to talk."

Instead of agreeing, Cristine let loose a string of curses.

Again, Zoe had to try to intervene. "Cristine, listen to me. I want you to wait until I get there. Don't do anything foolish."

"You don't even know where I live."

"You put your address on the flyer. Isn't that near the high school?"

When Cristine answered in the affirmative, Zoe pressed the accelerator and headed that way. She figured it would be safer if she kept Cristine on the phone all the way there.

Even as she cast about for something to say, Cristine started sobbing, great, hug-your-belly-with-your-arms-because-it-hurts-so-much sobs. In between these, she said something, but Zoe couldn't make it out.

Then, before Zoe could speak, Cristine ended the call.

Immediately, Zoe hit Redial. The call went to voice mail, which meant Cristine had turned the phone off.

Heartbeat kicking into overdrive, Zoe called 911. She reported what was going on to the dispatcher, a woman whose voice she vaguely recognized, giving her the general address. "You need to get Roger Giles," Zoe ordered. "He'll know where this is. Tell him to send someone over here." Then, despite the dispatcher's request to remain on the line, Zoe hung up.

She broke every speed limit on the way to Cristine's.

Chapter 15

Pulling up in front of the redbrick ranch house, Zoe took a deep breath. Did Cristine have a gun? Should she wait for the police? Since she only had a split second to decide, Zoe elected to go inside.

When she reached the front entrance, she knocked softly, and then tried the doorknob. Unlocked, it turned in her hand. Safe or not, she took a deep breath and stepped inside.

As she closed the door behind her, she stopped, blinking as her eyes tried to adjust to the light. Or lack of, to be more specific. Cristine had closed the heavy drapes and sat in as much darkness as could be managed in the middle of the day.

"Hey." Zoe moved closer. Cristine barely looked up or acknowledged her presence. She was sprawled in an armchair, her hair and clothing in total disarray.

"Are you all right?" Zoe asked.

Cristine grunted. "I will be soon." As she shifted her weight in the chair and faced Zoe, Zoe realized something else.

Cristine had a gun. Zoe's heart stuttered.

"What are you doing?" she asked gently, trying not to startle the other woman.

Lower lip trembling, Cristine lifted her head. She looked from her pistol to Zoe, and then back again. "Trying to get up the courage to end all this nonsense."

Swallowing, Zoe tried to figure out what to say. Well aware the wrong words could cause Cristine to do something they'd both regret, Zoe knew she had to try anyway.

"Why?" She made her voice soft and caring, that of a true friend, trying to understand. Her chest ached for the other woman's pain. If she'd known sooner, she might have been able to help, even if it meant involving a professional.

Instead of answering, Cristine looked up at Zoe and frowned. "Did you know I had an affair with Marshall Bell? He won't even talk to me now."

Was *that* what this was about?

"What about Shayna?" Zoe asked. "How is it you two were still friends after she walked in on you?"

Wiping away tears, Cristine continued. "I told her he raped me. I lied to protect myself and made my best friend hate her own father." At that, she started wailing again.

Zoe crouched down next to Cristine, wondering if she should try to take the weapon away. A sideways glance showed Cristine had her finger curled around the trigger. The wrong move could cause the gun to go off.

"I miss her so much," Cristine wailed. "She was special."

"Shayna was amazing," Zoe agreed, trying to ease the tightness in her chest as she exhaled. She couldn't stop trembling, and even had to curl her hands into fists so Cristine wouldn't notice. Where in the hell were the police? "I loved Shayna like a sister, too. I know how you feel."

Cristine's expression darkened, letting Zoe know she'd said the wrong thing. "You absolutely do not know how I feel."

While Zoe watched, her heart in her throat, Cristine lifted her pistol. She cocked her head and studied it as if she expected the weapon to give her the answers she clearly needed.

Making little moaning sounds of deep distress, Cristine raised the gun to her head, and then swiveled and pointed it directly at Zoe.

Crap. Zoe froze. For the first time Zoe realized Cristine could shoot her, too. Nothing like a little murder-suicide to make a statement.

"Please don't aim that at me," she said, keeping her voice soft. "It scares me."

To her relief, Cristine lowered the pistol back to her lap, though she kept it in a tight grip.

Heart pounding, Zoe tried to think, aware she had to do her absolute best to defuse the situation. "You're right. I have no idea how you feel," Zoe agreed quietly. "You and Shayna were extraordinarily close. I hadn't seen her in five years. I just meant…well, that I loved her."

Just like that, Cristine deflated. "I loved her more," she said in a broken whisper, hanging her head. "Shayna was everything to me. We were more than best friends. She was my…idol. I would have done anything for her. I never wanted her to get hurt. The thing with Marshall was just a fling. I wasn't serious. I felt awful, you have to believe me."

"Yet not awful enough to tell her the truth?"

Cristine stared at her, eyes narrowed. "Don't judge me. You don't know anything about me."

"Sorry." Zoe kept her tone mild. "I know Shayna cared about you, and that's good enough for me," she lied.

Apparently mollified, Cristine nodded. "My poor, sweet Shayna. What happened was an accident. I never wanted her to die."

At the choice of phrase, a sickening suspicion made Zoe's stomach lurch. Cristine spoke like a woman on the verge of making a confession. Had she been the one who'd killed Shayna? Surely not.

Still, stranger things had happened.

Gripping her hands tightly together, Zoe took a deep breath and waited. She didn't want to risk ruining the moment.

But instead of elaborating, Cristine began weeping again, the same great gulping sobs that sounded as if her heart were being ripped from her body. "I miss her so damn much."

Zoe let her cry, her own eyes filling at the raw emotion. She'd never liked Cristine much, but she could definitely empathize with the other woman's pain.

Eventually, though, it became clear if she wanted to hear more, she'd have to prod Cristine. Carefully.

"I wonder what actually happened to our Shayna," Zoe mused. "Mama Bell has been beside herself. This not knowing is killing her. All the medical examiner has been able to determine is that she died of blunt-force trauma. Like she was run over by a car or something."

At Zoe's words, which were absolutely true, Cristine winced and began sobbing even harder. "I'm so sorry," she wailed. "I didn't mean to do it."

"What did you do?" Zoe asked, praying she was wrong. For a few moments, Cristine continued to cry, too distraught to talk.

Briefly, Zoe again considered trying to take the pistol away from her but discarded the idea as too dangerous. Instead, she let Cristine cry it out, praying she wouldn't do anything foolish.

Finally, her sobs began to decrease in intensity. Wiping at her mascara-rimmed eyes with her free hand, she sniffled. "Honest to God, I didn't mean to hurt her. She called me from the lake, after she and Mike hooked up. I was drunk. Too drunk to drive. I realize that now. But she needed a ride home, so I drove out to get her."

"But her cell phone didn't show any calls," Zoe put in.

"I erased them from her phone," Cristine managed. "I'm sure Roger's office must have subpoenaed the records. It's only a matter of time until he figures out I was the last person to see Shayna alive."

Dizzy, Zoe clutched the door frame. She swallowed hard. "After you picked her up, what happened?"

In the distance, a siren sounded. About damn time, Zoe thought. What had taken them so long?

The siren grew closer. Louder. Unmistakably on the way there, to Cristine's house.

Immediately, Cristine stiffened. "Did you call the police?" she asked, her voice suddenly dangerously level.

"Yes. I didn't want you to hurt yourself," Zoe answered. "I called 911 on the way over here."

"Call them back," Cristine ordered, her monotone voice more worrisome than if she'd been screaming.

"And tell them what?" Zoe asked, hoping that meant Cristine was giving up the idea of suicide.

"Tell them to stay away." Raising the pistol, Cristine pointed it directly at Zoe. "This is loaded and the safety is off. Tell them to stay outside, or I'll kill you."

After Zoe had gotten into her car, Brock had turned and gone back into the sheriff's office. Agnes didn't even look up as he passed the front desk. There were a few more things he wanted to discuss with the sheriff.

As far as Brock was concerned, Roger Giles had better get on the ball and find Shayna's killer. Hell, now that he had whoever had shot at Zoe and Brock, Roger should be able to find out who had hired the guy and why.

Roger needed to do his damn job. Brock tried to put aside his personal feelings about the other man. If he could temporarily forget that the sheriff had hit on Zoe, he could admit he'd always thought Roger did a pretty good job as an officer of the law.

Until now. This entire Shayna thing had lots of town folks doubting their sheriff's abilities. Brock knew how their old sheriff Renee would have handled it. She'd have called a press conference, invited some of the bigger news stations from Dallas, and even Houston, and subtly put the heat on the killer.

Roger preferred a more understated method, apparently.

And the way Brock felt, they'd just about run out

of time. No way was he letting Zoe risk her life doing something the elected sheriff should be able to do.

He found Roger still in his office, going over paperwork. Not only did the sheriff have a large stack in front of him, but his in-box was overflowing, as well.

"Hey."

Roger looked up from his desk but didn't stand. Judging from the dark circles under his eyes, the sheriff hadn't been getting much sleep.

"What can I do for you, Brock?" Roger asked. "I thought we were done."

"We were, but I got to thinking. I have a couple of scenarios I wanted to run by you. Do you have a minute? I'd like to go over the case with you."

"Sure." Indicating a chair, Roger grimaced. "We'll have to make it short. I'm pretty busy."

Brock had just taken a seat and was about to start talking when Agnes rushed into the room.

"Sheriff," she said, wide-eyed. "Zoe Onella just called. Cristine Haywood is threatening to commit suicide. Zoe's on her way there now. I've sent a patrol car, but I thought you'd want to know."

"Damn it." Roger jumped to his feet. "Call the patrol and tell them to wait outside until I get there. Tell them I'm on my way."

"I'm going with you," Brock said, his tone leaving no room for disagreement.

Roger took one look at his face and nodded. "Come on. Let's go."

Sirens blaring and lights flashing, they made it across town in ten minutes. The marked patrol car had already arrived and sat parked in front of Cristine

Haywood's trim brick house. Both uniformed officers emerged from the car as the Sheriff screeched to a halt.

"Have you made contact?" Roger barked.

"No, sir. We tried the house phone and it just rings, unanswered. Her cell goes directly to voice mail."

Brock stepped forward. "Call Zoe," he said. "Or let me. She can fill us in on what's going on."

Jaw tight, Roger jerked his head toward Brock. "You call her. She'll feel more comfortable talking to you."

Immediately, Brock pulled out his phone and dialed Zoe's number.

After four rings, Zoe answered. She sounded tentative, nervous and stressed.

"Is everything all right in there?" Brock asked.

"No."

Swallowing hard, Brock inhaled. "The sheriff and his men are here. Can we come in?"

"I—" In the background, Brock could hear Cristine demanding Zoe hand her the phone.

Then Cristine came on the line. "Who is this?"

Brock identified himself.

"You tell the cops to stay outside, do you understand?" she said, her tone even and composed. "I'm armed. If they even try to come in, I'll shoot your girlfriend." She ended the call before he could respond.

"Dammit." Dragging his hand through his hair, Brock suppressed the urge to storm the front door.

"What did she say?" Roger asked, eyeing him as though bracing for bad news. "Judging from your expression, it wasn't good."

"She threatened Zoe." Grimly, Brock considered his options. "Said we need to stay out here or she'll shoot her."

"Shoot her?" Roger's brows rose. "She's armed?"

At the word, both of his officers stiffened, standing at attention.

"It sounds so." Brock glanced from Roger to the house and back again.

"Don't even think about it," Roger cautioned. "For now, it's best to let Zoe try to defuse the situation. If you go in there blazing, she's likely to shoot you, too."

Jaw set, Brock nodded. "I don't want Zoe hurt."

"None of us does."

"Sheriff," one of the deputies interrupted. "If this is a hostage situation, we need to call for backup."

"Not yet," Roger barked. "Call and tell the other deputies to be on standby."

The man nodded and returned to his car to do exactly that.

"What next?" Brock asked, itching to do something—anything—to make sure Zoe was safe.

"We wait." Roger took his arm, making him realize he'd instinctively started to move forward. Out of reflex, Brock shook the other man's grip off.

"Don't make me cuff you," Roger threatened. "You need to stay right here."

Brock snorted. "I'd like to see you try."

At that, one of the uniformed officers rested his hand on the butt of his gun.

"Stand down." Shaking his head, Roger glanced at the house.

An uneasy silence fell. Several of the neighbors grew curious and came outside to see what was going on. Roger motioned to one of his men to keep them back.

"It's too quiet," Roger mused. "I don't like not being able to hear what's going on inside."

"Me, either. Hey, look. There aren't any windows on the south side," Brock pointed out. "I could go around that way without anyone seeing me."

Roger considered. "You're a civilian," he argued. "I can't let you put your life in danger. I'll do it."

"No." Prepared to plead his case any way he had to, Brock stepped forward. "That's my Zoe in there. I can't let Cristine hurt her."

"*Your* Zoe?"

"That's right." Brock shot him a look, daring him to contradict him.

"So that's how it is." Roger grimaced. "I sort of suspected when you got so pissed that I took her to dinner." He sighed. "Look, I can't let you help. It would put my office in all kinds of lawsuit danger sending a civilian into a building where a woman is already holding one woman at gunpoint."

"Then turn your back. You don't have to know."

"That's not how it works." Roger spread his hands. "Sorry." His walkie-talkie squawked and he turned his attention to that.

Brock began moving. He strolled to the driveway, pretending to be focused on the fire truck that had just pulled up, lights flashing. Then he sprinted off, hoping to make it before the other man saw him.

When he reached the house, he hurried around to the back. From the layout, the kitchen was probably there, and would have a window over the sink. Since Zoe hadn't indicated what room she and Cristine were in, he'd need to be careful.

To his surprise, the back door was unlocked. Almost as if Cristine wanted someone to come in and stop her from whatever she planned to do. Once he was inside, he closed the door quietly and stood listening.

The murmur of feminine voices came from the front of the house, where the living room would be.

Moving quietly, he continued on.

The room was dark, with all the curtains and blinds closed. Cristine sat with her back to him, in the high-backed chair that faced the front window. Zoe crouched on the floor in front of her, keeping very still, as if afraid to move. Though she gave no visible indication, he knew she saw him immediately.

"Cristine," Zoe said. "Nothing will be accomplished by doing this."

"Justice." Again Cristine's flat voice made his gut clench. At least she was semilucid, he told himself, deciding to count his blessings. Though that could change at any moment, he knew.

"Not this way," Zoe argued. "Think of your mother."

"I *have* thought of her." Now Cristine displayed some agitation, waving something that looked a hell of a lot like a pistol in front of her. He couldn't see what it was since her body blocked it, but judging from the way Zoe's gaze tracked the thing, his guess was correct.

In the space of an afternoon, things had gone from bad to worse. Just freaking fantastic.

Edging closer, he ignored Zoe's wide-eyed look of warning. He needed to try to find out what had set Cristine off.

"I can't stand it." Now Cristine had begun crying. Damn. He'd rather she be calm and monotone. High emotions could lead to outbursts.

"Yes, you can," Zoe said. "You're a strong woman. When you tell them it was an accident—"

"That doesn't matter."

"Yes, it—"

"I was *drunk,* don't you understand?" Spraying spittle, Cristine stood. Brock froze, well aware all she had to do was turn around and she'd see him.

"It's a manslaughter charge. Vehicular manslaughter. They'll send me away. I can't go to prison. I'll never survive that." Her hysteria was rising.

Manslaughter charge? What the hell?

"Please. Sit back down. Tell me what happened." Still the quiet voice of reason, Zoe attempted to calm the other woman down.

To Brock's relief, Cristine sat. "I've lied about so many things," she said. "Shayna lied about everything and I, well, I just sort of started imitating her. It started out like a game, but once you start doing that, you forget what's real and what's not." She took a deep breath. "Like when I told you she and Brock were lovers at the end. They weren't. There never was a video."

Zoe nodded. "That's okay."

"Is it? You knew." Cristine gave a short bark of laughter. "Well, how about this then? I hired some druggie to shoot you in the Hitching Post parking lot."

Sucking her breath, Zoe revealed her shock. "Why?"

"I didn't want you poking around. Until you showed up again, I planned to frame the whole thing on Mike."

"I see." Zoe sounded calm. "You were about to tell me about Shayna."

While Cristine had been talking, Brock had dropped to the floor, crawling over to the back of her chair. Now, if Cristine stood, she wouldn't see him without gripping the top of her seat and peering down.

"That night, Shayna and I had started partying at

home. We did that a lot, to save money. We were drinking vodka and Diet Coke. I was totally wasted even before we got to the bar," Cristine said. "So was she. But we were laughing and having such a good time, I didn't worry about it."

She fell silent.

After a moment, Zoe prodded her. "Then she hooked up with Mike, right?"

"Exactly." Cristine went from listless sorrow to furious anger with that one word. "I couldn't believe she did that! I was seriously pissed when Shayna left with Mike. She knew damn good and well that I've been after him for months. And then she swooped in and took him, just like that. I think she did it to pay me back for sleeping with her father."

The vitriol in her voice worried Brock. He stayed put, trying to decide on his next course of action.

Zoe tried to speak, but Cristine told her to be quiet.

"Sorry," Zoe said. "You were saying?"

"After they left the bar together, I went home. And imagine how I felt when she had the nerve to call me to come pick her up at the lake after she and he were finished."

"Pretty awful." Zoe ventured a guess.

"Damn right. But we were friends and I saw the perfect opportunity to let her have a piece of my mind. So I went and got her."

Brock couldn't believe what he was hearing. It was beginning to sound like Cristine had killed Shayna. Never in a hundred years would he have guessed.

"And then what happened?" Zoe again, keeping her voice calm.

"I picked her up." Leaning over and giving him a

clear view of her, Cristine took a long drink from a tall plastic glass on the side table next to her. "There's not enough vodka in the world to erase what happened after that."

This time, Zoe didn't prod. She simply waited, like Brock, to hear the rest of the story of the end of Shayna's too short life.

Chapter 16

"We argued. Shayna started screaming at me to stop the car and let her out. I refused." Cristine began crying again, loudly. "Shayna opened her door and jumped. I had to be going at least fifty-five. I slammed on my breaks and put the car in Reverse. I was only going back to look for her, I swear. But instead I…"

"You ran over her," Zoe finished, sounding grim. "Oh, Cristine."

At that, Cristine stood, wiping at her eyes with one hand and brandishing her pistol with the other. "See? That's why I've got to end it," she said. "This town is my home. I can't bear knowing everyone is going to hate me."

Unbelievably, Zoe stood, too, facing off with Cristine. Brock clenched his jaw, mentally ordering her to sit back down.

"You need to get help," Zoe said. "I can't imagine carrying this burden around with you for so long."

"Yes. Exactly. It has been a burden." Clearly, Cristine hadn't expected sympathy. Though she still held the pistol carefully, she kept the muzzle down, aimed at the floor rather than Zoe or herself.

"A terrible thing to bear alone." Zoe reached out and enveloped the other woman in a hug.

For a second Cristine resisted, standing stiffly. Then, she relaxed into Zoe's embrace and let herself be comforted.

Now or never. Pushing to his feet, Brock grabbed Cristine's arm and twisted it. "Drop the gun."

Cristine shrieked in pain. "What the—" Reflexively, she squeezed the trigger. The gun went off, the bullet going into the wood floor.

Outside, hearing the shot, Roger and his men took action.

They smashed the front door in, weapons drawn.

"Don't move."

Brock gingerly took Cristine's pistol from her. "Thank you," he said, stepping back so Roger and his men could take charge of her.

"Arrest her," he told the sheriff. "She just confessed to killing Shayna Bell."

With the arrest of Cristine Haywood, the entire town of Anniversary was talking. Mama Bell even came out of hiding. Not to celebrate, but to request a meeting with the woman who'd been the last person to see her daughter alive.

Roger Giles had to ask Cristine, who was being detained in a holding cell until the bail hearing, if she was willing. He'd made it clear he hadn't wanted to but, as an officer of the law, he had no choice.

To Zoe's surprise, Cristine agreed.

Mama Bell dressed with great care. She put on one of her best church dresses, a pale cream chiffon with swirly blue flowers. Zoe had asked to accompany her, mainly to drive. She understood Mama's need to have a private talk with Cristine.

When they reached the sheriff's office, Roger came out to greet them before Zoe had time to help Mama out of the car.

Expression somber, Roger held out his arm. Mama Bell took it and, head held high, allowed him to escort her inside. Zoe followed, blinking back tears.

She waited in Roger's office while he and Mama went back to the holding cell. She had no idea what Mama wanted to ask Cristine or what the two of them would have to say to each other.

She only knew that here finally was closure. While it hadn't been the ending she'd expected, or even wanted, they'd all gotten what they'd needed. Shayna's killer had been caught. Remorseful, Cristine had made a full confession. It would only be a matter of time before she had her trial and received her sentence. Zoe had even heard that she'd requested the death penalty. Whether or not that was true, she didn't know.

Finally, Mama and Roger emerged. Mama Bell wept, hiding her face with a lace-edged handkerchief. Roger handed her over to Zoe, looking ashen as he hurried back to his office.

Without speaking, Zoe got her out to the car and in. After she'd buckled the seat belt and started the car, Mama's sobs quieted.

They'd nearly reached the house when Mama turned to her. "She was sorry, you know. Cristine. She didn't mean to kill Shayna. Though she's a thoroughly mixed-up girl, she has a lot of remorse. She loved Shayna, too. Somehow, that makes it a bit easier to bear."

Zoe nodded, not sure how to respond. In the time since Shayna's body had been found, the older woman seemed to have shrunk. Not only had she lost a lot of weight, but she'd turned inward, almost as if she'd mentally checked out.

After they'd made it home and parked, Zoe went around and helped Mama out of the car.

Once they were back inside the house, tears streaming unheeded down her weathered face, Mama turned to Zoe and held out her arms. As they embraced, Zoe felt her own eyes fill.

"I forgave her." Mama spoke in a low, shaky voice. "It wasn't easy—in fact, it was probably one of the most difficult things I've ever done."

Zoe didn't know how to respond, so she simply nodded.

"She was sorry, you know," Mama continued. "And not just because she's going to prison."

Zoe nodded again.

Finally, Mama released her. "Zoe, I have a favor to ask you," she said. "Please, sit." She patted the couch.

Zoe sat. "If you're wanting to talk to me about forgiving Cristine, I've already done so."

Mama smiled. "I'm glad, but that's not what I wanted to discuss with you." She took a seat on the couch next to Zoe and reached over to clasp Zoe's hand.

"I know it's none of my business," Mama started.

Zoe braced herself. Nothing that began like that could ever be good.

"But life's too short. It seems to me the only way you can find happiness is if you reach out and grab it with both hands."

Now confused, Zoe nodded. "I'm not really sure what you mean."

"Brock." Mama flashed a smile full of pain and love. "Both of you deserve a chance. I know that man still loves you and I'm guessing you still haven't told him why you keep pushing him away."

"I'll think about it," Zoe lied. While the older woman made sense, she didn't want Brock sacrificing his future happiness. Sure, right now he might say or think or believe he could live without children of his own, but over time he'd come to resent her for his lack. She knew. There'd been a time when she'd managed to convince herself that she was fine without kids. Yet look at her now. She could hardly stand to be around other people's children, aware her envy and grief and pain would eventually manifest itself.

She would not do that to Brock. She loved him far too much for that.

Now that Cristine had confessed to Shayna's killing, Brock knew Zoe would soon be making plans to leave Anniversary. He imagined she couldn't wait to get out of town and back in her precious city.

Despite that, he couldn't live with himself if he didn't give it one more shot. Give *them* one more shot. Because in his foolish heart, he couldn't accept that she'd willingly give it up. Not this time, now that they'd been given a second chance.

He called her and asked her to meet him in the park. If they got hungry, Sue's was a short distance away. To his surprise, she readily agreed. It was only after he'd hung up the phone that it dawned on him she'd probably agreed to see him so she could tell him goodbye.

Well, he'd just have to see about that. Damned if he'd spend the rest of his life yearning for a woman who didn't want him.

He waited for her on the painted metal bench near the end of the walking trail. Watching as she got out of Mrs. Bell's old car, he tried to quiet the thrumming feeling of love as she approached.

"So what are your plans now?" he asked, keeping his voice deliberately casual.

Zoe looked pensive. With the sunlight making copper hightlights in her long dark hair and highlighting her exotic cheekbones and creamy skin, she looked so beautiful he could hardly stand to look at her.

"I'm not sure," she answered carefully. "Eventually I'll probably head back to New York."

Just like that, she stomped on his hopes and crushed them underfoot. Doggedly, he continued, still refusing to abandon the battle before it even got started.

"Why? You don't have to run now," he said, afraid to breathe, afraid to hope. "This is where you belong, here in Anniversary. Here with me."

She wouldn't look at him. Never a good sign.

"All my things are there, in my apartment. Plus, I love New York," she said.

"As much as you love it here?" *As much as you love me?*

Slowly, she shook her head, but not to answer him. "This isn't going to work out, you know. It can't."

That hurt so much he had to close his eyes and swallow hard to keep his composure. He wouldn't beg, he had that much pride at least. But he would make sure she understood he'd welcome her back, arms wide open, if she was willing to give their relationship another go.

"Oh, Brock." When she lifted her face to his, her anguished expression tore at his heart. "There's nothing I'd love more than to stay here in Anniversary and make a life with you."

But.

No. He refused to let there be a but.

"If that's true, then why won't you stay?"

She only shook her head. "I can't, Brock. I just can't. Let's leave it at that."

Again with the secrets. About to demand she stop hiding from him, he paused when she held up her hand to silence him.

"Please. Don't make this any more difficult than it already is." And then, just as she'd done many times before, she turned her back on him and walked out of his life.

And, as he'd done so many times before, he let her go, hating himself and wishing like hell he could hate her.

This time, he swore to himself, he was finished. A man could only take so much. Clearly, she'd made her choice.

And once again, she hadn't chosen him.

Somehow he made it through the rest of the day. He went back to work, kept busy. When he wasn't helping customers, he took an impromptu and completely unnecessary inventory, restocking shelves, sweeping up and doing any kind of busywork he could find. Anything to keep him from thinking. Or feeling.

Finally, closing time arrived. Turning the lock, Brock heaved a sigh. He faced an extremely long night alone at home. Never had the idea of heading to JT's and having a drink sounded better. Maybe he'd do that, minus the alcohol.

"Brock, what is this?" Eve called him from his office. Something sounded off in her voice.

He hurried back, worried. She sat at his desk, peering intently at the computer. When she looked up, he was startled to realize she had tears running down her cheeks.

"Eve, what is it? What's wrong?"

She sniffed, making a vague gesture toward the screen. "This website. I found the paper where you'd written down the address, so I checked it out. This blog is fabulous. I even went back in the archives and started reading. Whoever this woman is, she pours her soul out on her blog."

At first, he had no idea what she meant. Then he saw the napkin with the words *City Girl* scrawled in Marshall Bell's handwriting.

Zoe's website. His baby sister had been reading Zoe's blog. His chest constricted.

"It's Zoe's. But it can't be too great," he pointed out. "Especially if it's making you cry."

"Ah, now I understand." Grinning through her tears, she grabbed a tissue and blew her nose, then another to mop at her eyes. "You've got to read it. I guarantee you'll learn things about Zoe that will break your heart. And maybe, just maybe, you'll understand why she keeps running away from you."

With those cryptic words, she pushed up from the desk and headed back out to the store.

"I've already locked up," he said absently, staring at the computer as if he expected it to jump up and bite him.

She nodded. "See you in the morning." She lifted her hand in a wave and let herself out.

Grabbing a diet cola from the fridge, Brock sat down to take a look at Zoe's blog.

Though she knew she needed to go online and purchase her airline tickets for the return trip to New York, Zoe couldn't make herself. Not yet. She wasn't ready. She finally told Mama Bell that she wanted to stay for a little while longer and, when the older woman expressed happiness at the idea, Zoe took to her blog, writing about her indecision. And, because she held nothing back on her blog, she finally opened up about her love for a man she couldn't have, and why.

The response was instantaneous. Within twenty minutes, she had over nine hundred comments. She got up to make a mug of hot tea and, while she was busy doing that, the number climbed to over fifteen hundred. Stunned, Zoe couldn't believe it. Her blog had always been popular and she had hundreds of subscribers and thousands of followers, but she couldn't remember a single post generating this kind of interest.

Even though they were still coming in faster than she could believe, she sat down at her laptop and began to read, tea in hand.

There were so many, the vast majority of them encouraging. As she read, a bit of the darkness lifted.

When the occasional internet troll popped up, spewing vitriol, she did as she always had and hit the delete key.

Luckily most of the comments weren't more than a sentence or two. Some of them were a single word. There were a lot of hugs and <3, which made a heart. There was advice and prayers, cheering and offering advice.

She made it through the first thousand or so before her head started to ache. She started to close the laptop and go do something else, but she decided to try to make it through as many as she could—not an easy feat since the number of comments was still climbing.

Still, she continued to read, wiping away the odd tear, shaking her head and smiling at the outpouring of love. Generally, the consensus seemed to be that she should fight for the chance at happiness. Stop running, stop hiding—those two phrases appeared over and over.

All her loyal readers thought she was giving up too easily. While she appreciated their opinions, she knew she wasn't. Because this had never been about her own happiness, but Brock's.

Let him have the chance to make his choice—this comment, from someone called Eve5466, had been followed by a row of hearts. Again, this made Zoe smile.

But the next comment nearly stopped her heart.

Do you really think a life without you is better than a life without children? What happened to being in it together, forever and ever, like you promised when you agreed to be my wife, five long years ago? Baby, you're not alone. You were never alone. We've been given this second chance and we're awfully close to blowing it. I don't care if we can't have children—there's adoption for that. I do care about not losing you. I love you. You, not some idea of the perfect family. That said, come find me if you're willing to take a leap of faith. I'm taking my own, by hoping we can have this one last chance. I'll be waiting with open arms, on the same park bench.

It was signed simply, B.

She couldn't breathe. Brock. Somehow he'd found her blog. And read it, or at least this most recent entry, which happened to be about him and the reason she'd turned him down yet again.

The rest of the comments blurred as her eyes filled. Shakily, she wiped the tears away, squinting and trying to focus on the screen.

Last chance. Open arms. Not alone. Love.

He was right. He'd tried and tried to tell her so. If she left this time, she'd be condemning them both to a barren, lonely future. Together, they at least stood a chance at happiness.

Crying, hiccupping, grinning foolishly, she ran to the car.

Brock was waiting, exactly as he'd promised, sitting on the metal park bench with the breeze ruffling his blond hair. At this time of the day the park was crowded. People had gotten off work and gone for the evening run. Young couples, children in tow, stood around the playground, letting their kids play. Out of habit, she avoided glancing over there, the high-pitched laughter and joyous voices piercing at her heart.

Then Brock's gaze caught and held hers, and she forgot about anything else. Hope, unfamiliar and dizzying, crowded out everything except the rapid beat of her heart.

He stood, big and powerful, and so damn handsome

her throat began to ache. She wavered, then lifted her chin and continued moving. This time, rather than meeting her halfway, he let her go to him. Symbolic, yes, because he'd already let her know what he wanted. Now it was up to her to make the choice.

As she approached him, she held out her hands. He took them in his, holding on tight.

Despite what he'd written and said, she had to be certain. She couldn't do this if there was the slightest chance he'd have regrets.

"Are you sure?" Tilting her head, she searched his beloved face. "Because you always said you wanted a family. You wanted six children, we compromised on three, a house with some land, the whole deal. I can't..." Swallowing, she cleared her throat and forced herself to go on. "I can't give you that. Since you read my blog, you know I can never have children."

"Do you think any of that matters to me now?" He shook his head. To her shock, his eyes appeared shiny with tears. "You're the greatest thing that ever happened to me. You're my heart and my soul and my life. Living without you is like living someone else's life, like trying to function with a giant hole inside me."

Her knees buckled, threatening to give out on her. After so many years of denying the possibility, of trying to close her heart off from love, she wasn't sure she could absorb it all.

Blue eyes full of love and determination, Brock watched her. She realized he was still waiting, that there was something she still needed to say.

No matter what else she'd been, she'd never been a coward. Taking a deep breath, she lifted her chin, smiled and dropped to one knee. "Brock McCauley, I love you. Will you marry me and spend the rest of your life with me?"

As a joyous smile spread across his face, lighting up his gaze, she felt warmth flow through her.

"Of course," he said quietly, pulling her to her feet, pulling her up against him. "With love, we can work anything out. I just had to know you were positive."

So much love shone in his face. She felt gloriously, blissfully happy. All her doubts had vanished. Because Brock was right. With love, anything was possible.

Epilogue

"This is exactly what the town needs." Mama Bell smiled, leaning in to make a last-minute adjustment to Zoe's veil. Her eyes appeared a bit watery, as if she might be on the verge of tears. "Healing and happiness after a time of so much sorrow."

"Stop." Smiling back, Zoe sniffed. "You're going to make me cry and ruin my makeup."

"And we definitely don't want that." Hands on Zoe's shoulders, Mama turned her to face the mirror. "Look at you. You practically radiate happiness. You're so beautiful."

Eyeing her reflection in the formfitting white dress, Zoe's eyes again began to sting. "Dang it," she whispered, fanning her face with her hand. "I honestly never imagined I'd see this day."

Mama nodded. Zoe knew she understood what Zoe

meant. Past and present and future all coming together at once. Zoe's only regret was that Shayna wasn't here to see it.

"She's here in spirit," Mama said, letting Zoe know that they'd been thinking the same thing.

"She was supposed to be my maid of honor, before everything went crazy."

Mama hugged her, careful not to disturb her veil. "I know, sweetheart. I know."

A discreet tap on the door startled them. The signal to let them know it was time for Zoe to walk down the aisle.

Her heart rate tripled. As she inhaled, trying to calm herself, she almost swore she heard Shayna's voice whisper in her ear. *Finally.*

Just like that, a calm strength settled over Zoe. Shayna was here, in spirit, exactly as Mama Bell had said.

Heart full, Zoe squared her shoulders, lifted her chin and moved forward to embrace her future.

* * * * *

COMING NEXT MONTH FROM

H HARLEQUIN®

ROMANTIC suspense

Available November 5, 2013

#1775 COURSE OF ACTION
by Lindsay McKenna and Merline Lovelace
Two deadly missions have these men in uniform putting their lives and their hearts on the line for service, duty and love.

#1776 THE COLTON HEIR
The Coltons of Wyoming • by Colleen Thompson
Ranch hand Dylan Frick threatens to turn in a gorgeous intruder, but Hope begs him to keep her deadly secret. She isn't the only one whose identity is under wraps. Will the truth set them free?

#1777 PROTECTING HIS PRINCESS
by C.J. Miller
When Arabian princess Laila agrees to help stop a terrorist group within her country's borders, she never expects to find love with the distrusting FBI agent who will do anything to keep her safe.

#1778 DEADLY CONTACT
by Lara Lacombe
Working to stop a bioterror attack in D.C., Special Agent James Reynolds is shocked to find his ex, microbiologist Kelly Jarvis, mixed up with the extremists—and worse, she's in danger.

YOU CAN FIND MORE INFORMATION ON UPCOMING HARLEQUIN® TITLES, FREE EXCERPTS AND MORE AT WWW.HARLEQUIN.COM.

HRSCNM1013

REQUEST YOUR FREE BOOKS!
2 FREE NOVELS PLUS 2 FREE GIFTS!

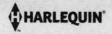

ROMANTIC suspense

Sparked by danger, fueled by passion

YES! Please send me 2 FREE Harlequin® Romantic Suspense novels and my 2 FREE gifts (gifts are worth about $10). After receiving them, if I don't wish to receive any more books, I can return the shipping statement marked "cancel." If I don't cancel, I will receive 4 brand-new novels every month and be billed just $4.74 per book in the U.S. or $5.24 per book in Canada. That's a savings of at least 14% off the cover price! It's quite a bargain! Shipping and handling is just 50¢ per book in the U.S. and 75¢ per book in Canada.* I understand that accepting the 2 free books and gifts places me under no obligation to buy anything. I can always return a shipment and cancel at any time. Even if I never buy another book, the two free books and gifts are mine to keep forever.

240/340 HDN F45N

Name	(PLEASE PRINT)	
Address		Apt. #
City	State/Prov.	Zip/Postal Code

Signature (if under 18, a parent or guardian must sign)

Mail to the Harlequin® Reader Service:
IN U.S.A.: P.O. Box 1867, Buffalo, NY 14240-1867
IN CANADA: P.O. Box 609, Fort Erie, Ontario L2A 5X3

Want to try two free books from another line?
Call 1-800-873-8635 or visit www.ReaderService.com.

* Terms and prices subject to change without notice. Prices do not include applicable taxes. Sales tax applicable in N.Y. Canadian residents will be charged applicable taxes. Offer not valid in Quebec. This offer is limited to one order per household. Not valid for current subscribers to Harlequin Romantic Suspense books. All orders subject to credit approval. Credit or debit balances in a customer's account(s) may be offset by any other outstanding balance owed by or to the customer. Please allow 4 to 6 weeks for delivery. Offer available while quantities last.

Your Privacy—The Harlequin® Reader Service is committed to protecting your privacy. Our Privacy Policy is available online at www.ReaderService.com or upon request from the Harlequin Reader Service.

We make a portion of our mailing list available to reputable third parties that offer products we believe may interest you. If you prefer that we not exchange your name with third parties, or if you wish to clarify or modify your communication preferences, please visit us at www.ReaderService.com/consumerschoice or write to us at Harlequin Reader Service Preference Service, P.O. Box 9062, Buffalo, NY 14269. Include your complete name and address.

HRS13R

SPECIAL EXCERPT FROM

H HARLEQUIN®

™

ROMANTIC suspense

When Arabian princess Laila agrees to help stop a
terrorist group within her country's borders, she never
expects to find love with the distrusting FBI agent who
will do anything to keep her safe.

Read on for a sneak peek of

PROTECTING HIS PRINCESS

by C.J. Miller, available November 2013 from
Harlequin® Romantic Suspense.

"What are you doing?" Laila asked, taking his arm.

Harris stared at her. "Why didn't you go with your family?"

"And leave you here alone?" Laila asked.

He didn't want Laila in the thick of this. An attempt had
been made on her life in America and he didn't know if she
had been one of the targets of the bombing here. "You need
to be somewhere safe."

She gripped his arm harder. "I am safest with you."

Another explosion boomed through the air. Harris grabbed
Laila and shielded her with his body, pulling them to the
ground. Was the sound a building collapsing from the damage
or another bomb? Harris guessed another bomb. Laila was
shaking in his arms. Harris waited for the noise around him to
quiet and concentrated on listening for the rat-tat-tat of gun
shots or another bomb.

His protective instincts roared louder. He wouldn't let anything happen to Laila. "I'm going to help where I can."

Her eyes widened with fear. "What if there is another bomb—"

He had some basic first-aid training and he'd been a marine. Dealing with difficult situations had been part of his training. "There might be another one. There's no time to wait for help."

"I can help, too," Laila said, lifting her chin.

"You aren't trained for this," he said.

"No, but I'm capable and smart. I will be useful. Don't treat me like a crystal vase."

Laila wouldn't back down. She wouldn't leave the scene, not when her countrymen needed help. Arguing wouldn't get him anywhere. He'd seen her strength many times before. She might act like a shrinking violet in front of her brother or other males, but she had an iron core. "You're stubborn when you want something."

"So are you," Laila said, giving him a small smile.

Don't miss
PROTECTING HIS PRINCESS
by C.J. Miller,
available November 2013 from
Harlequin® Romantic Suspense.

pyright © 2013 by Cynthia Miller

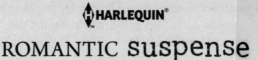

ROMANTIC suspense

THE COLTON HEIR

Ranch hand Dylan Frick threatens to turn
in a gorgeous intruder, but Hope begs him
to keep her deadly secret. She isn't the only
one whose identity is under wraps.
Will the truth set them free?

Look for the next installment of the
Coltons of Wyoming miniseries
next month from Colleen Thompson.

Only from Harlequin® Romantic Suspense!

Wherever books and ebooks are sold.

Heart-racing romance, high-stakes suspense!

www.Harlequin.com

HRS2